MAEZE:

RETURNING FROM AMERICA

Dr. Gabriel C. Onyekuru

This book represents a picturesque view of a victim of cross-cultural fertilization. In a very clear narrative, the author succeeded in showcasing his protagonist; Maeze and his tireless determination for survival in the midst and background of two somewhat conflicting socio-cultural environments. The story is endearing and book highly recommendable to all and sundry.

Chief Pius Uchenna Okoye, National President – IGBOEZUE INTERNATIONAL.

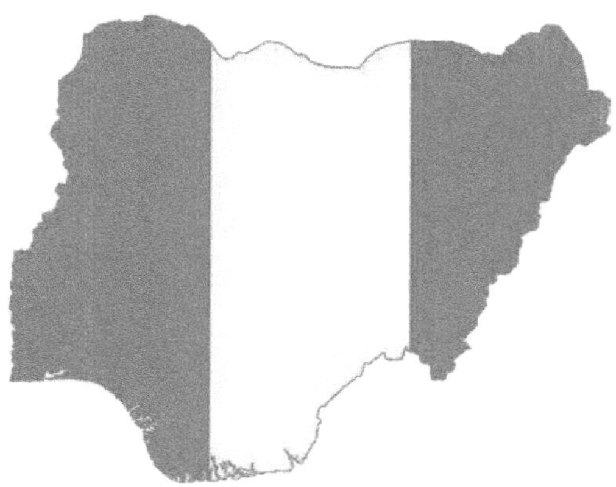

TABLE OF CONTENTS

PART I

1. CHILDHOOD

As a child, Maeze continually fantasized over distinguishing himself spectacularly. He did not dream of untold riches or power. However, he harbored an "inner man" that was certain he was destined for special achievements.

He remembered himself as a child just after the war, trudging to and from his elementary school. The trendy cars then were Peugeot 403 and 404. The lucky pupils were those whose parents had those cars. Maeze dreamed of growing up to become successful, like those who drove about in Peugeot cars with their wives and children. He imagined how blissful an existence he would have.

Maeze was certain he would achieve his dream if he worked very hard at his studies and remained a "good boy" –

obeying his teachers and respecting his parents and seniors. His humble background, however, belied his lofty ambitions.

Even in his deprived circumstances, he and his companions heard much of America and its marvels. The stories were as astonishing as the Bible stories taught in both school and catechism classes. They described a world that seemed unattainable in the present life. Living in America was the exclusive privilege of extraordinarily gilded beings, not for persons of his ilk. No, America was definitely not for people of his lowly background.

A few people from their town were known to have been educated abroad. Maeze and his fellows did not quite understand the difference between America and Europe, or any other foreign country for that matter. Secondly, it made no difference in their minds whether their highly educated townspeople received their academic laurels from America or any other part of the world. What was known was that they had studied abroad, and for the villagers, it invested them with splendor.

In that small community, those who had been abroad were deified. Although termed a town, theirs was a village devoid of "government presence" – no water pipes, good roads and similar amenities. The educated people were the few who had alternative electricity supply, a very privileged acquisition at the time. They visited the "town" occasionally from their places of residence in the big cities. Young people like Maeze would then converge at their homes to watch television in the evenings, usually through the windows. The offspring of those rich families were of course fortunate at that stage in life. They did not attend the same schools as impoverished children. However, whenever they visited home, they were virtually worshipped by other children. Some of the local children cherished their association with the wealthy, city-dwelling visitors, kowtowing unabashedly to them. Maeze's elder brother determinedly followed and fawned over those children of the affluent, while Maeze stayed away. On occasion, the sycophancy caused ruptures! Maeze's parents received messages that their toadying son had damaged expensive items in rich homes. They of course castigated their son.

Maeze, however, intent on achieving much in life, was utterly dedicated to his studies. He scored among the best in his internal examinations, receiving a certificate after passing his first school and then getting admitted into secondary school. At the time, the secondary school for some villages seemed very far away from home. In adulthood, he reflected that the distance was somewhat negligible! After his secondary school education, Maeze again sat for and passed his entrance examination to study at an institution of higher learning. His decisions and actions over continuing his education were his alone. His parents had no part in them. Lacking the means to finance Maeze's further education, they were much concerned with the training of his younger siblings. They could not continue to educate Maeze while fending for their younger offspring. They simply lacked the resources to train him at a higher institution.

Maeze's lot appeared clear. He would find a clerical job while assisting his parents in the education of his younger siblings. A miracle occurred. When he completed his secondary education, his cousin offered to take him to the city where she and her husband lived. It was in the oil-producing zone of the Niger Delta. Two weeks after moving in with his cousin and her husband in the city of Warri, Maeze got a job with a French Multi-National Mechanical Servicing Company.

2.   A YOUNG WORKER

In that city job, Maeze's life proved amazing. He found himself moving from the lowliest post of time-keeper to undreamed heights.   Maeze became an achiever in various aspects of life – personal, professional, and societal. He noted his transformation from a naïve village urchin to a man of consequence in the city. He became the first Nigerian to be employed in the administrative office of that multi-national company. Hitherto, most people employed to work with the expatriate staff were from Francophone West African countries. The company appeared to be experimenting by employing a Nigerian as a clerical assistant to comply with the legal dictates of affirmative action for foreign companies operating in Nigeria. Maeze started as a time-keeper initially and rose to become an office clerk. He simultaneously worked as a janitor in the general administration office, the mechanic workshop and the fabrication workshop. Shortly afterwards, the British administration manager of the French company decided he was fit to serve as a "utility employee." That meant that Maeze worked for the company in various capacities. About one year later, the administration manager invited him to his office for an inspiring, fatherly discussion. Maeze, he declared gleefully, was a boy he could train and promised that he would shortly start to train him in that company. That meeting motivated Maeze to work harder, certain that his exertion would ensure his growth in the company.

That momentous meeting was, in fact, Maeze's first close encounter with a white man, and he found the man's speech hard to grasp. When foreigners spoke, he understood some of the words and used his intuition to fathom the rest. The expatriated bosses obviously noted Maeze's difficulty in understanding them, a deficiency which many other Nigerians suffered.   They overlooked that "shortcoming" and continually expressed their satisfaction with Maeze, who was always keen to learn. This was his early odyssey in the company, a venture that would last for eighteen years.

Maeze literally grew from one position to another, from one level to another, and from one beautiful story in the company to another. It was not long before the administration manager had to leave the organization because recession had set in. That was Nigeria in 1984. That recession affected the fortunes and operational activities of the company. Almost all the employees were disengaged. Ten Africans remained to maintain the company's yard, and Maeze was among those who survived the sweeping retrenchment. The company had foundry machines that could be employed in miscellaneous jobs. So, rather than pass the day in idleness, those survivors of the mass dismissal bought used steel pipes from the many dealers found all over the city of Warri. As iron and steel stockings formed the main business of some private enterprises in the city, those used pipes were converted to flat sheets. Alternatively, they bought flat sheets and rolled them to produce pipes according to demands in the steel market.

Those activities sustained the company during that period of inactivity and averted its dismissal of the remaining employees. The only expatriate left was Mr. Jean, the company's Base Manager. The recession lasted until about 1985 when the parent company of the multi-national in France secured its breakthrough contract from Warri Refinery and Petro-Chemical Company. This new contract reinvigorated the company, prompting the advent of a crop of young expatriate engineers and professionals, employed to change the entire management system of the company.

Mr. Jean and the few other employees left in the company were available to receive the new expatriates sent from France for the big project. He had enjoyed the "lull" in activities in the life of the company. As chief custodian of the company's property, he had been notorious among staff and contractors for looting the stores of equipment and selling them to his friends. As Mr. Jean was close to retirement, he decided to steal as much as he could. In fact, Maeze was surprised to see that a white man could do what he considered unimaginably deplorable.

However, the new set of young technocrats came into the organization primed with computers and new technology for their work. It was fascinating for Maeze to participate in the deployment of unknown technologies by young French engineers. He loved them with everything in him. He yearned to learn from them.

Meanwhile, Maeze had not been in the good books of Mr. Jean. The aversion might have been caused by Maeze's inability to speak French, or the fact that Mr. Jean was not the person who employed Maeze in the company. He tried his utmost to have Maeze sacked, but curiously, his bids always failed. Sheer luck, it seemed, kept Maeze in the company long enough to witness the new dawn in its life. It seemed that what saved Maeze was that the payroll and taxation system were not quite simple for Mr. Jean and his friends who concentrated on operations, logistics and purchasing. That fact, Maeze felt, might have kept him in the company until the start of its new phase.

Mr. Jean had enjoyed the security and distinction of being the only expatriate, a commander-in-chief who could do whatever he pleased. He was solely responsible for processing requests to his head office in Paris. He had begun to implement his bids at self-enrichment. He knew all the suppliers and users of steel products in Warri, and the company had many iron and steel products in stock. He was the manager, purchaser, store keeper, cashier and played other undefined roles. This man was at liberty to do whatever pleased him with the resources of the company, as there were neither other expatriates to monitor his activities nor control measures in the system. Consequently, to steal was an easy task.

When the new expatriated staff arrived, he was loath to cooperate with them. It was at that stage that Maeze's new rise began. Mr. Pierre was at the head of the new team as Operations Manager. His efforts to effect immediate organizational change met a brick wall in the person of Mr. Jean and his associates. Mr. Pierre needed everybody around to tell him about the company's activities in order to restructure and computerize the entire system. Mr. Jean was not prepared to divulge such information. Maeze still remembered vividly the mockery of farting on machines in the absence of the young technocrats. Maeze was interested in those machines and liked the way Mr. Pierre carried them with him everywhere. Mr. Pierre used them to take note of every discussion, report, complaint or query. In fact, they appeared mystical as Mr. Pierre bore them on his rounds.

Maeze was the only staff who was always in the office from very early in the mornings to late in the evenings doing all the clerical work. Consequently, despite Mr. Jean's obduracy, Mr. Pierre found Maeze virtually indispensable. That professional association proved of immense mutual benefit. Mr. Pierre had a wealth of experience in management of organizations. He readily gave Maeze valuable training in the course of their working relationship. Maeze supplied Mr. Pierre with all the necessary information he and his team needed for their work, an information channel Mr. Jean and his acolytes strove to block. Maeze, defying them, struggled continually to assist Mr. Pierre.

In later years, Maeze proudly reflected that his relationship with Mr. Pierre helped him to not only develop himself but be recognized as a successful person in the country. His association with Mr. Pierre's team provided Maeze with quality life experience, knowledge, wealth and healthy relationship with people. It was in the process of helping the new set of managers to develop their organizational structure that Maeze was exposed to all areas of management principles and activities.

Mr. Pierre would gather all the information needed in order to fashion a workable process, piece them together, do all the modifications to an existing reporting system, and hand over to the personnel who would be responsible for that duty. He would pick up the administration system, sit down with the gathered information as necessary, fathom the modifications needed, and develop a process of handling correspondence. The out-going reports from operations sites, policy dissemination, and transmission of documents from clients, vendors, and telecommunication messages, he handed over to secretaries and administrative officers in charge. He addressed the personnel system, developed the process of advertising for vacant positions, organized recruitment, selection, interview, documentation and general personnel policy for the personnel department. He would also review the stores and purchasing sub-system, develop the stock cards, the requisition forms, purchasing process, approvals, method of keeping retrievable records and hand over everything to the purchasing department.

Mr. Pierre delved into the accounts sub-system with receivables, payables, cash account keeping, bank accounts keeping, and their records and handed them over to the personnel in the department. Likewise, he addressed the health, safety and environmental policies and updated them to required standards, handing over same to the personnel in that department. He worked on logistics, maintenance, security and finally, fabrication, developing a workable system in all the departments and handing over to the personnel in those departments. Maeze worked ceaselessly with Mr. Pierre as he strove to reorganize various departments. In fact, Maeze became the trainer of most of the personnel in those departments. As an engineer, it was easy for Mr. Pierre and his team to modify the template previously used and integrate the entire company management system. Thanks to Mr. Pierre's presence, computerization and sound management pervaded the company. Prior to that, it appeared to be Mr. Jean's one-man operation.

A new phase was firmly established. Before Mr. Pierre's arrival with his team, the company was generating an annual turnover of approximately one hundred and sixty thousand naira, mainly from converting pipes to flat sheets and flat sheets to pipes in the local market. The situation changed with Mr. Pierre's arrival.

3. THE NEW ERA

A new era began for the company -- multimillion dollar projects going on all over the country. Maeze was happy to meet a set of young company managers. That encounter changed his world view, providing a new experience and the prospects to develop himself in the field of management. Being close to the Operations Manager, Mr. Pierre, he found himself in a position to help others by recommendations to work positions as opportunities arose. As a young man unsullied with the attitudes that tribal and sectional affiliations would later rouse, Maeze opened his heart and hands, assisting people from all parts of Nigeria. Free of discrimination, his open mindedness and good heart endeared him to a wide range of persons as he worked for the company's interest.

The first person Maeze helped was a younger brother to his friend who was a welder in the organization. That younger brother had just graduated from the University of Benin's Mathematics Department. The French were naturally pleasant and easy going, esteeming practical knowledge above certificates. They did not care much about the education as long as one was willing to learn and fulfill the requirements of one's employment. Maeze observed that they appreciated character and willingness to learn on the job. More people were employed in personnel, Health, Safety and Environment (HSE), and the commercial and fabrication departments as operational demands increased. Many of those new employees had higher educational qualifications than Maeze – a factor that would be used against him.

The degreed employees began to mock Maeze for possessing only a secondary school education! They gossiped about him. Some were more confrontational, calling him "mediocre" to his face. They even strove to thwart his growth in the company because of his assumed deficient qualifications. Those fierce foes were people he had helped to gain employment and trained in their respective duties. Maeze's saving grace was that Mr. Pierre himself, who eventually became the Managing Director of the company, needed nobody to vouch for Maeze's character and capabilities. He had, of course, worked directly with Maeze during his early days in Africa and through the enormous difficulties of assuming control of company operations.

As there were many projects thriving in Nigeria, the company had expanded, its employees numbering over a thousand. Maeze was definitely a key staff to Mr. Pierre, with all the billions of Dollars now at his disposal. As the company expanded, so did the number of personnel, experts and Nigerians alike. Maeze was unflagging in his zeal, leaving home sometimes at 5:30 in the mornings and often working late into the night, even on Sundays and holidays. Maeze's dedication and efficiency were second to none, a fact acknowledged by the Managing Director. Some of the newly employed people in the company were not interested or willing to emulate Maeze's commitment. They only wished to get him dismissed in order to occupy his position.

The arrival in the organization of a certain Mr. Sedrob in about 1987/88 compounded Maeze's woes. Mr. Sedrob was among the expatriates Mr. Pierre brought to Nigeria from the United Arab Emirates (UAE) where they had previously worked. He was a highly experienced man in finance and administration. However, he disliked seeing black people around him. The man came in and was introduced as the head of the administrative department. At first, he pretended to be well disposed towards Maeze. Maeze, young and naïve, felt he had found a father figure to learn from as they were in the same office. He resolved to serve the man diligently. He also imagined that Mr. Jean had told Mr. Sedrob what a conscientious worker he was.

Maeze provided the new Administration Manager with all the information he required in accounts and administration. For the first few months of Mr. Sedrob's employment in the company, he and Maeze worked together. Sedrob continually expressed his satisfaction to Maeze. The compliments would soon be proved insincere. The trickery was revealed when Mr. Sedrob decided to send Maeze on annual leave in order to bring in his very close friend, an Indian who had worked with him in the United Arab Emirates. Mr. Sedrob decided to remove Maeze from his office.

Maeze was euphoric at the prospect of ranking just below Mr. Sebrob in the company hierarchy. He never imagined the old man had ignoble intentions. Indeed, he realized later that the old man had hoped to find him out in an incriminating deed and failed. However, he remained intent on executing his wicked plan. That was why he recommended Maeze to proceed on annual leave. As Maeze began his holiday, Mr. Sedrob's Indian friend started work in his stead.

When word reached Maeze that a new expatriate had taken over his job, he prayed his heart out, calling fervently on God. He realized the new Administrative Manager was merely executing his nefarious plans. Just before Maeze left for his leave, Mr. Sedrob had employed an assistant. This new Nigerian employee had an office next to Maeze's. With the arrival of Mr. Sedrob's Indian friend in Maeze's office, there was a complete reorganization that seemed only to achieve the ulterior motive of keeping Maeze out of the inner functioning of the administration and finance of the company. Maeze was incredulous. A set of managers that he had helped to establish in their tasks were rewarding his loyalty and hard work with evil. His only offences were that he was black and a Nigerian who knew more than he was supposed to know. Maeze pondered, "Is this how I'll end up in a company I serve with all in me?"

This was a company that had seemed ineffectual and was now executing multi-billion-dollar projects. Where exactly had he gone wrong? How had he offended the company management? Was it an offence to be Nigerian? Mr. Sedrob reassigned Maeze's assistant to work with the new Indian man, while the Indian would be reporting to him. Maeze believed that Mr. Pierre must have been advised to terminate his employment while he was still on leave. Out of Mr. Pierre's good nature and considering the good service Maeze had rendered him in the past, he could not accede to that request from Mr. Sedrob. Meanwhile, Maeze was on leave and had not yet learned what was happening in his office.

From the grapevine, Maeze realized that Mr. Sedrob's sole purpose was to take him out as a Nigerian who was naturally smart and had known much. According to the gossip, he had observed during his short interaction with Maeze that the young man was courageous and could ask probing questions, not having any course to fear anything. So, replacing him with a mere jolly good fellow, a non-national who would concur with everything they were to do in the company was the most desirable thing the management sought at that very time money was coming from all directions in the company's history.

Now, the problem was what to do with Maeze--to discard or to keep him. Mr. Sedrob decided to relocate his office, with the other two associates, to a contractor's office some miles outside the company's premises. They would merely receive cash vouchers from Maeze, while important financial reports would be forwarded directly to them in the accounts department. Maeze was effectively removed from the company's accounts department. He felt more humiliated and frustrated than he had ever been in his life.

He realized that Mr. Sedrob's aim was to impel him to leave the company of his own accord. However, that harrowing experience nerved Maeze to fight relentlessly whenever he found his rights trampled upon. He reflected that discrimination was heinous. Merely because Mr. Sedrob wished to conceal financial transactions from Nigerians, he was prepared to destroy and turn all white people against a young man of irreproachable loyalty and dedication. Maeze felt he was encountering a situation akin to the apartheid of South Africa that he had only read about. Discrimination could wreck one's emotional wholeness. Mr. Sedrob was an expert at disrupting young people's psychological tranquility. He expertly perpetrated his viciousness on Maeze.

Maeze faced two options: to resign from his job or to stay away from the financial activities of the company. If he resigned, where would he find a job? If he left the finance and administration department of the company, where else would he work? Positions in other departments were filled. Maeze decided that his employment should be terminated by the company's management, or his obvious victimization stopped, and his rightful position given to him. He was not prepared to relinquish his position to the Indian.

Maeze reasoned that it didn't make any sense trying to impress anybody anymore, for that would not change the situation. He had tried to work with everything youthful in him to prove he was a good man, but that wasn't accepted. So, what sense did it really make anymore to continue his striving that meant nothing to those white people? As a young man brimful of strength and administrative talent, he was resolved to take his complaint to whomever cared to hear his voice. In his native community's parlance, the chicken said that she was shouting, not for the predator to leave her alone, but for the whole world to at least hear her cries.

Maeze reasoned that it would be appropriate to meet with Mr. Pierre and discuss those gnawing issues with him before confronting Mr. Sedrob. After all, he had worked with Mr. Pierre when Pierre first arrived in Nigeria, and now Maeze badly needed help. Pierre's home office had rewarded him by promoting him from the Operations Manager position to becoming the Managing Director (MD).

For a while, Maeze pondered how to face him but could not muster sufficient boldness for the interview with the Managing Director. It would be hard to express his grief and disappointment at being the butt of cruelty despite his loyalty and hard work. Mr. Sedrob, he was certain, could not be acting alone. It was unbelievable, indeed impossible, that Mr. Pierre did not know what Mr. Sedrob was doing, or what Maeze was suffering at the hands of his new Finance Manager. Maeze considered writing down his complaints.

Eventually, he went to the Managing Director's office to bare his mind. He told Pierre distinctly that he was not happy with the treatment he was receiving from the management. He stated that he was ready to resign in the face of the humiliation. He reminded the Managing Director that he had worked for him with all dedication and loyalty and asked whether he had decided to reward him with persecution. Mr. Pierre just looked into Maeze's face, smiled and said, "I know what you are talking about. Maeze do not worry; I will send you to Port Harcourt." Maeze was the happiest person in the world at that moment. He went back to his lonely office and relished his relief.

His short dialogue with Mr. Pierre effected miraculous change. In an instant, the anger in him yielded to hope, and his frustration was replaced by a new zeal. Mr. Pierre truly realized how much young Maeze had contributed to his own elevation and to the company's success. He knew all that Maeze was going through at Mr. Sedrob's hands. Mr. Pierre needed the experience and expertise of Mr. Sedrob in his new structure for the company, and at the same time did not wish to dismiss this young African man who had manifested amazing self-motivation and loyalty over the affairs of the organization. If Maeze had left at that moment, he would have found it impossible to forgive all the French for the rest of his life. However, Mr. Pierre's singular humane action reinforced his earlier perception of the French as good and compassionate.

Maeze began to imagine his future ambience. Taking up residence in Warri had been his first contact with city life, and now he would move to the garden city of Port Harcourt! Never in his wildest imagination did Maeze dream of becoming a Port Harcourt boy. And now, the Managing Director had declared to him that he would be transferring to Port Harcourt. For Maeze, it was like winning a power-ball grand prize. The thought alone intoxicated him. He was overwhelmed. From the depths of his heart, he was grateful to Mr. Pierre and to his God and even to Mr. Sedrob for beginning the nightmarish episode. "See where all his torture has taken me – to Port Harcourt," he mused. It had never featured in his dreams, even when he had acute malaria accompanied by wild dreams. He kept asking himself: "Could this be real?" It was just too huge a prospect for Maeze to grasp.

He continued working, marking time, waiting for the day the promise would materialize. Mr. Pierre had not been in Nigeria for weeks. He had traveled around the world; Europe today, South America the next, North America, the Middle East, and finally back in Nigeria. Even when in Nigeria, Mr. Pierre and Maeze could hardly meet because the MD was very busy. He was always visiting one project site or the other. There were just too many projects for the company at the same time. Maeze was proud that in any case, he was part of the whole story of getting contracts from the giant oil and gas companies in Nigeria. Mr. Sedrob of course was blatantly discriminating, but there were clear legal provisions for the protection of Nigerian employees in companies which also hired expatriates.

Days turned into weeks, and weeks became months after Mr. Pierre's promise that Maeze would be transferred to the Port Harcourt office. None of the managers in Nigeria said anything about Maeze and the transfer. Rather, they started mobilizing other staff to Port Harcourt. Again, Maeze began to wonder whether the entire plan had changed. He didn't know what else Mr. Sedrob planned beyond the frustration being inflicted on him. There was a certain Michel, a young Frenchman who arrived in Nigeria for his country's compulsory national service after graduation. He was the person Mr. Sedrob decided to send to Port Harcourt instead of Maeze to start the company's new office. Michel was sent to work with a newly engaged General Manager. That General Manager undertook numerous trips to Port Harcourt. Michel was stationed there in a hotel. The company was spending huge amounts of money for their upkeep and rent in one of the most expensive hotels in Port Harcourt, whereas they could have moved instead into the company's own already paid for office. Michel was grossly lacking in the necessary experience to handle an office on his own.

4. TRANSFER TO PORT HARCOURT

When Mr. Pierre was next in Nigeria, he was dismayed to find that the Port Harcourt staff roamed about rather than settle down to work. They seemed to shuttle ceaselessly between Port Harcourt and Warri, mindless of the risks of travel and hotel expenses. Some of the staff overheard him express his anger on the expatriate management team led by the new General Manager and Mr. Sedrob. He was irked that they were unable to establish an office in Port Harcourt, despite the fact that office premises had been paid for several months earlier. Obviously remembering Maeze's ability and how hard and successfully they had worked together, he summoned Maeze to his office. There, in the presence of the Base Manager, he declared: "Maeze be ready tomorrow; you are going to Port Harcourt."

Thus, was Maeze effectively transferred to Port Harcourt. Transfer to Port Harcourt held an added attraction. Maeze longed to attend a university, and that city had university programs in which he could enroll. When Maeze arrived in Port Harcourt, it was August and admission processes at the university were almost completed. By divine intervention, he managed to secure a place at the College of Continuing Education of the University. Nobody would have believed that someone in Maeze's position at the company, with his enervating workload, and considering too the huge distance between the lecture center and his office, could attempt to combine his work with studies. Maeze, however, was determined to rise from the derision of his colleagues over his lack of higher education. Those he had helped employ and trained had of course not hesitated to mock him.

Maeze was brisk. He had only been in Port Harcourt for a while when he established the office. That Port Harcourt branch was meant to send all its reports to Mr. Sedrob through Michel.

All the documents that Michel and the General Manager were carrying about in their suitcases, not knowing what to do with them, were bundled to Maeze. He had to sort and arrange them properly for documentation. Maeze created the Port Harcourt office records and accounts and transmitted all the reports needed by Mr. Sedrob. Mr. Sedrob was not one readily to drop his ideas. He strove to use Michel to frustrate Maeze in his new position. Whenever Maeze prepared and handed his report to Michel to be passed to Mr. Sedrob in Warri, Michel would instead recopy the report in his own hand writing, verbatim, and transmit it to Sedrob. Maeze decided not to let that practice bother him, as he was left in the company to continue his work. So, just as Maeze had from the British administrator, he was now training the young Michel from France, who was not ashamed to recopy what was meant to be sent without alteration to their Finance Manager. Michel was happy to be given the position of supervisor. Thus, Maeze was his administrative assistant.

Maeze was not surprised when, on one occasion, he presented his expense report for approval and reimbursement of his hotel and transportation bills as contained in the company's general conditions of service, and Michel refused to approve it. Maeze had joined other junior employees in one of the cheapest hotels in the city of Port Harcourt. Yet, Michel turned down his request for approval. When Maeze sought an explanation, Michel simply informed him: "Mr. Sedrob instructed me not to approve it." That report covered about two months of Maeze's stay in Port Harcourt. Some people had been in the hotel for over six months, and yet their expense reports were being approved by the same Michel.

Maeze silently pondered how the pair of Mr. Sedrob and Michel could continue to mete out such wickedness to him. He wondered for how long he was going to be troubling the

Managing Director over little matters that their office in Port Harcourt could handle. His frustration was growing. How could Michel not approve his expenses while Michel and other expatriates staying at Hotel Presidential, a five-star facility, had theirs paid? There and then, Maeze decided to end the oppression and ruthlessness of Mr. Sedrob, once and for all. He promised Michel, "Before the end of this day, you will hear my story with Mr. Sedrob." Maeze drove straight from his office to Mr. Sedrob in Warri. He marched straight to the "oppressor's" office and confronted him.

Mr. Sedrob must have seen and been unnerved by Maeze's raging fury. Maeze was obviously the last person he expected to see at that time of day. As soon as Maeze got into his office and Mr. Sedrob observed the anger in his face, he knew instantly that Maeze came to make trouble. Maeze was really aggravated. Maeze took a quick gaze around the office and thought, "So, this is where this oppressor issues his obnoxious directives and instructions from."

Mr. Sedrob tried to be charming and conciliatory. "Hi! Sit down Mr. Maeze."
Maeze ignored him and remained standing for a few seconds.

For the second time, "Could you sit down so that we can talk, Okay!" He beckoned Maeze.

Maeze asked him, "Mr. Sedrob, I have come to ask you what I did to you to warrant all the victimizations you have been visiting on my person."

"What happened, Mr. Maeze?" he asked.

"What have I done to you since you came into this company?" Maeze asked.

"What happened? Did Michel know you were coming?" Maeze ignored him.

Maeze said, "I have come to warn you to leave me alone in this company."

Again, he asked Maeze calmly, "Could you sit down, Mr. Maeze?"

When Mr. Sedrob saw that his bids at mollifying Maeze had failed, he turned aggressive, shouting at Maeze to leave his office. Rather than exit, Maeze leapt onto his desk, facing him directly.

Mr. Sedrob raised his voice and shouted, "Help! Help!! Help!!!"

Workers and company security men from every part of the premises streamed into the office. They evinced shock at Maeze's strange position. Some of those employees must have thought Maeze was having a psychotic phase. No black Nigerian in his right mind could confront a white person in that manner.

Maeze issued his warning to Mr. Sedrob: "If you don't leave me alone in this company, the next time I visit you, you won't have the chance to call for help and our story will be on national television."

Before the alarmed throng in the office could learn what had happened, Maeze strode from the scene. He drove straight back to Port Harcourt without visiting the main operational base where Mr. Sedrob had originally abandoned him before his transfer to Port Harcourt.

Maeze was to learn from Michel that before he could return to Port Harcourt, the Managing Director had called him to ask Maeze to return to Warri to see him. That was early the next morning. Of course, Maeze had to go back to Warri to meet the Managing Director. Deciding that the meeting signified the end of his employment, Maeze prepared himself.

And, the story spread across all the branches and sites in Nigeria and abroad that a black Nigerian man went into confrontation with one of the untouchable expatriates. When he marched into the MD's office, the high officials were seated and waiting for him – MD, General Manager, the new Operations Manager and Base Manager.

The MD asked him, "Why did you travel to Warri to meet with Mr. Sedrob?"

Maeze answered, "I don't think there's a need for such a question. What use is it you pretending you'd give a fair judgment in an issue between a black African and a French expatriate? By the way, where is the said Mr. Sedrob in this meeting?"

The men were manifestly astounded at Maeze's audacity. They looked at Maeze, then at one another. The silence in the room was deafening! Mr. Pierre then asked Maeze to leave the office, saying he would invite him later. Maeze told him that he would not leave until they gave him his termination letter. Mr. Pierre, for the second time, asked Maeze to give the management some time to discuss and call him back. He was later handed a query. He had already written his version of the incident and handed that over to the MD.

5. MR. SEDROB MOVED TO LAGOS

That same day, Maeze learned that Mr. Sedrob had hired a moving truck to move his office to the company's Head Office in Lagos while together with his deputy, Kumar, they had flown by air. The two had wished never to set their eyes again on Maeze the rest of their life. Thus, they declared a full-fledged war against Maeze from the comfort of their luxury office, hundreds of miles away from the operational sites of the company.

By this time, Mr. Sedrob started launching his administrative missiles against Maeze. He swore never to let Maeze settle down in the company no matter how dedicated and hard working the young man might be. And, Maeze swore that Mr. Sedrob was his enemy number one, and nothing could make both of them reconcile again. Maeze knew that his days in the company were numbered since all the White men would naturally see him as their enemy. The Managing Director warned him never to meet Mr. Sedrob directly for anything again but communicate through the General Manager or any other supervisor in his team.

Surprisingly, Maeze worked with the company for another ten years before he decided to quit. He grew to become the Site Administration Manager of the company, notwithstanding the position of Mr. Sedrob over finance and administration for the company in Nigeria. To show he needed his own job, Mr. Sedrob also did not quit the company with his friend, Kumar. The question Maeze kept asking himself was if Mr. Sedrob loved his job and didn't want to lose it, why then did he want Maeze to leave the company? Afterall, nobody is happy to be unemployed.

So, while Maeze was in charge of all the company's sites in Bonny, Eleme, Port Harcourt, Obirikom/Obiafu (OB/OB), Qua Ibom terminal, Eket, Warri, Escravos, Forcados, and Kaduna, Mr. Sedrob was the overall Head of Finance and Administration in Lagos. For Mr. Sedrob, Maeze's punishment was the fact that he was shut out of the headquarters of the company in Lagos. In as much as that would have been the most desirable accomplishment, nevertheless, it didn't bother Maeze much, since he was also a boss in his own right. Mr. Sedrob never stopped antagonizing Maeze through his proxies. He would use willing young French people who were in the company to victimize Maeze all over the sites. He would always send queries for everything he received. And of course, Maeze was bound to answer all of them.

The advantage of their relationship to Maeze was that everybody in the company knew that there was an existing quarrel between the Finance and Administration Manager and the Nigerian Site Administration Manager. Whereas the bulk of the work was done on sites supervised by Maeze, Mr. Sedrob and Kumar were in an exclusive area in Lagos where they could manipulate the entire reports of the company to the advantage of their home office. Maeze, and indeed Nigerians, were totally disconnected from whatever forgery that was going on. In a way, that was good for Maeze, because he didn't want to be part of the stealing of his country's income. It was better that they managed their way with the statutory watch dogs, as long as he didn't know what they were all doing with the company. Even in that quarrel, Maeze learned a lot from Mr. Sedrob, both in the queries he continuously issued and the ways to respond to them.

Sometimes, Mr. Sedrob would use company auditors to torment Maeze. It was shameful to see external auditors of the company making themselves willing tools in the hands of people working against the economic establishment of the country. As a reward, the auditors converted some of their employees to Mr. Sedrob's assistants. But our people said, "The person pursuing a little bird is only training it on how to fly." The queries kept Maeze on his toes, knowing that some people were after him.

On one of those occasions, Maeze had to fight it out with one of the young overzealous French expatriates. The man's name was Cent. He seemed to have made a promise to Mr. Sedrob to take Maeze out of the company. Cent had worked in Africa over time and had acquired the requisite experience to deal with non-conforming attitudes like Maeze's. He looked like while he was still on his way to Port Harcourt, Mr. Sedrob had given him his version of the story. The young Cent could not stand the thought of a Nigerian standing up against the "almighty" French head of Finance and decided to continue the challenge to take Maeze out.

In his first week, Cent arrived at Port Harcourt Office, not very interested in his assignment. He asked Maeze to write all sorts of things in the form of familiarization. Maeze, knowing the bond between the expatriates, took time to cooperate with Cent. After testing Maeze, he must have realized he had nothing to nail him.

At first, Cent pretended to be friendly, but Maeze could not be fooled by such a cheap smartness. He also pretended to be cooperative, but deep inside he knew that Cent was looking for a way to nail him. Their pseudo friendship even caused Maeze to buy some of the toy computer accessories that Cent had brought from France at that time, even at exorbitant prices. They both played along.

When Cent could not find anything incriminating, he lost his cool and launched his childish attacks. He decided to remove the computer provided for Maeze by the Base Manager from his office in his absence without his consent. Maeze suspected that Cent must have searched through the computer's memory for anything that could incriminate him. Well, Maeze wasn't much of a computer expert, but he did not think that there could be something of special note saved in his computer. Why would Cent want to move another employee's desktop to his own office without any information? Although he had pretended to mean no harm by only showing that he was a workaholic, Maeze knew that there was more to his disposition than met ordinary eyes.

Gradually, Cent began to show himself as the authentic Mr. Sedrob. He had approached Maeze's assistants to promise them he would give them promotions if they would help him remove Maeze. He didn't know that Africans were trained to read moods and body cues at a young age. The weakest animals' survival in the wild is not always by chance. Their parents had tutored them well. Cent's several attempts to break Maeze's strong relationship with his associates failed him woefully. He didn't know that Maeze was receiving all the information. He must have thought he was a very smart person. While trying to cunningly disgrace Maeze out of office, he had become frustrated himself.

One day, he lost his composure and confronted Maeze physically. In an attempt by Maeze to face him squarely, an office accident occurred. He had left Maeze's office in anger after a shout out. On his way out, a cleaner who was incidentally entering at that same time had caused him to step back. It was during that process that the door he had slammed behind him in annoyance hit him on his head. He fell on the ground and was quickly rushed to the hospital. The bad news spread around town that Maeze had hit Cent with an object on the head. Maeze was really terrified.

In all the milieu between Mr. Sedrob and Maeze on one hand, and the current one between Maeze and Cent, some other people who felt that Maeze's position was enticing were always on the prowl. Of course, there were some Nigerians who used that opportunity to perpetuate their own game plan too. They constantly fed the whites with lies about Maeze so that he would be sacked. One African adage says, "Anyone surrounded by enemies always watches his back."

When Maeze had acquired his first degree and an MBA to crown it in a quick succession, it became clear that Maeze had been preparing to leave the company. He didn't want to leave without a good education. There were many ex-employees who used to seek either re-employment or contracts. Maeze didn't want to ever come to ask for employment or contract. He didn't like how some former employees were treated when they needed help. Maeze was a proud man. He didn't quite see himself fitting into that beggarly ex-employee status. With what Mr. Sedrob was doing to his reputation among the expatriate staff, Maeze thought it would be futile to come back to face these people.

As coalition forces of Mr. Sedrob spread, one of the Nigerian directors decided to play along with them. Maeze knew immediately that the time was up for him to leave the company. The director would call Maeze to arrange logistics and accommodation for his visits. When he arrived in Port Harcourt, he would invite Maeze for discussion in his hotel room. Therein, the big shot would try to get Maeze to discuss the wrongs the white people were doing in the company with an assurance to deal with them. Maeze was smarter than that. He would respectfully provide all the Chairman's needs but would remain exceptionally careful in discussing anything bad about the expatriates. The more the old man tried to lure him into such commitments, the more that Maeze withdrew from such discussions with him. In the process, he would be frustrated until he left Port Harcourt. Maeze was not in a position to decline to meet him. So, he would play along with reasonable caution. The same gullible old man would go to the white men to ask them to remove Maeze from his administration manager position. But, the white people, knowing how much they needed the services of Maeze, used caution instead. They let him know that he had always mounted pressure on them to sack him. Thus, Maeze was extremely careful but courteous each time he interacted with the big shot, whether physically or over the telephone.

Mr. Pierre and his team had left the company and the country. The new Managing Director called for negotiation with the Nigerian Managers for which Maeze was the arrow head. He called for downward renegotiation of their entitlements. Maeze didn't waste time to tell the new MD that he did not accept a downward renegotiation. He opted to receive his entitlements as of that date, according to the existing conditions of service between management and the employees and was not prepared for anything less. Maeze's decision was essentially as a result of the macabre dance by the aforementioned Nigerian director.

By this time, Maeze had saved some money to start his own personal business. He had acquired an MBA and was contemplating going further for doctoral studies overseas. He had also registered and was gradually setting up his private business. He had even been appointed as a coordinator of programs in a federal university in the city. He asked himself, "Why can't I pursue my further studies?" What other place could have been more alluring than the United States of America? With all the childhood fantasies and imagination, that was how Maeze headed to the United States of America for his doctoral studies.

PART II

6. MAEZE TRAVELS TO AMERICA

Maeze's first stop in America was the O'Hare International Airport, Chicago, Illinois in October 2001. His expectations about the United States were not fulfilled when he reached that airport. His challenges in America began immediately. Maeze was to travel by road to his final destination, St. Louis, Missouri. His friend, Chima, who was scheduled to meet him, was not at the airport when Maeze arrived. He joined other passengers at the arrival area waiting for their relatives and friends. He received his first shock when he asked someone for help, and everyone around, hearing his accent, shrank from him. Everyone he approached avoided him. He would later reflect that many in the Western world failed to realize that much they took for granted seemed unfathomable to people from other places. Maeze, despite all his work experience, had never used a phone in a booth.

On the day of his arrival, he stood fumbling with the phone's receiver, desperate for assistance. A certain young woman who must have been in her early twenties finally approached and offered help. She used her own coin to call Maeze's friend, Chima, and helped Maeze get a cab to take him to Chima in River Forest, where he spent the night.

Chima and Maeze had been good friends in Nigeria before Chima left for studies in the United States about four months earlier. That night, he gave Maeze a brief orientation on American life. The next morning, Maeze proceeded to his final destination, St. Louis. After boarding a Greyhound bus, Maeze realized that it was really a long distance to travel by road from Chicago to St. Louis. There were kilometers-long expanses of modern agricultural farms on both sides of the highway. They stopped twice to rest on their way before arriving at St. Louis in the evening. With other incoming students, Maeze was received at the international students' office for the fall semester the next morning. They already had Maeze's details and were expecting him. The documentations were quickly done. The incoming students were taken around the school on a familiarization tour by the international school's officer. An academic adviser was appointed, and normal orientation was scheduled for the next day. The officials were all pleasant as they welcomed the new students into the university.

Another Nigerian student in the cohort met with Maeze. There were usually American families who voluntarily provided accommodation for arriving international students on a short-term basis, prior to the students getting their own permanent accommodation. Maeze and the other Nigerian student, Lawal, lived together for a week in a room provided by an American, James. The house was less than a five-minute walk to the university. He lived in the big house all by himself. He had a sparkling, beautiful compound. There were two Porsche cars parked there and a swimming pool that looked like it had not been in use for a long time. The American was about the same age as Maeze, but you could tell he had all the good things of life around him.

James told Maeze and Lawal that they were always welcome in his house. Maeze was impressed by Americans' hospitality. The university had arrangements with some American residents in the institution's neighborhood. They gave free accommodation for international students referred by the international students' office, mostly those arriving in America for the first time. The students would stay with the hosts for about a week before moving into their own places.

James proved very friendly. He took them out for dinner that first night. They had a good meal in a restaurant. "Wow! This America must be a paradise," Maeze thought. As they chatted that evening, James asked many questions about Maeze's personal life and family, and Nigeria's general political, economic and cultural life. Maeze and Lawal were impressed by their host's generosity in that transitional phase. They were truly in a new world. It was an unfamiliar situation-- someone sharing his home with total strangers. After about a week, Maeze and Lawal found their own apartments and left James'. They felt immensely grateful to James who wished to remain their friend. He gave them his phone number and encouraged them to always call him.

Maeze later strove to continue the association, but James proved unresponsive! He did not take Maeze's phone calls. Maeze considered that James was busy with an office to run. Then there was the incident of the black suit. Maeze had forgotten it in James' house. It was left in the closet in the visitor's room to which James had assigned him. Maeze returned to the house and fetched the house keys where they were usually kept, then went upstairs to get his suit. James called Maeze that evening and asked what he had gone to his house to do. Maeze explained to him that he had gone for his suit after many calls to James were not answered. James seemed unconvinced, impelling Maeze into a lengthy explanation. Fortunately, James appeared to remember seeing Maeze in that suit on one of their outings. Maeze realized that cameras were mounted all over James' premises.

Long afterwards he began to suspect that James had been a security agent in disguise, the kind of secret security agent that appraised new immigrants into the United States. Maeze never met James again throughout his sojourn in America. He could not drop his conviction that James had acted for the security agencies of America.

The university teemed with security checks and suspicion. In the restrooms, you were watched as though you had come to plant explosives. There were checks everywhere. As it was October, just one month after the terrorist incident in America, the tension and vigilance were not surprising.

Another early surprise for Maeze was that his bank was mailing the checks for his account. In his country, check books were not sent to account holders' apartments by mail. Maeze received a package by mail. He would not open it, wondering who could have sent him such a package just a few days after his arrival in the United States. Stories were rife of suspicious items being delivered to people through the post office. People learned to be cautious with packages. When Maeze finally mustered the courage to open the "parcel" and realized that it was the check book he had requested, he reflected on how different things were in his new country of residence.

His studies were going well, and the professors were very compassionate. Of course, Maeze had difficulties understanding American accents. American education was simplified. The course content of the semester's program would be given to students in advance. That "advance reinforcement" helped to counter the barriers of oral communication. The laboratories and computers were highly functional and readily available.

Having an MBA degree from Nigeria, Maeze was advised to do what was called a sequential Master of Arts degree in his chosen field of study. It consisted of studies to learn what was not featured in his MBA program, rather like a complementary or enrichment program.

There were very few Nigerians, mainly academics and medical personnel, living in St. Louis. Maeze met a few of them while working in the university's library. He virtually lived every day in the school. Where else could he have been? Where and who did he know in St. Louis? He started the day's program in the classroom, moved to the computer laboratory and ended in the library.

Maeze occasionally encountered a few of his countrymen. He knew of no church to attend and had begun to feel guilty about not going to church since he came to America. Shopping at the Walgreens one evening, he noticed a church called *Church of the Nazarene*. It was close to his house and looked welcoming. Maeze decided he would be worshipping there as he could not find a catholic church in his vicinity.

The following Sunday, Maeze was at the church. He was the only black person there. Their method of worship was unlike the Roman Catholic ritual to which he was accustomed. The Pastor was a big fellow and demonstrably warm to Maeze. Most of the members seemed pleased by his presence, although some were manifestly shocked to see a person of color and hear an alien accent in their midst.

Most of the congregation wished to know who introduced Maeze to the church. His explanation that he was passing by the Walgreens and responded to the general invitation on a banner did not seem convincing to them. The truth was that Maeze had come on his own volition. A certain family seemed greatly concerned for Maeze. He must have appeared forlorn and lonely to them. The family consisted of a man, his wife and two children. One Sunday after service, they offered Maeze a ride. As Maeze alighted from their car, the wife stepped forward to give him a hug and 'peck.' Maeze, lacking a certain social facility, went for a kiss instead. He noticed that her husband seemed appalled by his act, as it was more ardent than was expected. After that episode, the family became cold and distant to him. He felt the rest of the congregation become similarly aloof. During services, everyone sat as far away from him as possible. Maeze's loneliness and forlornness were acute; yet, he knew of nowhere else to go.

It was at this time that he met Mike, a Nigerian working with a Catholic church in the city. The meeting occurred at a session in the university's computer laboratory. They introduced themselves. Mike was studying for his Master's program in Information and Computer Technology (ICT). Their acquaintance provided the channel that Maeze needed to reach the other Africans in the city. Mike worked with Father Burg, a Parish Priest in a Catholic church in downtown St. Louis. He took Maeze to Rev. Father Burg, a nice person who loved everybody who came to him. He was delighted to meet Maeze.

Thus, Maeze found his first family in St. Louis. He started to attend their church and became part of the Parish family, involved in all the programs of the church, including Mike's

Charity Foundation attached to the church. Mike's charity was a well-established non-profit, 501(c)(3), organization that tried to help the disadvantaged populace with an adult literacy program. Part of the church's premises was used for classes to prepare people for their high school diploma examinations. The school found Maeze very useful in their system, because his MBA degree qualified him to teach mathematics and related subjects. The charitable organization sponsored him for a week's teacher qualification course at the state capital, Jefferson City. Part of the research block, previously not in use in the church, was converted into a set of classrooms. It was there that the adult education program blossomed. Maeze would join other staff members in purely voluntary work at the school. They cleaned the abandoned rooms, repainted them, brought in donated furniture and computers from across the city of St. Louis, and completely revamped the building by direct labor. The charitable organization helped Maeze greatly to develop his human potentials through several seminars. Maeze was happy because without the work at the charity and in the church, he had only his normal academic classes to attend. He worked in the church as a greeter on Sundays, helping the old and infirmed into the church and also serving at mass.

Maeze found a new family he could spend time with after school. From the church, he began to meet other Nigerians in that city. He also met visiting Nigerian priests, attending gatherings and functions of Nigerians in that city. He started to make new friends. He joined in soccer training on Saturday mornings. Thus, Maeze practically settled down in the true sense of the word during his one-year experience studying for his Master's.

St. Louis, however, was extremely cold, too chilly for Maeze's liking. When it was time to choose a place for his doctorate program, he decided to move to Texas where the weather was milder. On completion of his one-year sequential Master's Degree program, Maeze decided to move, notwithstanding that he was being pressured by the university to stay.

7.   FROM ST. LOUIS TO HOUSTON

Maeze had long dreamed of moving to Texas. He had visited it on three occasions and was in love with its weather and social life. There were many Nigerian families in Texas. Houston seemed to have become for them a home away from home. Literally every sphere of human endeavor featured Nigerians. They were found in businesses, universities, hospitals, transportation and sports. What fascinated Maeze most was the business community. Nigerians were in all known businesses: restaurants, African shops, auction dealers and auto shops. There were many social events to choose from every weekend. There were visiting Nigerian families, corporate entities and government representatives year-round. While St. Louis seemed to have attracted mostly academics and health professionals, Houston drew everybody, big and small. Maeze felt very much at home in Texas.

While in Texas, Maeze enrolled in Master's/Doctorate classes, since he was changing to a new area of study – from business studies to an education major. In the big city, Houston, with its large Nigerian population, Maeze found it easy to settle down. He made supportive Nigerian friends. The weather was not unduly challenging. So, Maeze quickly enrolled and did many leveling classes for the first year. He also visited Nigeria that year – his second since coming to America. He had visited during the Easter break of 2002, a mere five months from his first arrival.

Maeze had struggled with depression during his year in St Louis. At some stage, he had begun to consider ending his studies in America and returning to Nigeria for a fresh PhD admission. It was for that reason that he travelled home. Maeze stayed in Nigeria for three months. He wondered continually if the suffering in America was worth the education and qualification received. He considered his young family, children, the many growing business opportunities at that particular period of his career and, on the other side, the suffering he had exposed himself to in America. Maeze had married at a young age, given his ethnic background, and was blessed with four children. His wife was equally young. Together, they had been through the challenge of young couples, and holding on in the struggle to build a family independent of their parents. Maeze loved his children with everything a father could be. He devoted time to take them to school, church and social functions. He ensured they had the best picnics and outing any father could afford for his loved ones. And now, he has left them in the hands of only their mother for America. He asked himself, "Why should I abandon these things for America?"

He was in prolonged pondering of his options when his wife advised him not to end his studies so abruptly. She maintained that abandoning the doctorate program that everyone in Nigeria knew about would be a massive embarrassment. He would be widely mocked if he did not return to America to complete his program. After long and careful thought, Maeze decided the reasonable course for him was to return to his university in America. It was indeed imperative. All his Port Harcourt acquaintances knew that he, a man who had occupied many lofty posts, had gone for a PhD in the United States. To hear later that he could not complete his program would prompt defamatory conjecture. Maeze decided to return to America, if only to complete his program. That was the second time he returned to Nigeria, eleven months after he had first left for his academic pursuit in the United States of America.

Maeze left determined to avoid the shame of not completing doctoral studies. He was worried he might not be allowed to continue with his program because of his lengthy absence. The university had written many letters asking why he had not returned. Consequently, Maeze had to go to the graduate school to clarify his academic status with the office. While there, he was advised to go back to the full Master's Degree program which he had rejected before it was changed to the Master's/Doctorate in Education. He was obliged to do many leveling courses in the Master's program for one year, before continuing to the doctoral courses. Consequently, his doctoral program required a greater number of credit hours instead of about sixty. Maeze eventually did one hundred and four credit hours before completing his doctorate program with the University.

When he left the airport upon returning to America, Maeze did not know where to go. He finally decided to live with a Nigerian family for a few months before sharing an apartment with a friend. Maeze was not allowed to work outside the University while receiving studies as a student. Yet, in the United States, one had to pay for courses to remain a student in good standing and, therefore, in good immigration status.

It was surprising for Maeze to observe that as a Nigerian student, he had only two years of stay approved by immigration in his entry visa, while students from other parts of Africa had five years of student visa approval from embassies in their respective countries. The difference was baffling. As a Nigerian student, if he went to his country after the two-year term, he would not be allowed into the United States without another round of visa-processing. Obtaining a visa from the American Embassy in Nigeria was an indescribably enervating process. A student could, however, decide to continue with his studies after the expiration of his two-year visa period, provided he did not leave the United States. If you stopped taking classes, you would automatically be out of status and would be declared as staying illegally in the country. It would be a dicey undertaking to begin to apply for a visa to return and continue to study in the United States when you had already been enrolled in a program. Usually, this condition made many Nigerians unable to travel to visit their families after two years of living in the United States on student visas. Maeze thought often of his options. If he travelled to Nigeria and the reentry visa was refused, he would lose all his previous payments, as well as the time and energy expended on his studies. He decided he must continue in the program until its completion.

He further reflected that most foreign students in the United States were fettered by immigration policies. They struggled to raise their status to permanent residency. If he had that, his tuition would be reduced. He would also have a work permit and be able to visit his family at will. Maeze was reminded by other Nigerians of an African adage: "You do not climb an Iroko tree two times in a lifetime. Once you climb up, you have to pick everything that you need from the tree top." It was important to regulate one's studies in order to enjoy the benefits of working to earn an income and travel in and out of the country at one's convenience. One also needed to be free of the psychological burdens borne of immigration restrictions.

Indeed, at this time, Maeze was psychologically and spiritually low. As his visa was virtually invalid for reentry, he could not visit his family, for he would lose all he had put into his studies. He felt himself in the middle of an ocean, yearning for dry land. His sole source of strength was that as he continued his studies at the University and took the minimum course load, he was still a legal resident by virtue of his student visa.

Maeze trudged on through this part of his life, hoping to complete his program and go home. At some stage, he considered transferring his studies to a university in Nigeria. He sought the opinions of some acquaintances who lectured at Nigerian universities, and they all urged him to complete his studies in America. They predicted that he would find the Nigerian system frustrating. Maeze was displeased by their counsel. He was weary of America and yearned for home. However, he reflected that his home community was intensely scornful of those who returned from abroad without finishing their studies. Maeze gritted his teeth and resolved to endure the trials of America. He knew his children missed him badly, and his parents too were worried. They knew he was always solicitous of them and were asking: "What could keep Maeze from coming home to shower us with love as usual?"

Maeze had become the main support of the extended family. By this time, his business was suffering from his absence, although he communicated daily with his employees by telephone and email. Maeze, however, knew he had no option but to remain in America.

Apart from his worries, Maeze was overwhelmed by loneliness. His growing depression was so obvious that people around him expressed concern. Maeze decided to seek a companion. A year after his return to Texas, a young woman was introduced to him by a Nigerian family. She was a dark-complexioned beautiful single mother about the same age as Maeze. She had a stable job and also desired a boyfriend.

Jenny was her name. She was lonely after a failed marriage and a few ultimately disappointing relationships. The Nigerian lady who introduced her to Maeze was her colleague at work and found her more dignified than many other women she had known in America. Maeze and Jenny started dating. Surprisingly, on one of their outings, Jenny told Maeze without mincing words that all she wanted was marriage. Maeze was not in a position to offer her that. It was the last thing he expected to hear from her. She had already mentioned her sixteen-year-old daughter to Maeze.

Jenny was dissatisfied with the neighborhood where her daughter attended school, feeling that her daughter would not go there if she had a choice. Jenny preferred the schools in the tranquil neighborhood where Maeze resided. She asked Maeze to include her in his tenancy agreement so that her daughter could benefit from a school in that district. Maeze was scared!

While pondering that issue, they undertook background checks of each other. Jenny then discovered that Maeze had had a failed marriage. Jenny's marriage proposal completely destroyed Maeze's affection for her. After his previous experience with a young woman who deceived him, Maeze dreaded marriage to any woman. He merely wanted a companion. Happily, as his relationship with Jenny was still in its early stages, he decided to bring it to a swift end.

When Jenny felt their relationship was coming to a close, she became very bitter. Maeze began to avoid seeing her, although he spoke occasionally to her on the phone. He ensured that all her offers to see him failed. Jenny proved more resourceful than he realized. One day after school, Maeze returned to his apartment at about eleven. He parked his car at the lot and climbed the stairs to his second-floor apartment. He was opening the door when someone suddenly appeared and called, "Maeze!" He was startled, even as he recognized the voice as Jenny's. Indeed, he was terrified. He had heard stories of American women shooting their partners. He felt Jenny had come to kill him. She craved a husband and was desperate to marry Maeze. Although beautiful, age was not on Jenny's side. Her yearning for marriage did not surprise Maeze. He had seen very successful women in Nigeria abase themselves to be married to some inconsequential man. Society's contempt for the unmarried woman was obviously overwhelming.

Scared, Maeze stood frozen with his hand on the key already inserted into the hole. He had no wish to open the door anymore but merely awaited his fate. She was asking, "Why are you behaving like this to me?" Then Maeze pleaded with her not to shoot him. She assured him that she had no plans to be violent, striving to convince him that she meant well. Maeze asked her to show him the contents of her bag. She opened it to prove she was not carrying a gun, then pleaded with him to open the door so that they could talk indoors rather than in the hallway.

Inside, they both sat on the double couch. Maeze told Jenny plainly that he had no interest in marriage, and since she desired marriage, they should end their relationship. Jenny employed blackmail! She threatened that if Maeze did not marry her, she would report him to the Immigration Service as someone who tried to buy her conscience and help him change his alien status to permanent residence. Maeze reminded her that she knew that was untrue, insisting he could not continue with the relationship. At the end, Maeze wrote Jenny a check for a thousand dollars to compensate her for any losses she had incurred, considering they had already spent money over background checks. He then urged her to leave.

However, Jenny had surprises up her sleeve. She collected the check but told Maeze that his wish was not her desire. She vowed to go to unimaginable lengths, including using the check against Maeze, if he ended their relationship. Maeze did not know what else to do but plead with her to drop her threats. By then, the discussion had gone on for about one and half hours. One thing led to another, and she virtually raped Maeze on that couch.

Maeze would not quickly forget that night. It marked him coming firmly into her power. The apartment complex was in big, beautiful premises with blocks laid out in one-bedroom, two-bedroom and three-bedroom sections. The parking lot was always orderly and spacious enough to accommodate up to a thousand cars. Jenny said Maeze should move from his one-bedroom apartment to a two-bedroomm one, and she would pay part of the rent. The plan was for her daughter to live with her. Maeze and Jenny duly occupied one room, while her daughter lived in the other.

Consequently, Maeze deserted all his contacts and they all deserted him, while he lived in hell with Jenny and her daughter. Maeze's fear was that if she carried out her threat to report him to Immigration, his entire career in the United States would be ruined. He knew Jenny was the kind of woman who would do anything if angered. As she was a citizen, the law would heed her. She had obviously gone to Maeze's on the fateful night determined to get her daughter to live in that school district.

Although Maeze had already divorced his wife down in Nigeria, he was lonely and truly needed a woman beside him. However, his present milieu was not what he longed for, but he felt utterly helpless and handicapped. He and Jenny lived together as man and wife, for Jenny also made him marry her. Maeze continually wondered why Jenny had been so keen on marrying him. Was it the beautiful environment she had seen him living in, or had the Nigerian family told her that Maeze was well-to-do in Africa, and could offer her enormous financial support?

8. LIVING WITH THE JENNYS

Like everyone else, Maeze had heard many stories about hell. He wondered sometimes how it must feel there. He was moved to conclude that calling his life with Jenny hell on earth would not be an exaggeration. Jenny did not know how to cook. He greatly minded that deficiency. Maeze loved his food, particularly African dishes. When hungry, he was not choosy over his food. African, American, Mexican or Caribbean fare would satisfy him. He avoided fast food. Whenever he ate fried food, the oil would show on his face as pimples. Upon arrival in America, he tried assorted body lotions and cleansing, but none could help him. No American over-the-counter products proved effective on his skin.

Jenny did not merely lack knowledge of cooking, but she also hated the process. She intensely disliked the aromas of African food. Jenny's daughter, Cynthia, openly despised Maeze's presence and food. It did not matter that she had the same humble background as Maeze, or that she had just emerged from an underprivileged Houston neighborhood. It did not matter to her that Maeze was the person who helped her mother raise her from existing in their former apartment to their present beautiful upscale apartment community.

Cynthia's presence in the house was a tremendous vexation to Maeze. Her self-contained room was seen first on the right as one entered the apartment. Of course, the dining section was an extension of the living room which made it difficult to avoid seeing Cynthia when all three were at home. Cynthia dropped out of school and was mostly at home playing music. Her room's door faced the kitchen directly. As the kitchen was merely a corner with no demarcations, anyone there would be assailed by the noise from her room. She loved to keep her door open as she chatted with her mother who might be in another part of the apartment.   If she noticed only Maeze was in the kitchen cooking or checking on the washer, she slammed the door as though saying, "I don't want to see you!" Cynthia had her own television and virtually all she needed right inside her room, but perhaps to maintain the normal daughter-mother contact, she would leave her room open most of the time. That was not an issue though. What irked was that she seemed to have forgotten that there was a third person living in the house with them. That attitude of hers, and the fact that Maeze wished to avoid any clashes with the minor, kept Maeze continually on guard.

Jenny wanted Maeze to be the man of the house, always at her side. She was a woman between 40 and 41years, who had not enjoyed that special life of a wife, the husband and daughter, all three living together under one roof. She craved it with all her heart. Maeze, for his part, also longed to make her happy. She found her handsome soul mate to be easygoing and respectful. Jenny longed to have Maeze for the twenty-four hours of the day, seven days a week, three sixty-five days of the year and for the rest of her life. She pretended that she loved Maeze but was only restraining herself in the expression of that love. Over time, she did not stop declaring that he was a jackpot to her. Jenny spoke often of her past relationships and disappointments and her resolve to have nothing to do with any man except Maeze.

Maeze began to feel smothered by Jenny. He learned that she had friends who told her how deceitful Nigerian men were in their relationships with American women. The suspicions roused were a challenge to their serenity. Jenny also loved her daughter dearly and wished Maeze to play the role of supportive father to her. That longing could not be realized, for Cynthia repulsed all of Maeze's paternal overtures. Maeze was, in fact, finding it impossible to feel free in the house and avoided using the living room as much as possible. Conflicts were inevitable, for the overlord role Jenny wanted Maeze to play was not accepted by her tempestuous daughter, Cynthia.

Jenny loved to watch African movies and would ask questions about African family life and village settings, African life styles, extended family system, African food and culture generally. She could go to any lengths to defend her husband's cause as long as Maeze supplied her needs. Jenny told Maeze of her medical history -- the challenges that made her incapable of having another baby since the birth of Cynthia. Maeze believed that she tried as hard as she could to reverse that situation during their marriage, but the situation didn't change. Maeze knew that she wanted to have children for him. She strove to hide some struggles from Maeze, but he knew she was depressed most of the time.

Maeze did his best to help her with physical and emotional support. She had spells of weeping and hysteria. Jenny loved shopping, eating out and going out. Consequently, when she received her pay every two weeks, she would embark on an orgy of spending, often buying things she already had. Maeze thought the spending sprees unnecessary, indeed foolish, but on her insistence would accompany her. They sometimes went to see movies or trained in the park. Jenny was a strong woman, conscious of her figure and sometimes bragged about it, especially her buttocks. In amorous moments in the bedroom, she would flaunt her body at Maeze, rousing him to ardent lovemaking.

She loved to eat out. At restaurants, she even ordered food she would not eat. When Maeze finished his meal, she would insist that he share hers. That to her was the joy of 'hanging out.' Maeze liked her to eat well, but Jenny invariably ate little! Maeze was appalled at her wastefulness, for he only ordered food he would eat. Jenny seemed to feel that plying him with food was indicative of deep love! She grew interested in African cuisine and began to eat rice and plantain and *garri* with soup. She liked having Maeze beside her as she engaged in her various activities.

Jenny dragged Maeze to church on some occasions and introduced him to her pastor. Their church was a small Pentecostal group that had many South American worshippers. It was basically a band of family friends. They often had choir practice. Maeze was uncomfortable on his few visits. A certain friend of Jenny's, slightly older than her, was trying to seduce him. Maeze shrank from the probable consequences of her attraction becoming widely known. It would unleash a scandal on the group, her husband might find out and pronounce Maeze guilty without a hearing, and the woman in her injured pride could cause untold harm to him and Jenny. The woman was influential in the group, an adviser to many of the younger women in their network of friends. Maeze tried a lot to avoid attending activities of Jenny's church, maintaining his normal worship with his traditional church as just a weekly Sunday church attendee. He duly wondered whether the woman was merely testing his faithfulness to Jenny.

Maeze wondered why many Christians would not adhere to the teachings of the gospel. The environment he had found godlike in his early days in the United States, participating in church activities, was Fr. Burg's Church in St. Louis. Father Burg's devoutness reflected the accounts of the zeal and piety of 19th century missionaries in Igbo land. He was a charming and charitable man who would receive everyone from the streets of St. Louis. Fr. Burg opened his door to the homeless, served food, and paid electricity, water and other bills of the indigent. He preached God's word with conviction, yet without attempts at coercion. Fr. Burg's was the only place where Maeze sometimes felt comfortable enough to sleep over.

Jenny sometimes joined Maeze in worship at Maeze's own church, now in Houston. Even as he was now living in Houston, far away from Fr. Burg's St. Louis parish, he remained a true man of God, accommodating visiting African priests and sojourners in the United States, making them feel they had a home at his church. Their church service was one hour long, short and direct, unlike the practice in his home country, Nigeria. Church services in Nigeria lasted for at least three hours. Maeze liked going to study at the University of Houston public library on Sundays. Consequently, after church service and his household chores, he would leave for studies and stay out until about eight o'clock at night. Going to his school or to study at the library gave Maeze much-needed relief from the company of Jenny and her daughter.

9. POOR ACADEMIC WORK

Maeze was determined to complete his studies and leave the United States after all the frustrations of failing to normalize his stay through marriage with Jenny. His life with Jenny remained a source of pain. Jenny's attachment to him was suffocating. Yet, she seemed to be working against his achieving the freedom to live in the United States – the very goal she had vowed to help him realize. It was clear for anyone who lived in the United States that, if you had no legal status there, you missed out on 'the dream' with its attendant liberty and happiness. It was unbelievable that Jenny, Maeze's wife who swore to love him, should not be working for his achievement of full legal residence.

Maeze could neither answer the question, nor even understand the essence of their union. He was confused, especially when Jenny sometimes threatened to report to the authorities that he was using her only to legalize his stay. Jenny's phone calls to Maeze were incessant and inconsiderate, without a thought to where he was or what he might be doing. He might be in class taking a lecture or making a presentation, at a church service or a meeting. If he failed or dawdled over taking a call, it prompted quarrels – a source of further stress for him. Jenny insisted that Maeze must set his phone on silence so that he would always take her calls, at least to be able to send her a short message saying he could not take her call.

Jenny had Maeze's class schedule in school, his unofficial schedule with his study group, and his library schedule. Even if Maeze were driving, he was required to answer Jenny's calls. He felt as though clamped in a monitoring device. If Jenny's last call was five minutes earlier, she would guess where her husband had reached on his route, and query him like a military commandant,

"Why have you not got to Gessner by 59?" Maeze would have to answer and explain that he had to detour to buy gas. He would be questioned further on how much gas he bought, then reminded of the last time he bought gas, all making Maeze feel he was under surveillance. If his voice betrayed irritation, that would draw more queries. If Maeze sounded pleasant, the question would be, "What could be making you so happy?"

Jenny was obviously insecure and obsessive, but Maeze was tortured. He had no one to bare his soul, none to soothe his strains, and he sank under the weight of psychological assaults. Maeze was simply alone and miserable. Jenny's nagging did not merely unsettle. It was totally blighting his life. He could not concentrate on his studies – his reason for going to the United States. He longed to achieve permanent legal residency in America, reducing the high cost of tuition and saving himself a rigorous session with an unpredictable interviewer at the American Embassy. Maeze now despaired of seeing the process through to the end. It certainly could not be achieved in his present crushing circumstances.

Sometimes, in somber retrospection, Maeze would ask himself why he ever decided to take his present route in life. He recalled that he had been doing well in Nigeria and castigated himself for not continuing his studies there. He had many university professors as friends in Nigeria and would have had no difficulties in completing his studies. He had the required resources, and his business had been thriving. Why on earth did he abandon his young family to undertake this tortuous journey? For three years, Maeze had not set eyes on his children, aged parents and the rest of the family members. What sort of irresponsible life had a grown man like him drifted into? The prolonged estrangement from his family was driving him mad.

Although they spoke regularly on the phone, the long-distance chats were not enough.

Maeze had to be furtive over communicating with his family. He usually did it while at school. If Jenny had known he spoke to them while at school, she would have become even more suffocating. She always watched him closely when he used the phone in her presence. If the conversation was with a family member, she would feign concern but might start an argument afterward.   She was jealous that Maeze paid more attention to his children than to her. As for his former wife, she could not even bear to hear Maeze speak to her. However, it was only on the phone that Maeze could reach his children.

Maeze's academic work suffered greatly on account of Jenny's nagging and obsessive behavior. That worried Maeze tremendously. Even if Jenny called him when he was in school studying with his group, he was bound to answer or send a message immediately to explain how he was engaged. That in itself was a distraction, because her calls would continue until she set eyes on him. At his final examination, Maeze had to repeat one of four courses that he needed to qualify as a doctoral candidate. If he failed at the second attempt, his dream would be shattered. For that second effort, he prayed hard to God and promised himself that it must be achieved, determinedly ignoring Jenny's nagging.

Ultimately, Maeze's plans of changing his immigration status from student visa (F1) to permanent stay seemed like medicine after death. He pondered his situation. He had seen God's favor in his life and was doing well in his career back in Nigeria. In America, his life had suddenly taken a dive. He decided his best course of action was to endeavor to complete his studies and leave America for good. Already, the immigration interview had proved unsuccessful. In America, if you have no permanent legal status, but just a student visa, you are half-existing. You have no right as you cannot defend your course freely. You are left with a feeling that something crucial is absent in your life.

How could you pay five times more for your education? You can't get a credit rating; so, you spend more on property and very many personal needs. It would not matter how many years you had lived in the country. If you are not an academic or medical professional, everyone in the streets would view you with suspicion and disrespect.

Maeze asked himself, "Why are you wasting your precious life living in America?" Fortunately, Jenny never tried to meet his classmates in the study group. Maeze was glad of that, for she would have destroyed the only relationships he had. Her low self-esteem and worldview seemed to have made her stay away from scholars. Sometimes, in happy moments, she would hail Maeze as an academic, lauding his achievements and acknowledging that they conferred status in American society. At such times, her respect for him was manifest.

10. A RECKLESS SPENDER

Prior to Maeze's cohabiting with Jenny, she had lived a humble life with her daughter. It seemed she devoted all her career earnings to looking after her daughter. They lived in a standard apartment complex, riding buses around the city, struggling to exist within Jenny's income. Maeze guessed she needed a husband figure, not just for the physical responsibilities but for overall emotional fulfillment. Now, having Maeze in her life seemed to have made Jenny feel that her life's ambition had been fulfilled. She was reveling in imperiousness.

Jenny seemed intent on garnering all the spousal care she and her daughter had lacked in her previous marriage. Maeze was surprised that Jenny expected him to meet her financial needs, as though from an unlimited pocket. He wondered if some people had told her he was affluent in Nigeria. He tried to make her realize he was struggling through tuition and feeling the pinch of paying those prohibitive fees as a poor immigrant without a work permit. Jenny, heedless of his cautionary words, continued to spend without restraint.

Maeze tried his hand as psycho technician and nurse assistant in some obscure hospitals, and even the business of auction car exports to Nigeria. He told Jenny of his struggles. Jenny would appear to listen, only to repeat her splurges whenever there was a little money in their account. They had opened a joint account – a condition for a married immigrant to change his immigration status. They agreed they would each pay one thousand, five hundred dollars into the account every month. Besides theevidence of a joint account, other documents evidencing joint payment of insurance, electricity, water, house and rent bills were required. Those documents would all prove that the two were living together, as required by Immigration and

Naturalization Service (INS) to determine Maeze's fitness for the status he wished to assume.

That was the hardest test of their marriage. In spite of all the declarations of love and eagerness to upgrade Maeze's status so that he could begin to enjoy the benefits of living in America (American Dream), Jenny seemed to be in conflict with herself over the realization of that goal. Maeze did not quite understand what she was struggling with inside. Being a psychotherapist, he knew of personality disorders or "behavioral quirkiness" which could be debilitating and render a sufferer helpless. He couldn't help in his own case with Jenny.

Consequent on their application for his change of status, she awaited an invitation to an interview from the Immigration and Naturalization Service. The interview date could be at any given time. Couples would attend the interview with all available documents to support the application. Just like when you submit an invoice for a service contract, you would be expected to attach the job order, certificates of job completion, waybill or delivery notes, and all justifications. The documentation for a marriage interview would include bank statements showing the spouses' home was run from a joint account. Bills like rent, water, tax returns, were all done together. Jenny was not forthcoming with her contributions as agreed. Maeze was bound to make those deposits if they really wanted to make a successful marriage interview. To make matters worse, monies paid into the accounts were not left there to service their expenses as at when due. While Maeze kept the checkbook used for payment of various bills, Jenny insisted on keeping the bank card. As soon as cash was deposited into the account, Jenny would start assailing the account with debits. When Maeze seized the bank card from her, she obtained another one without his consent. She seemed intoxicated by bank cards, like a child playing with a fascinating toy.

Jenny was utterly incapable of self-control over use of bank cards. Maeze had heard tales of people misusing money but could never have imagined the depth of that habit in Jenny. She spent from that joint account as though she had won a jackpot. Maeze remained alert over not falling behind in payments. He had seen the huge risks of falling behind with bills in America. The debtor would be like one stripped of rights and privileges and clamped up in a cage. Maeze had alarming hints of imminent doom but felt unable to avert the catastrophe. If they fell behind in payment of rent, they would be sent packing. The conditions were clearly stated in the rent agreement. The trouble of moving would be too much for anybody. Maeze had enjoyed every moment of his stay in their current apartment. Should their electricity supply be disconnected, they would be stricken with heavy colds and unable to cook. In America, there was no choice over utilities or means of making do if your supply was disconnected. Although she had full knowledge of the dire consequences of default in that system, Jenny remained nonchalant. When she acted wrongly, she would avoid Maeze and become very much attached to her daughter, Cynthia. They would both seem to be enjoying the episode, mocking him. The situation became a 'two versus one' or 'America versus Africa' or 'citizens versus immigrant.' Lacking a permanent stay in America was a huge disadvantage.

The interview date was fast approaching, and they had not prepared for it, the appointment that would procure or forbid his permanent residence in the country. Cynthia would join her mother to intensify their mockery of Maeze, while Jenny occasionally looked at Maeze to relish his reactions. To infuriate him further, she would ask annoying questions. However Maeze tried to avoid or ignore Jenny, it proved impossible not to answer her questions. She would prod: "Didn't you hear my questions?"

Sometimes, Maeze paid the rent twice. Although sufficient money would be in the account when the check was issued, the available funds would be greatly reduced by Jenny before the landlord received his due. The check would then be returned unpaid. Maeze learned to pay from some other sources, to avoid the penalties of non-payment.

That pattern continued over some months. All other bills suffered the same fate. Meanwhile, Maeze needed to prepare the immigration interview package against the fateful day. He valiantly bore his cross, thinking how disastrous it would be to appear at the immigration office with insufficient documentation, despite having truly lived with Jenny.

He had faced many challenges: meeting all the conditions stipulation by the Immigration and Naturalization office, suffering in his studies because of Jenny's nagging, losing contact with his associates and relatives, not seeing his family for years, and restricted in his phone conversations with them. Of course, peace still eluded him in his own house. Notwithstanding all these, Jenny was not taking much interest in assisting him to gain freedom and happiness. It began to appear unlikely that Maeze would gain his permanent residence. He began bitterly to regret coming to America.

He decided to endure to the end, the undeserved circumstances he had found himself in the hands of Jenny and Cynthia. They continually fell behind in paying bills, and he continued to augment the shortfalls, trying also to make deposits in their joint account whenever Jenny removed cash. That would be a determinant of his grant of his requested status. Jenny suddenly demanded a car! Lacking the good credit to buy one herself, she insisted her husband who did not have a credit history, good or bad, should stand in for her. She felt having a car was a widespread privilege enjoyed by many of her friends, which she too was entitled to. At first, Maeze thought the yearning for a car was only a momentary whim, but shortly realized she was serious,

Jenny nagged and threatened and raged. After a few weeks, Maeze knew to his dismay that she would not even attend the immigration interview with him unless he met her request. He made her a gift of a 1995 Ford Escort he bought when he first arrived in the United States. The car was in excellent condition. Jenny rejected it. She preferred Maeze's 2004 Nissan Xterra bought recently at an auction sale. The car had only five thousand miles of use and was in superb form having been carefully serviced and prepared to be sent to Nigeria. Maeze thought Jenny must be insane to even imagine he would give her that car. It had cost him much to put in its present enviable form, and ready for shipment.

However, the immigration interview was approaching fast, and Maeze knew he could not afford to trifle with Jenny. He feared the young woman might fail him when they were asked to come for the interview. He was not even sure that any deeds of his could make her see his residency project to its conclusion. Maeze considered his situation a coin with two heads, concluding that in both cases, Jenny would emerge winner. Jenny however made it clear that he should either accede to her demands or lose her cooperation.

Maeze knew that a disaster hung over his credit worthiness in America, a facility he absolutely needed for his future. He had always trusted himself over meeting his financial commitments. Jenny, of course, could not be trusted over issues of financial prudence or accountability. Yet they were on the brink of a long-term financial commitment, with Maeze's name in front of the contract.

Within a few days, Jenny had gone around and obtained quotes, deciding on a Nissan Altima. Maeze followed her reluctantly to the dealer. The 1995 Ford Escort was promptly traded in, and off Jenny went off with a new car. Her lifelong dream was realized. Her daughter could not contain her joy. They not only lived in a privileged environment, but also drove a new car. Their lives were completely transformed, thanks to Maeze's presence in their lives. They now ate out as a family, went to movie theatre, shops, and sometimes, church services.

Shortly afterwards, Cynthia wished to learn to drive. She had dreamt of it for a long time. Cynthia after all was now seventeen, and her mother had a car to herself, thanks to her African husband. Maeze, rather than gratify that desire wished to introduce placidity into Cynthia's life. Cynthia went berserk! She had a number of wild friends, and they were continually 'hanging out.' On occasions, returning late with her, the noise of their socializing would echo throughout the otherwise quiet apartment complex. The music from her room would blare while they danced all night long. Maeze would stay right inside the room on such occasions. The "mom" would alternate between their bedroom and Cynthia's, as though to ensure all was well in both rooms. She knew that Maeze detested both the din and Cynthia's unchecked rush into self-destruction. Cynthia, however, ruled her mother, not the other way around.

Maeze sometimes empathized with Jenny. A woman who had had no happiness in her life prior to this time, she appeared depressed every day of her life. Cynthia seemed her sole spur and tonic in life. She was invigorated whenever she saw Cynthia. She felt she should let her daughter live her life. The name of Cynthia's boyfriend duly slipped into Maeze's consciousness.

Maeze had long reflected on how teenagers in America did not hide their love affairs from parents. Parents claimed the openness enabled them to supervise their children and help them avoid mistakes that might mar their lives. He had concluded that the practice had its benefits.

Cynthia's boyfriend's name was Rex. Jenny and Cynthia talked incessantly of him. Maeze wondered if they had checked on the young man's character. They seemed consumed in the euphoria of the handsome young man in Cynthia's life. Maeze heard the name "Rex" over hundred times a day. It was disappointing to learn that Rex was a mere shift hand at the fast food restaurant. Cynthia was not working but depended on the mother for her needs. Jenny's strange decision to assume the financial responsibility of supporting Rex added immensely to Maeze's woes. Jenny defended Rex by protesting that he did not earn much in his job. Jenny and her daughter often bought clothes and other gifts for Rex, saying he had no family and was trying to return to school.

Cynthia became pregnant. Maeze was relieved, thinking that Cynthia would move in with her boyfriend. Jenny however decided on her own that Cynthia would remain with her. The bond between mother and daughter was very strong. Cynthia's pregnancy was fraught with complications. On several occasions, Maeze was called to help rush Cynthia to the hospital. Twice, she had to be carried from the third floor of the apartment to the car. On account of the solicitude showered on pregnant mothers in Africa, and the desire to give the best to an unborn baby, Maeze was unflagging in his devotion to Cynthia. An adage held by his community' was: "Whatever the situation, a pregnant woman must be attended to first." Maeze had no option but to assume the full role of father of the house. The pregnancy brought out

Cynthia's nature: She was often rude and ruthless. No kindnesses of Maeze's were appreciated.

Cynthia took advantage of her condition to perpetuate her dominance of the house. The mother became evermore deferential to her, Cynthia became increasingly messy and nasty. During the last trimester of her pregnancy, Rex disappeared from the scene. The name was no longer mentioned. Questions to Jenny as to Rex's whereabouts drew irritation and curtness. It was obvious that the relationship was foundering, although nobody told Maeze what the problem was. However, neither Rex nor even his shadow was seen! Jenny and Cynthia remained silent about the situation.

Maeze's immigration application was duly rejected for a second time. Now he asked himself: "Is this truly the best for me? Is this the best decision I have taken at this stage of my life, considering my age and family status? I have come very far considering my family background. God has been good to me in business, marriage, and health-wise. What exactly am I seeking in the United States that made me abandon my home and now go through this lengthy suffering?" There were no answers. Then an inner voice reminded him that he had not completed his doctorate degree. He reflected and counted again, ...2006!, 2007!!. At least, two more years of study. If all went well, he had about two more years to spend in his hellish relationship before he could leave. The immigration matter for him had become a forgotten issue. Indeed, Maeze felt himself tumbling into a deep sea.

He reflected on America's harsh weather. "In Nigeria, I would dress plainly as it pleased me no matter the time and day of the year and would move around freely anywhere in the country without any fear or thought of anybody going to ask me embarrassing questions. I know the police are the rude tormentors of our freedom of movement and there are criminal elements there, especially on the highways. Those are the everyday challenges of living in Nigeria. Yes, there is carnage on the highways because of non-adherence to traffic laws, yet the freedom is immeasurable beside the total lack of freedom, the rape and abuse being encountered here on a daily basis. What am I doing in the United States?" When Maeze first arrived in America, the weather had given him much thought. It was so cold that only the fittest could survive it. After battling the weather for months, he told himself the truth: that place was not meant for him.

However, Maeze considered that he had already left Nigeria, was enrolled in a programme, and that American qualifications were esteemed much higher than Nigerian ones across the globe. He resolved that he would at least complete the programme he had begun, avoiding that jeers that would certainly be roused if he failed to complete his course. He should certainly not return home without achieving the goal of a doctoral degree.

Over the years, he had of course experienced many summers. However, the agony of his first winter was never effaced from his memory. Maeze was allergic to the house-heater. He expected it would only warm the house to a comfortable temperature. Things reached a point where both the heater and the cold weather became intolerable to Maeze. With the heater, he felt suffocated, finding its warmth no substitute for sunlight's natural heat. Maeze had prepared for a class that was scheduled for 11:30am. Bus time at the bus stop nearest to his apartment was ten minutes to every hour. Maeze got to the bus stop at fifteen minutes to 9am. He waited in the chilling cold until 9:30 am, feeling there might have been a delay. There was no bus in sight and he was alone at the bus stop. It did not bother him much that there were no persons about, because that bus stop, and indeed, many others around St. Louis, were not patronized much. Most people drove their cars rather than use public transportation. Buses often had few passengers. From the bus stop to the university was less than a ten-minute ride. Therefore, rather than wait another hour for the next bus, and freeze whilst waiting, Maeze began to walk. His backpack hung, hands tucked into his pockets, he marched along. Maeze saw himself as a strong, young man who had overcome tremendous challenges at home, and would not be daunted by any obstacles America posed.

That walk proved a suicide mission. Maeze trudged through piles of snow. Not a soul was to be seen, but only a few vehicles. Only the good Lord knew what those drivers thought of the sanity of that lone pedestrian in the snow as they drove past him. Maeze did not try to imagine the thought of people indoors peering at him through their tightly locked windows. By the time he got to school, his neck felt stiff and hard as a stone. He was totally drenched. It proved his resilience and luck that he did not have to be rushed to the emergency department of the nearest medical facility on campus.

Maeze also remembered how he got lost on his first Independence Day holiday in the United States on November 4, 2001. It was just under three weeks since he arrived from Nigeria, and he had only been in his new apartment for a few days. He had boarded a bus from the University library, and for some reason passed his bus stop. The diction of the African American woman driver was incomprehensible to him. By the time Maeze realized they had passed his destination, the bus had gone far. Assuming the bus would turn and return on the same course, he relaxed. The bus was becoming empty. The driver must have surmised that Maeze was new to the country, given his deep African accent. She began to address Maeze as though she longed for revenge for some misdeeds suffered in the past from people of Maeze's ilk. Eventually, every other passenger left and she was alone with him. "Where you gonna stop?" she asked him. Maeze tried to explain his predicament. He did not quite know his way. She kept mute until she reached a certain point, parked the bus, and alighted saying, "The final destination of the bus! Get off I'm locking the bus!"

Maeze's bids to ask her questions were ignored. He had never felt so humiliated in his life. She was standing outside, and turned her face eloquently expressing that she was in no mood to waste her time by answering his questions. Perhaps she was mindful of her safety – Maeze could have been a terrorist or suicide bomber for all she knew. Maeze, tremulous, persisted: "Ma'am, please how can I get back to Webster University?" She pointed at the opposite direction dismissively. Maeze was dazed and confused. Even a fool could grasp the woman's feeling – she hated to see people like him in her country. The "Nine-Eleven" tragedy had occurred two months earlier. America was explosive. A call had been made on the patriotism of all American citizens, charging them to find the perpetrators of that monumental crime. Every immigrant was therefore a suspect, especially those whose behavior appeared odd to Westerners. It seemed that those with strong foreign accents like Maeze's topped the list of suspects! Wherever they went in America at that time, they were watched with suspicion and hostility. At the Webster University where he enrolled for a Masters' program, the Janitors habitually spied on international students. Maeze noted that whenever he entered the restroom, especially when no other persons were about, he would be trailed after suspiciously. On one occasion, Maeze felt very embarrassed when a young female cleaner who looked mentally challenged followed him about the restroom.

He thought of warning her to stop following him but feared doing so would somehow worsen his situation. If it had been in Nigeria, Maeze would have told her outright never to be seen within the male restroom when it was occupied; but here in America, he wouldn't try it. Even if his body language alone expressed his fury, the wrath of American security officials would have descended on him. Not even the international students' personnel would have sympathized with his behavior. They claimed that men in Africa were too overbearing and mistreated their womenfolk, and it was time African men were taught some hard lessons about feminism and equality.

Maeze felt compelled to tell the bus driver: "thank you ma'am!" She was silent and baleful as though asking him to go to blazes with his greeting. Maeze alighted from the bus and walked straight to the nearest restaurant which was by a plaza that was still open. He saw a sign on top of the restaurant "LOUISIANA FISH CUISINE." Maeze had heard much about Louisiana people and their fine food. He had some money, so ordered food and ate. After eating, Maeze politely showed the owner of the restaurant the address of his apartment. That African American woman, the opposite of the bus driver, was soft-spoken and friendly. She urged Maeze not to worry, picked up her yellow pages book, and dialed a cab number. A few minutes later, a cab arrived. On their way back, the cab driver chatted with Maeze.

"Where you from"? He asked

"Nigeria," Maeze answered.

"Okay, I'm from Egypt."

"How long you been here?" He asked.

"Couple of Days," Maeze answered.

"And you?" Asked Maeze.

"Twenty-two years," He answered.

Maeze, already becoming Americanized, exclaimed "wow!"

"What you come for? Visiting or staying?" the cab driver queried, and Maeze told him he had come to study.

"Oh! You're an international student?" Maeze confirmed that he was. The inquisitive man wished to know the university Maeze was attending, and when told remarked, "That's interesting!"

They continued their conversation along the streets of St. Louis. From their discussion, Maeze learned that many foreigners were not happy in America. The driver related a tale of woe: his odyssey in America, now in its third decade. Maeze was rapt, even as he gazed through the windows at a beautiful city adorned with neon lights. The car meandered through the lovely city, along highways and past blocks of nice neighbourhoods, and finally stopped at the door of Maeze's apartment.

Maeze was thankful to have reached home without incident. He placed the five-dollar turkey he had bought at the restaurant on the table. It was purchased in the spirit of celebration and not because he had any craving for turkey. He was incredulous that such a big chunk of meat had been sold for five dollars. He reflected that it might take him weeks to finish the turkey, then thought of the poverty at home. 'So much food in America, and food so scarce in my country!"

Their immigration interview date finally arrived. Maeze had taken days to arrange the required documents: evidence of house rent payments, contracts, telephone bills, electricity bills, water bills, insurance and bank account statements, and tax returns. By this time, Jenny and her daughter were acting as though they were about to hand Maeze a jackpot win. Jenny moved about with more boldness than he had ever seen in her. She addressed Maeze in the tones of a commander addressing his subordinates. Her demands became just too much for Maeze.

She wanted a gold wedding ring. All the beautiful things of life Jenny had dreamt for, but lacked in her entire life, were presented to Maeze. She wanted all sorts of expensive clothes. She wanted her car fixed with alloyed wheels and some spectacular fittings. She wanted her daughter to be taught how to drive and gave Maeze that assignment. Those driving lessons became the hardest task of Maeze's life. Cynthia was impatient, rude and careless. Maeze tried to endure her insolence for the first two days of the training but could not continue to tolerate it. On their third lesson day, Cynthia was speeding to the back of a Mercedes car in front, when Maeze who was seated next to her called her gently to attention. She was obviously offended at how she had been addressed, perhaps not with the deference to which she had grown accustomed from Maeze.

Cynthia hurriedly applied the brakes just inches away from the Mercedes. She then opened the door and left Maeze in the middle of the road, angrily walking away. In fact, the car was still in motion. She had not bothered to engage the gear lever in "park" position. Maeze had to disengage his seatbelt and leap into the driver's seat to avert the car colliding with another car. He called to Cynthia to please return and continue with their training. The saving grace for him that day was that the learners "L" sign was on the car number plate. Other drivers manifested angelic patience throughout the episode. The shame of facing all the surprised and curious faces on the busy road was crushing.

That incident was a big trial for Maeze. He considered telling his wife about it, then decided against it. He knew she would hold that her daughter had done no wrong, and even castigate Maeze for rousing Cynthia to rage in the streets.

Maeze drove to the nearest gas station, bought some petrol and drove straight to the University of Houston Library. He had become addicted to that library, the environment infusing his soul with serenity. He could study and print as many papers as he wished there, without paying anything. Whilst there, he also managed to bury the gnawing questions as to why and how he drifted into his present hell. Those thoughts continually plagued Maeze.

Maeze no longer saw his Nigerian community. In his early years in Houston, he had made friends, both in the city and at the university center. Now, he was in contact with only a few and only on the phone. Efe was the only person from home that he knew.

Efe's story was fascinating and representative of the intriguing realities encountered by many Nigerian immigrants. Efe had been in the United States for about thirty-one years. To many Nigerians, he was a very "big shot" considering his foreign exposure, and the fact that he had helped numerous family members come to the United States. Efe had also built a big family house in his fast-growing hometown in western Nigeria. On one of his memorable visits to his motherland, when things were still going well in his home country, Efe had been celebrated by family, friends and community as a successful "son of the soil." He kept tactfully silent about his experience with his divorced wife.

He brought his wife to America from Nigeria and helped her to be trained as a nurse. Maeze never met Efe's former wife throughout his stay in the city. However, the two pretty daughters she had with Efe and abandoned, proved that their mother was strikingly beautiful. The story was that the woman had arrived in the United States, uneducated and uncouth, but expecting bliss and fulfillment. Of course, like many people arriving in "God's own country", she realized that her husband was not quite the dazzling success she had thought him when he sought her hand in Nigeria. She realized rather late that her husband, like any immigrant, was struggling with life in the plainest sense of the phrase. Efe was working with the city of Houston. However, his promotion and opportunities were not what they would have been in the United States. He was merely living from hand to mouth, from pay-check to pay-check. In fact, he was barely surviving on his meagre earning. The house he built down in Nigeria was financed by the student loans he obtained while studying for his undergraduate program. Like most people, he had acquired property with part of the loan and would repay the loan for the rest of his working life. His people in Nigeria thought he built it from his earnings. Families in Africa were delighted by the material acquisitions of their relatives in the United States. They expected those who went to America to be transformed into millionaires, buying opulent cars and garnering qualifications along the way.

Efe's wife found on arrival in America that he was struggling with two jobs to continue to defray a huge debt burden. He had lost his credit worthiness and was faced with bills on his little monthly income. Their apartment was in a deprived neighborhood. When she arrived, she had liked the house and the euphoria of living in the U.S did not let her realize how downtrodden they were. After all, everywhere looked beautiful with all the amenities of water and electricity. As years went by, she had two girls in quick succession, passed her nurse certification examination, and began to regret rejecting some wealthy suitors who had sought her before Efe came from America. Her work as a nurse earned her far more than her husband's combined earnings in the two jobs he was doing. She had come to terms with the reality of working and raising her daughters all by herself, and of operating a joint bank account with her husband. The husband's bank account was subject to regular huge, mandatory loan repayment deductions. She did not envisage the deductions. The husband had filed for change of immigration status as married dependent relative and they needed the evidence of a joint bank account to show they both lived together. Immigration and naturalization service needed the evidence to justify the approval of their application. Efe, like most Nigerians living in America, had hoped that after sponsoring his wife through the nursing certification program, and with the added income, he would be in a position to repay his long-outstanding loans. That, hopefully, would help him to regain his greatly eroded freedom in the United States. The wife on the other hand could simply not come to terms with the hardships of existence in America, considering the grand dreams she had before following Efe to the United States. She felt she had been played false, as she remembered the rich and handsome men who had pursued her. One of those suitors had promised to make her a royal highness attended by numerous servants. Those missed opportunities were recalled with choking bitterness.

Efe had taken her to Nigerian parties, showing off his beautiful wife to friends. Nigerian men seemed to be competing among themselves as to who married the most beautiful woman from Nigeria. Many of them had left home when their communities were backward, but the situation had changed greatly over the years. They failed to realize how advanced many African communities had become over use of modern communications. Africans arriving newly in America soon realized that life was not exactly as they had watched on television. The weather, culture, hard work, and lack of financial help when in need were some of the hard facts they learned only when they were in America.

Efe's former wife was disappointed by the time she understood the true life of America. Not long after her arrival, she began to interact with neighbors. When Efe left for work, she mixed freely with the men around the apartment complex, just as was done in Africa. Efe learnt about the new life his wife had found with his friends and set a wiretap around their house. Its revelations about his wife were revolting. Efe confronted her with the outrage of an African "head of the home," and she fought back. She had been tutored by her numerous nurse/colleagues that women had power in America. The family feud had worsened and become public. They finally ended their young marriage at the county court. The wife was freed from bondage by the court, while Efe was to keep the two girls because he had proved his wife's life of irresponsibility to the court. She was rather to pay alimony to Efe. For a man, the physical and emotional burden of raising two girls was enormous, but he soldiered on in his task. He went virtually everywhere with his two little girls and grew accustomed to strangers' questions as to their mother's whereabouts. "She's at work," he would say briefly.

For fifteen years, he raised his daughters all by himself. It was not an uncommon situation in America. In Nigeria, their mother would have been ashamed and hidden her face from her relatives and friends. In America, it was a commonplace situation. Countless Nigerian marriages failed in America. There had been frustration, divorces, suicides and homicides all in the quest of the American dream. The two different cultures met and clashed continually in the new world of diversity and multiculturalism.

Maeze's friendship with Efe flourished. Maeze worked on his doctorate degree, while Efe concentrated on his masters and certification. Efe hoped to retire soon from his job at the county and practice. He loved going to clubs and Nigerian parties, womanizing and drinking. Efe's townspeople reveled in partying and merriment while Maeze's were chronic business people who could make money from inconsequential objects. While Maeze could make more money than Efe, Efe showed him that life was sweeter when the money was spent.

Efe loved women a lot but always had difficulty in wooing them. He often started his gestures with boyish excitement, then would suddenly fail. Efe related how, lacking a woman in his life, he often masturbated for sexual satisfaction. He sometimes expressed his crushing frustration and loneliness.

Maeze was not often keen on listening to Efe's tales of woe. He kept his own marital frustrations to himself. His sufferings at the hands of Jenny and Cynthia were like weights strapped to his chest. Maeze was often depressed. On occasion, he would begin to discuss the problem with Efe, then stop abruptly. He did not trust Efe sufficiently to share his secrets. Every Nigerian in America was agog to know if his fellow Nigerian had permanent residency or citizenship, family status and employment, and whether the person had to return to Nigeria soon. Those returning to Nigeria were deemed not to have legal status or to have lots of cash in Nigeria. All others remained in America. Some tried to live partly in Nigeria and partly in America.

The day of the immigration interview finally arrived. Maeze had assembled all the necessary documents relating to their marriage showing that they were living together. You could never be sure with interviewers of INS, whether the visa interview was in one's home country in Africa or inside America, no matter your level of preparation and sense of sincerity. The interviewers called in Jenny and Maeze separately. Maeze had all the facts to show their marriage was genuine, but only the Almighty knew what Jenny would say inside. When she emerged from the interview, she seemed uneasy. Maeze was called in and the interviewer, a woman, was brisk. When Maeze said "thank you" after the short interview, she did not answer him. He felt her attitude boded ill. Americans are business-minded, abjuring Africans' lengthy pleasantries and small talk. Maeze felt that if they had decided to reject his application, they would not waste their time and his on what they knew to be only futile chatter. The woman only took Maeze into the room, then brought him out without any questions. That was the end of the interview!

Now Maeze was convinced that Jenny had ruined his case. He had heard of an African living with his American wife, whose wife testified against him in court when he was being prosecuted. The man was shocked to learn his own wife was working for the security agency investigating him.

Maeze was dejected by the interview experience. He lost all hope. Jenny's behavior worsened his misgivings. As she came out of the interview chamber, she was alluding to Maeze's first marriage as the cause of their problems! Stories abounded of interviews of people who had had a failed marriage. The onus was usually on the sponsor, who in Maeze's case was Jenny, to present a powerful argument in defence of her husband. She would state how she would suffer if the application for resident status was denied her husband. Maeze would not be permitted to work and support the family financially.

Maeze suspected that the interviewer had tried to convince Jenny that he was not marrying her out of a genuine wish but merely in order to secure permanent residence approval, and that once he got that with its benefits, he would terminate the union. Jenny, he knew, had always feared that Maeze would leave her. He had after all not married her voluntarily. It appeared probable that the interviewer worked on her psyche, and she somehow agreed with her that Maeze should not be given the approval to change his status from student to permanent resident.

At home, she would not discuss her interview session. Maeze concluded there was no cause to hope.

Jenny curiously began to smother Maeze with affection. He was suspicious of her sudden warmth. A month after the interview, the decisive letter arrived. Maeze had been denied a change of status. Maeze was wrecked and sunk in misery. He again brooded over his estrangement from the Nigerian community in the United States and alienation from his family in Nigeria, his secretiveness with his close pal, Efe, hoping eventually to surprise him when his approval came. Maeze had lost a lot financially, and his credit standing in the U.S. In addition to accustomed abuse from Jenny and Cynthia, he now had a bad record with the INS, all in the quest for a green card. He felt his life in utter ruins, a building on the brink of crumbling on him. He writhed in unspeakable self-contempt.

To make matters worse, he had no one with whom to share his agony. Jenny was around him, trying to be loving, but she disgusted him as phony. He merely kept quiet.

He again reflected that merely to visit America was considered a huge achievement by many in Nigeria. America could make one, and America could also destroy one. A popular adage of his people held: "if you succeed in hunting down a snake for pepper soup with your family, everyone wishes to enjoy it with you; but if in the process of hunting, the snake turns around and bits you, you die, and your family mourns you." Consequently, if your life is marred in the pursuit of the "American dream" you are mocked for the rest of your life. Maeze considered that in his situation, the dream was shattered. He was like a boxer just received a 'killer' jab from his sparring mate. Such a boxer is knocked unconscious. When he regains consciousness and finds he had been on the floor all along, he realizes all is lost. He and his supporters are sunk in shame.

He again mused on his past, and his previous prospects. A responsible and progressive young man he had been, coming to America to pursue his dream. He had been succeeding. If he had confined himself to education, he would have completed his studies and returned to his country to continue to advance in his lofty career.

He would have been able to visit America with pride whenever he wished without being denied a visa. Trying to contract a new marriage and have a change of status had entangled him in a mess. He considered he would not be able to receive an entry visa into America in the future. In fact, had his student visa not been in good standing all along, immigration authorities would have sought him for deportation. It would affect not only his life in America, but in his home country and other countries around the world. The world had become a global village. He would be vulnerable to denial of entry by embassies in future. The mere existence of that damning record was a grave smear on pride and integrity.

Maeze repeatedly asked himself what led him into his present muddle. Yes, he had not been lucky. Why had others succeeded, and his attempt failed? Was it truly God's plan for him to have a huge setback and return home? Did God wish him to go home and help rebuild his own country? So many people, including close friends whose own applications had succeeded, were not better persons than Maeze. Some had arrived years after him and started their applications almost on arrival through exactly the same channel as Maeze. Why did their applications succeed and his fail? Perhaps he had most grievously sinned against God by divorcing his wife and remarrying. How would his children, the people he hoped would be the ultimate beneficiaries of his reckless venture, feel about their father when they learned of his disgrace? How would other Nigerians, both home and in the United States, judge his person and character? Many of them got their change of status through the method he had employed but hated and even worked overtly to make others fail. Many of them maintained an information network, to know how others' bids for change of status ended. It appeared that discrimination against nonpermanent Africans in the United States was more grievous within African groups than among non-Africans in America. They insulted their fellows openly, shouting that they were aliens. Those who became green card holders or citizens sometimes exuded arrogance and disdain for others. That contempt of compatriots prompted zeal or desperation on non-residents to acquire their own "freedom cards."

If it were only for work and social benefits, many people would not bother with the tortuous process of change of status with the attendant risks of failure.

Jenny's voice suddenly intruded into Maeze's mournful thoughts: "What you doing? Is it because of the green card? Never mind I'll send an objection letter. My attorney says they can change their decision if I have a good reason!" Maeze was silent as she spoke, and she came to sit beside him on the couch. "Whenever you begin to shake your legs in this mood, I know you are thinking deeply about something. It's either about your children you have not visited for a long time or now, about your immigration application that has been denied."

She seemed to wish to cheer him up, but Maeze could not force a smile to his face. She persisted: "I brought one of these Nollywood videos from my friend at the work place. She said it's very interesting. It's not one of those friends of yours though, but this is also good. C'mon babe what's going on?" He knew that when Jenny spoke of his "friend," she meant Maeze's favourite actor, Osuofia. Maeze found the man's dressing, walking and acting all hilarious. When in a bad mood, an Osuofia movie would infuse his soul with gladness.

Jenny slotted her movie into the movie player and began to watch it. Maeze pretended he was watching it with her, but his thoughts were far away. He was thinking: "I have two years before my doctorate program is completed. Though I am in good standing with immigration service, courtesy of my student visa, inwardly, I want to be free. This dream doesn't look realizable with the way things have turned out. My people say, "A woman who has reached puberty, is not supposed to go about without clothes." Again, "A runner does not have to stop running unless he reaches the end of the race or the thing pursuing him stops pursuing him." Maeze realized his only option was to finish the race.

He was now like a beautiful woman stripped naked in the marketplace. The upper cloth of the person nearest to her must be grabbed to hide her nakedness. Jenny was his last hope in his endeavour. They must send a letter giving reasons for a reversal of the verdict in his application. No action was taken on that objection letter. The officials, he knew, often used their "discretion" over such matters, a discretion often biased where Africans were concerned. The law was clear over conditions for change of status. In Maeze's case, he and Jenny were married and lived together, and provided all the documentary requirements. Why then was the application denied? Maeze simply decided to pursue his doctorate program to its conclusion while waiting for a reply from the immigration and naturalization services. To hunt down an antelope in a hunting expedition was determined by the first sighting. Once that chance was missed, it might never come again.

Maeze made sure he never missed his classes or any events necessary for the pursuit and award of his diploma. The library in fact became his second home. On most days, he left only when the library was about to close. His world was dominated by the computer and the internet. He soldiered on, remembering sometimes how he missed his children, and hoping he would see them someday.

By this time, he had become familiar with and fond of the professors and staff of his faculty. His course mates were friendly. A certain professor who later became chair of his dissertation, showed love and concern to all his students. Nerved by that professor's conviviality, Maeze requested a work position in the man's practice firm. Maeze wished to gain reasonable practical experience in his course of study before finally returning to his home country. The professor promptly gave Maeze the golden opportunity sought.

Though Maeze was not paid a salary, it proved a wonderful working experience in his career. Whereas he did twenty hours of work as stipulated by immigration service for fulltime students, he was also able to pursue his personal venture: scouting for goods to ship to Nigeria. His practicum for both the masters and doctorate degrees was done in the professor's firm. Maeze wondered where else he would have had the opportunity to fulfill this important aspect of his academic work. It was not easy to find a place to work in America. Before getting the opportunity to work at the professor's office, Maeze had worked for a Nigerian woman as a Psytech (Psychiatric Technician).

The Nigerian woman that Maeze worked for inorder to obtain his assistant nurse certification was ruthless. She had about three foster homes in different parts of the city for people living with disabilities. They all met at a central place during the day, and engaged in such activities as handicrafts, storytelling, sightseeing, dancing and music. For sightseeing activity, they would be driven around the city. The woman employed mainly

Africans who had no employment authorization. This group had no protection and rights of theirs, continually hiding from agents of government. They would present their employers with employment authorization of their relatives and friends and the employers would pretend they did not know that those brandishing the authorization cards were not the owners. The usual background checks were ignored or done in half measure. This vulnerable group, "working under the table", was poorly paid and viciously abused, as employers knew they only wanted some form of income to stay alive, burdened that they were under risk of exposure from the United States authorities. It was an exposure that could result in deportation.

This particular woman employer was unaware that Maeze had received authorization from the international student's office of his university as part of his academic work, although not the official employment authorization from Immigration and Naturalization Service (INS) known generally by employers. She saw him as her regular immigrant employees. She had come to the office that morning on account of an incident the previous day involving some of her clients. She might have been displeased by the education and erudition reflected in Maeze's written report and wished to diminish him before her visiting friends and staff. She made the usually terrifying demand for Maeze's "immigration papers" and documentation of employment. She was informed at that time that Maeze was in good status to be engaged in work because the university documented his work engagement with her organization. She then demanded the printed document and it was produced. The woman went berserk, tore the paper and rained curses on Maeze. When Maeze would not be prostrate or ask her forgiveness, she raised her hand to slap him. He ducked, successfully avoiding the "smack." She then rose from her seat. Maeze, not wanting to learn what she planned to do, rushed from the office.

By then, all the people in her office had begun to plead with her to calm down. They were cautious, anxious not to receive her transferred aggression. The raging woman was well-known in the African community for exacting courtesy from others. She instructed people on politeness and decent speech yet did not care how she addressed "nobodies." She shouted at Maeze to return to his "useless university" and remove her business name from their records, or she would "deal" with him. She stopped Maeze's employment in her organization, refusing to pay his salary for the three weeks he had worked in that month. Maeze sent several letters and reminders for months before she reluctantly paid part of what was outstanding.

Prior to that, Maeze had once worked for Dong, a white man and his wife in the status of an undocumented worker ("under the table employee"). They had met at one of their church outings. When the man realized that Maeze was enduring years of inability to see his loved ones, all because he wished to acquire a good education, he took pity on Maeze and hired him temporarily to work around his house. He had paid him handsomely and regularly.

Dong, thickset and in his mid-fifties, lived with only his wife and their little pet dog. Maeze sensed that the man must have discussed and agreed with the wife to employ him. This man had a good heart. In the first few days of working with them at their home, the little dog disappeared. It was painful to watch the wife sorrow as the publicity over the missing puppy spread in their neighborhood. Feeling that his presence had scared the pet away, Maeze felt guilty when the woman could not hold back her tears over the canine's disappearance. The pet fortunately was found seven days after its disappearance.

Dong and his wife gave Maeze special hospitality as part of their family, perhaps to soothe his agony over his own family's absence. Maeze worked for them in their garden and environment. From Dong, he learned how to mow fields and construct wooden fences. He and Dong would measure, prepare schedules and drive to the Home Depot to buy their requirements. The wife would go to the kitchen and make lunch. Then, all three would sit at table eating and telling stories. Afterwards, Dong and Maeze would return to work while the wife did the household chores. Dong worked from home as a stockbroker. In the three months he worked for them, Maeze enjoyed his life as he never did throughout his stay in the United States.

Dong would introduce Maeze to "Toastmasters International," a social group that helped members develop public speaking and leadership skills through practice and feedback. Maeze became a very active member, contesting in speechmaking, administration and timekeeping, then held an executive position. That particular unit used to meet in a local library in Houston every Wednesday morning. It comprised many retired but highly successful men and women. Maeze was also active as a moderator in debates. He remained in that unit for the rest of his time in America.

It was sad to compare his idyllic association with that white American family with his harrowing experience with a Nigerian employer. He reflected that an African would have expected kindliness and assistance from a fellow African.

While at lunch, Dong and wife often asked many questions about Maeze's family, and life on the African continent. Some of the enquiries about his family opened wounds in Maeze's heart. However, he hid his American remarriage from the couple. He did not want to be termed a character that ended his former marriage for another one in America. He thanked the

Almighty he had ceased to live with Jenny by then. They would definitely have found out he was married and asked more questions. Jenny could not spend thirty minutes without phoning him to ask some question or other.

11. INSIDE PROFESSOR ROBERT'S CLASS

Maeze found Dr. Robert's benevolence uplifting. It was instrumental in Maeze's ability to complete his studies. If Dr. Robert found one's academic work brilliant, he proclaimed it to other students in order to motivate them. He would publicly express his pride to have one as his student. Such attitudes were uncharacteristic of student-lecturer relationships in Nigeria. When you are under performing, Dr. Robert was fond of his red pen. He could use it all over your work, yet he would find the right words to encourage you to work harder; and you would never feel bad at his remarks. His approach was so fatherly that all his students were charmed by him.

For this reason, students were always around him. He remembered the names of both current and previous students. He was remarkable as a motivator and leader. For many international students challenged by cultural adjustment, Dr. Robert had invigorating words. He appeared to relish those discussion classes where students felt like members of one family at a dinner table, savouring a sumptuous meal. To miss Dr. Robert's class was like missing the repose and invigoration of a good night's sleep after days of stressful work. Some professors envied him for his cordial relationship with his students, yet his life was worth imitating by all leaders. It was only in his classes that one found many single women happy and rejuvenated in spirit.

Maeze sometimes wondered how a changing world with so many educated people in top positions could have so many single people, men and women remaining unmarried. When met walking to the car park alone or in their respective offices, they would smile. A stranger would suppose their smile to be genuine, but Maeze felt it indicated distrust or a shield from fear. He believed people longed to settle down in families, but many lacked the patience, or could simply not endure the upheavals of married life. Many would be enraged at the slightest provocation. Moreover, many men, for their social reputations, would be impeccably pleasant in public, but in private unleash beastliness on the women in their lives.

Maeze saw that many had grown used to single lives. Men and women were living out a new global culture of individualism. In Africa, men worked hard to support their families while their wives cared for the children and home. In America, both spouses worked for the family's upkeep, and also for the children's care and household chores. In Nigerian culture, the man was deemed responsible for the family's material needs. It was widely considered normal for a wife to stay at home while her husband supplied her financial needs. Single mothers were openly despised and defamed.

Dr. Robert's large heart embraced everyone. It was no surprise when he took student groups on outings, or asked Maeze to his family house for dinner.

As Dr. Robert was among the world's best professional counselors, his students sometimes remained after his class to interact on a range of issues: family, work, and academic life. On a certain day, as his students engaged in their accustomed after-class discourse, one of Dr. Robert's numerous professor friends peeped in, and was welcomed by Dr. Robert: "come right in." The students were relaxed, exchanging information on what they would do when they acquired their doctorate degrees. Various answers came: "I am going to become a professor. I am going to sit for the professional certification examination and seek a well-paid job after I pass. I am going to settle down to marry, I am going to be a coach, I am going to write for my promotion." Then it was the turn of Maeze, the only African in the class. He declared: "I'm going to leave immediately for my country. In fact, the day after our commencement in May."

It seemed everyone had been waiting for Maeze's answer. They openly doubted and debated his statement. The guest professor started to mock Maeze's country men: "I've known a lot of Nigerians. If they are out of status after completing their studies, they move to another city outside the state they graduated from and would never return to Nigeria until they have finally changed their immigration status to become citizens." Jeers and jests upon Nigerians rained from all sides. They were from a poor country where people lived in dirt, yet whose leaders came to America to flaunt their wealth, even trying to outspend the wealthiest Americans."

Maeze heard of Nigerian fraud, the '419,' and was surprised that the group knew of that infamous term, 419. Almost everyone in the class claimed to have received 419 email messages on some occasion. One of Maeze's course mates launched into a disquisition on the perpetration of 419. He said ABC Television news had carried a documentary on the activities of those criminals and their network in Nigeria, Asia, Europe and across the United States. The 419 operators did not know that the FBI was following them. They were trailed from some of their introductory letters to their victims in the United States, through telephone monitoring, recorded at their expensive hotels, offices and homes, international airports, through banking transactions and lavish parties, and even through their immediate and extended families and friends, until they were exposed across the globe. When the gang's arrow head and chief negotiator was caught in his luxury hotel suite in New York by ABC television crew, he was informed that he was on live television and that his associates similarly were facing the world at that material time.

At first, the criminal tried to appear unflustered, asking: "What are all these cameras for?" His smile was unconvincing.

The crew told him he was being watched on television worldwide. They went ahead to mention his associates real names and pseudonyms to convince him that they knew all about him, his track of movements, dates, transit of airports, airlines' schedules and even clothes he wore on his movement across the world, his office, residential and family country home, his wife, girlfriends' and children's names and addresses, the cars, parties and favorite meals…

He was then convinced that he was routed. He duly feigned remorse, weeping and covering his face, begging for the filming to end. He was shown clips of his associates in Lagos, Malaysia, Spain and the United States. Questions were asked about his profession of deception, and its implications for a holder of the United States' citizenship. The man duly confessed his numerous criminal activities. Officers of banks and staff of other institutions he had used were also being interviewed and shown on live television.

The suspect proceeded to give further information on members of his criminal gang not already exposed by the police. Indeed, it seemed Maeze's class had rehearsed stories about Nigerian criminality and had awaited the opportunity to relate them in chilling detail.

Another person told how some Nigerians had come to America without any form of passport or identification at the airport but claimed they were Liberians who managed to escape the devastation of war in their country and were adopted by wealthy Americans, including some celebrities. Those criminal elements would declare themselves to be teenagers – although some were above twenty-five years old – and tell heartbreaking tales of losing their parents to the insurrection, managing to escape by the help of some international intervention agencies, and eventually finding their way onto American soil as refuges. Another course mate told the story of another Nigerian 419 activity. It was of a medical supply chain that specialized in violating provisions of the United States Disability Act over the provision of wheelchairs and regular medical supplies and equipping of unqualified Americans with benefits. The upshot was that the criminals would end up with millions of dollars in their pockets.

As Maeze squirmed, another student told of abuse of immigration laws by coming into America with pregnancies to enjoy free medical treatment and automatic citizenship for the newborn, easing the mother's path to future citizenship. Maeze heard of sham marriages, where the foreigner would pay for the services of the American spouses, endure the false marriage from six months to a year, claim their green card, go for their citizenship, divorce, and finally work to bring their original family over to live their American dream. That speaker concluded that was the means by which the majority of Nigerians in America obtained their stay.

A conspicuous feature of American education was that learning was not strictly confined to the curriculum and course outline. Any source of information or awareness was considered enriching by professor and students alike. Now everyone wished to hear more of the exploits of Nigerian fraudsters. Dr. Robert stated: "Not all Nigerians are criminals. I've enjoyed the many that I met both in my student days and as professor in many universities across the United States. In fact, I'm proud to say that they are some of the brightest people I've come across in academics. Statistics show that Nigerians are the highest and fastest educated group in this country. Listen, let me tell you something; Nigerian brothers are hardworking people. They have shown resilience and capacity to combine work with study. Each family living in the US has someone with a minimum of a master's degree. I love them"

The class knew that Dr. Robert loved everybody and would not discriminate in spite of the stories being told. He probably held that Maeze could not be part of the criminal pack. Professor Robert told how he used to give his ATM card with its code to Maeze to buy lunch for the office. His visitors sometimes tried to dissuade him from letting Maeze, a Nigerian, be privy to such personal and tempting information, but he ignored them.

Maeze was hurt by the stories and moved to educate the class about his country. They were looking at him with the mocking expression *well, what could you say in answer to all these stories?* Maeze was about to speak when another student began her own story. It was an American who said she had been married to a Nigerian, and the relationship had been so blissful that she would go through it again. She said that when her former husband wished to return to Nigeria for good, she refused to go with him. The man had been bequeathed his father's extensive auto parts business in present Anambra-State of Nigeria. His father's only surviving brother had died and he had no choice but to return to Nigeria.

The former husband's family had much property in various parts of Nigeria, but she had been influenced by stories of insecurity and fetish rituals seen in Nollywood movies. She had chosen to remain in America with their two sons rather than follow her husband to Nigeria. After two years' separation, she divorced him. The woman told the class that she communicated with the man and his new family, was totally proud of him, and wished she had continued to live with him. She declared that she could never meet a more loving or hardworking man than her former Nigerian husband. She had not been surprised to learn in the Nigerian Wives' Association that in Nigeria the women were mostly not expected to work, the man being responsible for providing for his wife and children. If the wife decided to work, her income was exclusively for her, the husband forbidden to touch her money. She learnt that was African culture.

She imparted that she had learned further that among the Igbos of Eastern Nigeria, before undergoing rites for initiation into manhood, a man should prove himself capable of maintaining not only his nuclear but his extended family. He would shower gifts and a high bride-price on his prospective in-laws. The man's kinsmen and his wife's family alike would be satisfied that he was mature, responsible, loving and fit to take a wife. The new wife would visit her husband's family for four days' trial or familiarization.

After the four-day marriage assessment test, the bride would return to her parents' home and await the groom's family's reaction. The groom's mother or aunts would give their verdict on the prospective bride, based on efficiency or ineptitude over housekeeping and cookery, generosity or meanness over serving meals to guests, hospitality to extended family members and ability to work under pressure. If the groom's family sent men with kegs of palm wine to the bride's father, it signified that the man's family had found her fit to marry, and marriage preparations would progress. If on the other hand, no messengers appeared after eight market days, it meant the marriage plans were cancelled.

Maeze was surprised at how much of African culture that American woman knew. Dr. Robert's professor friend was leaving to continue his own class down the hallway and delivered a comment: "Maeze is not going back to Nigeria on completion of his program. He's moving over to Florida or New York. Bet me if you doubt that."

The class exclaimed in unison, "Yes we agree with you." Maeze explained that he was tired of the half-freedom and second-class life he was experiencing in the United States of America. He stated that with his doctorate degree, he would surely be at the upper rungs of the social pyramid in Nigeria. The professor said that he had a former student friend from one of the Northern states of Nigeria who, having obtained a doctorate in America, spent years wandering in Nigeria without a job. He later joined politics and became a federal cabinet minister. He said too that a few of his ex-students returned to the South Eastern part of the country and never found jobs, and some returned to the United States after a while to begin a new life. He left the class at that stage. The American ex-wife of a Nigerian began another absorbing tale about Nigeria. "Bring it on," urged the class, particularly the ladies.

She said she had been told of a new trend. "Nigerian parents are investing in their American children. I know many of you are wondering what I mean by investing. Yes, parents are supposed to invest everything they can afford into the training of their children.

"But that is not quite what I mean," She stated, then explained that the American passport was of course considered a guarantee of wealth and a grand future by many Nigerian families. It had been compared to merchandise. When you buy wares for resale, you would enhance their value and display them on a shelf. If you took a product in high demand to the market place, you were certain to make a handsome profit. Young Nigeria-American parents took good care of their children when they were young, worked hard to provide them with all the good things of life they might desire, were vigilant over their associates so that they would not be corrupted by objectionable friends and associates, and helped them to toil towards acquiring a good education.

As soon as they were through the undergraduate phase, and had attained some maturity, the parents would take them to the motherland at festive periods like Christmas. Rather than stay in their traditional big homes in the countryside, they would lodge at expensive hotels in the big cities. The situation was akin to taking a bitch to a dog park to mate with a special breed of male canine. Convincing reasons were voiced for staying in those city hotels rather than in the villages: kidnappings, robberies, ritual murders, actions of university cult gangs with their attendant violence, and general security flaws. An accomplishment of those visiting Nigerian families, prized by the untraveled Nigerians, was an American accent. Wealthy Nigerian parents, drawn to that intimation of foreign sophistication, endeavoured to keep their offspring in the same grand hotels. The hotels became veritable dating parks. The visiting mothers, feigning disinterest, watched the courtships with eagle eyes. They effected and fostered desirable liaisons.

The mothers of course enquired into the desirable families' backgrounds and finances. Those matchmakers naturally craved families of big corporation directors, political leaders, celebrities, and legends of the business and social worlds in Nigeria. The offspring were the bait for 'netting' the big fish of Nigeria and being in control of Nigeria's financial and social edifices. The woman remarked: "That's the power of the American international passport and accent. You know that young people in Africa are crazy about the American accent. So, these Nigerian couples toiling and doing two or three jobs at the same time, with all the attendant bills they are struggling to pay monthly, believe that their investment returns await them as their children get married to the children of 'big shots.'"

"Oh! I see," exclaimed a single mother sitting in front of the class. "So that's why they don't like to marry us. These crazy Nigerians, they better don't mess with us in Texas anymore."
"These guys are never in short supply of their game. How can somebody not have love, but because of money, go to marry an innocent woman?"

I don't like them" declared another single mother in the class.

Dr. Robert. Said: "But there are some that are not in this game. Certainly, Maeze is a good guy. He can't be involved in this kind of business."

Some supported him, "No, he can't."   Other voices dissented: "Yes, he can!"

The lady continued her story: "You know, for every good business, there is a risk. The more rewarding a business is, the riskier and more attractive it is for many copy cats."

She continued: "Over time, people get to know about the game and the predator may become the prey." She proceeded to explain that bigger and smarter fraudsters had penetrated the hotel dating parks, and the cover the hotels gave those American fortune seekers also became a nest for the professional fraudsters' activities. Some of these American women were also recording losses. Conmen had elevated the game and joined the spree. "Often, very poor youngsters would clean themselves up and rent good clothes, learn the accent, learn the game and etiquette and mingle in such high places acting up all the big attractive things those ambitious women dreamed about too. As we speak, it has become a 'dog eat dog' affair. There are young people who borrow money to prey around airports with the sole aim of making a kill.

As Nigerian roads were death traps, kidnappers prowling by the highways to inflict calamity on hapless motorists, and since the local airlines had high fares, it became the norm that rich people travelled by air while poor citizens opted for road transport. .

The woman disclosed further: "More young people are joining the business: just dress fine, wear some expensive cologne, act American from one local airport to another, and do your professional job of scamming. More young women with foreign passports are ending up joining fake young men in Europe and America, only to realize their folly too late. Do you wonder why there are many broken marriages in this generation, especially Nigerians in Diaspora?" The woman also told how young, female Africans tried to come into America in the last trimester of their pregnancies, just to have their baby born in America, and automatically qualify for an American passport. They hoped that when the newborn turned eighteen, that young adult would file for change of status for the parents no matter their country of residency.

It was Maeze's turn to contribute to the conversation. Many obviously wondered what his reactions would be. Nobody loved to hear their country's nationals ridiculed and defamed by foreigners, no matter how flawed they might be. Maeze's classmates had long considered him a good teacher. While most of his course mates were exasperated by some topics, he introduced some techniques to the group. Those simple but effective methods turned many who disliked figures into enthusiasts for figures! Maeze was indeed respected.

He started his remarks by condemning what deserved condemnation in the remarks made in class. Remarking the Americanization of American children learned in American history classes, he reminded the group of the hordes of immigrants who flocked to America from various parts of Europe in the 17th and 18th centuries, declaring that countless Americans were once immigrants. Maeze also reminded them of how America was, indeed, in existence, even before the arrival of Christopher Columbus. He recalled the slavery era when the West pretended to be teaching civilization but was rather more interested in human exploitation. The deceit, exploitation, and degradation that attended nearly three centuries of slavery left in its trail poverty, wars and bitterness that lasted up to the present day. Africa's natural resources – gold, ivory, and humans – were used to enrich Europe and America in their industrial revolution. Africans, Maeze said, were rightly angered by negative press commentaries on reparation. It was regrettable that issues of reparation had not been resolved. The dehumanization and exploitation of persons of African descent in order to develop the West could never be denounced enough. The fittest men and women were carted off and taken across the Atlantic in the unspeakable "Middle Passage," to spend their lives and energies in slavery.

Those who died on the voyage were fed to the beasts of the sea. To ensure the continuance of slavery, ethnic groups were incited into inter-tribal frays which decimated their populations. As the battles raged, the westerners supplied weapons whilst persisting with their trade.

Maeze told how, when colonial rule was being established, diverse nationalities were merged for the cheaper administrative convenience of the colonial headquarters. It resulted in the annihilation of the cultures and looting of the art treasures of colonized territories. Rather than bring machines and technologies to sources of raw materials as dictated by simple economic principles, the colonialists preferred to send those raw materials to their home countries. A one-off sourcing and transportation of machines to Africa would have been much cheaper than the continuous shipment of raw materials to the western world. The obvious aim was to perpetually deny the people of the colonies employment, value chain in wealth creation, technical skill and overall development. The colonialists, Maeze raged, did not need entry visas or regulations for their citizens to work or engage in business in any part of Africa. Africans had continually been cut off from technologies ranging from simple manufacturing to high grade nuclear processes, so that the populace might remain in want.

That, Maeze declared, was the only way to ensure the west remained wealthy and vibrant. Beggarly African countries were indirectly bound to the political leadership of western powers, for protection from external aggressors. Emerging African leaders grasped the subtle warning – remain loyal to colonial masters and be assured of peace, or rebel against the West and lose your political power.

Countries like Iraq, Libya and Syria could only offer their bitter stories to nations that nursed the ambition to change the world's equation. During the Nigeria-Biafra war, the Igbos suffered genocide. What could have made many world powers back the Nigerian State in that brazen destruction of Biafrans? It was rumoured that the West was determined that a strong power should not be allowed to emerge from the indigenous people of Eastern Nigeria.

It was a case of "Are we going to let the only continent at our disposal be taken over by this richly endowed but special indigenous people of Biafra off the hook? Hence, the torrent of bombardments, aided by the combined forces of world powers, to the decapitation and rape of a people. They rained bombs on civilian targets at markets, hospitals and churches killing over three million people in the war. Not for the instigation and support, the Biafra secession would have been peacefully negotiated decades ago in Aburi.

Like other African countries, Nigeria still depends on the west for financial aid, manufacturing, technology, human capital development and virtually all imports. What stops Europe and America from expanding their industrial capacity to African cities if not to continue to keep them under perpetual bondage? A mere accusation by president George W. Bush of piling weapons of mass destruction led to the destruction of once burgeoning economics of Libya and Iraq. Today their people are refuges spilling into other countries and causing further devastation of poor countries surrounding them. Consider the cost of execution of American invasion of these countries in socio-cultural, economic and human losses. And consider the transformation in Africa if the amount was otherwise used to provide employment and wealth in form of industries in a peaceful Libya, nay Africa. Immigration and Customs regulations are meant to provide security for the home country so that her citizens can continue to plan and provide quality life for her people. The question is, "What do you want these Africans to do?"

In exploiting their natural resources, refusing to pay due reparations to help the countries rise from past exploitations and violations, and making ever stricter immigration laws to stop them from entering wealthy economies, you were simply saying "go-and die in your country." As though to ensure their complete destruction, the wicked and oppressive regimes of African countries were ironically accommodated in the west. Families of the looters and despots lived, studied, holidayed and received medical treatment and virtually everything in the West with monies stolen from their ravaged economies. The economic principle of autonomous consumption would always impel the hungry and dying people of Africa into seeking employment and nourishment wherever they were available in the world, to save their families from starvation. Maeze emphasized to the class that seeking survival wherever it could be found was not deemed criminal by Africans. The weather and culture of the West alone would keep Africans back in Africa if they could find their needs in their own countries. Western leaders understood and accommodated the feelings and needs of their diversified populations, but not the feelings of Africans over immigration issues. Therefore, whether or not they found it acceptable, the development of Africa was directly related to the interest showed by the West in its survival. Maeze conceded that the importance of immigration control cannot be undermined in a country's national security, especially in times of global terrorism when satanic creatures prowled across nations. He maintained however that greater world peace could be achieved when wealth was spread across the globe.

Capitalism was intertwined with ruthless competitiveness that continually strengthened some, whilst destroying weaker others. Although acknowledging the adage "East or West home is best," no spirited humans would fecklessly let themselves be effaced by disease or poverty if they could find some nurturing realms. Disobedience to the law should not be justified, yet everyone should pause to ask, "What would make someone undertake an arduous and hazardous trip across the Sahara, then try to cross the Mediterranean from North Africa to Europe?" Countless stories of horrible deaths had not deterred numerous people from embarking on the same perilous venture. Reports of the International Organization on Migration, governments, and survivors of the terrible voyage had all failed to halt those trips of desperate Africans and Asians.

Maeze continued, his passion unabated: "We have heard many heart-breaking stories of rape, prostitution rings, kidnapping, robbery, terrorism, rituals and others caused by hooligans on those routes. Youths are lured into crimes with promises of future wealth, only to realize how cleverly they had been fooled." On those journeys, withdrawal became more dangerous than advancing. Half of those able-bodied men, women and teenagers died. Those who arrived in Europe ended up as international criminals. Their suffering and encounters stripped them of their consciences and all decent instincts. They proceeded to try to recruit others into their lives of crime and grime. Policing has failed to end that trend.

Maeze stated that peace would come to the world when governments had mutually beneficial relationships. When countries could boast of infrastructures and productive capacity to provide their citizens with employment and opportunities for wealth creation, citizens would naturally – and gladly – engage in rewarding ventures in their native lands, surrounded by their families and support groups. That was the ultimate freedom a normal human being yearned for.

Many Africans sought freedom and fulfillment in America because of the deprivations in their own states. For some immigrants, their journey to a good life began with travel from North African countries with boundaries with Europe and the Middle East. There were mafias facilitating international trafficking, hiring professional traffickers, recruiters, transporters, kidnappers, informants and contacts in governments.

Recruiters operated in cities in all the countries along the trafficking route. They often deceived vulnerable youths and their parents with promises of help towards employment and a comfortable life outside the country. Gullibility and neediness make those issue of poor households drop all their work or studies in their home countries to "heed the call!" Oftentimes, the poor families borrowed or sold all their possessions to enable their children make the trip to the West. Some packs, who facilitated prostitution and terrorism even offered to sponsor the trips, with the understanding that they would be repaid when the travelers reached their destination. The parents would be flush with hope and joy. Some would die when their children disappeared, especially when baffling stories began to reach them about the casualties and fatalities of such trips. Of the few that reached Europe and made money, their sudden wealth prompted whispers and slanders and innuendo in their neighborhoods at home.

Maeze reflected on the journey, modern Africa's Middle Passage. The recruits were assembled and smuggled through criminal routes. Human struggling documentaries are strewn with the horrifying encounters of that journey. Wild animals, armed jobbers, kidnappers and ritualists all assailed those adventurers. On arrival at any of their departure points at the horn of Africa, those fortune seekers were camped and trained on survival techniques, language and counter actions, taking into account their probable safe journey through various nations, or failing and falling into the hands of security agents. Many of the victims were used to peddle hard and illicit drugs. Stories abounded of some caught at borders excreting kilograms of the deadly drugs they had swallowed. Those immigrants were sometimes made to spend long periods in their bay countries learning the basic languages of some friendly countries. When sweeping arrests were made, some security agents had been known to be lenient to nationals of countries which were not on their nations' security watch list. Tales were heard of travelers arriving at entry points of some wealthy countries and rushing into restrooms to tear their international passports so that they could assume citizenship of stable and prosperous countries, or of war-torn nations in order to qualify for refugee status. It would become impossible to trace and document their original names and biological data. Terrorists could be absorbed into countries through such means. They might initially keep the proverbial "low profile" until they deemed it right to unleash death upon their host countries. Transporters, informants and smugglers were masters of the deadly routes used by traffickers for their illicit trade. They would casually violate laws – traffic, maritime, immigration, and customs. They sometimes liaised with security personnel and spies, who aided them to their final destination. On those journeys, there were sometimes armed clashes, the shooting of course often causing fatalities. In times of danger, immigrants were used as physical shields. The operational vehicles of the criminals often broke down with no rescue plans. There were frequent stories of rickety and overloaded boats sinking and of course passengers drowning. Horrifying too were the many stories of women and children floundering on the high seas for days without nourishment, under inhuman conditions. Sometimes, the dead were left on board the embattled boats, and at other times they were thrown overboard.

Maeze was concluding his presentation. "As I said, most of the few who make it to Europe are received by agents and mafia groups. They are quickly mostly dispatched to illegal jobs that remain undocumented. The 'big bosses' use them for the continuous expansion of their criminal network. Those without criminal tendencies sometimes become good citizens. They might even fight the same crimes they had been involved in, and become ambassadors of peace, turning over a new leaf, doing good works. Some become advocates for justice in countries around the world. Yet, most of the victims are brainwashed and they hook deeper with the mafia gang. They are then sent across the world to join other networks across continents to violate laws and wreak havoc on humanity.

"Point here is that global peace is achievable when sovereign nations cooperate and support poorer countries to develop their economic potential. The cost of doing that is far less than the current budgets for enforcement of border security or fighting wars across continents." The class roared its unreserved agreement and admiration for Maeze.

12. SEPARATING FROM JENNY

Jenny and Cynthia retained their stranglehold on Maeze's life. He was constantly reminded of the outstanding matter with Immigration and Naturalization Service. Maeze however by now was no longer worried about the approval or denial of his immigration application, or his continuous stay in America, or lack of the freedom he had been seeking. What hurt was that his name had been discredited. It meant he would find it hard to obtain an entry visa to America in future. This was a country where he had spent many vigorous years of his youth in pursuit of education. Maeze had spent considerable time at universities in America, made firm friends, and had enriching career opportunities. The smear consequent on the rejection of his application for permanent stay was indeed grievous.

Resolving to pursue the matter further, he worked with Jenny to send an appeal to INS to rescind its decision. INS did not reply to their letter. The young female attorney representing him in the pursuit of his application seemed indifferent to its outcome. Her detachment appalled Maeze. How could someone employed to fight his cause be so lukewarm in the task? He was however familiar with such professionals, who seemed to resent the idea of granting permanent immigration status to the likes of Maeze. At his meetings with the attorney, she treated him as an irritant. If she had not charged and been paid huge attorney's fees, he would have acted differently. Rather than ask for a change of status, he would simply have applied for travelling documents to visit his home country or delayed the application for some time.

Maeze however held on to his fate, waiting for INS to consider the numerous facts presented in support of his application. He was forlorn, feeling there was no one to help him, including the lawyer. Jenny and Cynthia of course were not helpful. They remained his relentless tormenters. Maeze expected that the INS, deciding to reconsider his application, would invite them for another interview at short notice. Consequently, he continued to pay money into his joint account with Jenny, from which Jenny as before continually siphoned funds.

As was her won't, she often made withdrawals before check issued for bills were paid. Consequently, the money in the bank was always insufficient and Maeze had continually to strive to maintain financial obligations. His credit credibility was being effaced by Jenny's profligacy. After many months of fruitless waiting to hear from the immigration office, prolonged financial loss and psychological torment, Maeze resolved to end his punishment. He stopped paying into that joint account, and paid bills directly from his personal account. Jenny was angered, and her abusiveness intensified

Their joint existence became the proverbial "cat and mouse". Cynthia had reconciled with Rex and lived with him in a distant part of the city. Jenny liked to visit them weekly, going straight from work and returning late at night. By then, whatever affection he had left for Jenny was dead. Their relationship, it seemed, had been determined by their joint account and anticipated immigration interview. Maeze now felt that the less contact they had, the better. He consequently devoted more time to his studies, staying at the university for as long as he could. Jenny continued with her telephone monitoring, but Maeze now usually ignored her tantrums.

The situation exploded in an incident of slapping. Maeze was cooking in the kitchen when Jenny returned late. After greetings, Jenny complained about the aroma of Maeze's *egusi* soup, something she had never done in the past. Maeze merely continued to cook.

Jenny marched up to him: "Are you not the one I'm speaking to?" He stayed silent and she said after a few seconds: "I'm asking you a question." Maeze still did not speak and she removed the pot from the gas cooker.

As she made her way into the bedroom, Maeze relit the burner and replaced the pot on the hob.

Jenny returned. "Can't you answer a question?" She stood waiting for an answer. Maeze was mute, thinking he had already done about seventy percent of the cooking of the soup. He could not throw it away or start to explain why he was making a dish she had seen him cook and enjoy on innumerable occasions. He felt she simply wanted to be unpleasant.

"No, No, you have to answer me." She insisted. As Maeze hesitantly made some sounds, she slapped him hard. Twice.

Maeze felt like his world had come to an end. Thoughts whirled within him. *A woman slapping me? With all this woman has been doing to me! Now, physical abuse! This can't happen in Africa – a woman physically abusing the husband ... impossible. Any ear that hears this in Africa will burn.*

In Maeze's native community, no woman no matter how demented would have dared commit that assault, even in jest. The gods of the land would be incensed by such abomination. There would be no grounds for concealment either. It was believed that if the victim, or any other grown-up who witnessed the incident did not report it to the local chief for cleansing of the land, calamities would definitely befall the community.

It was also believed that a woman who could perpetrate such a deed must be possessed by an evil spirit. Indeed, it would be a smear on her family, deterring men from marrying her sisters. All prospective suitors of theirs would be told the family was evil.

Maeze stood reflecting on his life. He knew the law in America was severe on a man raising his hand against a woman. Jenny, he felt, must truly be possessed of the devil to rouse him to an act that might lead to imprisonment and ruin of his entire life. Maeze's inner voice reminded him of self-control as a characteristic of emotional intelligence. He went into the bedroom. Jenny was now vaunting herself and threatening further assaults, even promising him another slap.

Maeze closed the bedroom door, sat on his bed and tried to take stock of his life in America. "What's really happening to me?" He queried himself. "Who can I share this experience with? Should I call her bluff and end this relationship?"
Jenny flung the door open, pronounced "You suck," then, walked away when she realized Maeze was actually crying.

Maeze picked a hand towel from the table and wiped the tears dropping down his cheeks. He lay back in bed, brooding, concluding he had no one to advise him over his plight. If he called his friends in America, they could do little to help. They would merely repeat the story to others. He knew how swiftly gossip was circulated in America. Telephone calls were free from 7pm to 7am, and all weekend. Nigerians spent hours on the phone tattling about one another. A tale like his slapping by Jenny would spread as fast as a wild fire in California. Rather than sympathize, fellow Nigerians would embellish and even send it to some blogs. They might not state the names of the persons involved, but the story would be told in such a way that acquaintances could tell the personae. The Nigerian community was close-knit, and a story about someone studying for a doctorate would be relished by many.

"How about sharing with some friends down in motherland; at least, somebody to talk to just to ease the stress right now?" Maeze mused. Then, he concluded that people at home even spread tales faster on local blogs. Many graduates were jobless, relying on politicians for survival. Many of those political 'godfathers' were educationally and professional deficient. Their moral flexibility affected their deprived disciples.

Internet platforms and groups through Facebook, WhatsApp, Instagram, Twitter and the numerous free online media enabled those idlers to live virtually on computers and mobile phones, all day and every day. The story of a woman slapping her husband would make a succulent item for their group chats and spread rapidly. Maeze, dreading such embarrassment, concluded that he had no one to share his experience with.

He castigated himself for the ugly developments in his life. If only he had stayed away from American women! But how could he when his body pined for a woman?

His hormones had been surging and steaming. If he had found no proper outlet for his ferment, he would have killed himself with masturbation or grabbed a prostitute or raped a lunatic. Maeze had encountered many African women in America. Some whose husbands were not in America were often lonely, and craved companionship and sex. Maeze shrank from such furtive relationships.

The single ones yearned for marriage, but not to a divorcee with young children to care for. Although Maeze had never regretted coming to America for educational advancement, he knew the decision to remarry had been a mistake.

He again thought of his country and it's apparently incurable bad governments. If only the leaders had not failed, many citizens would have loved to remain in the country, proud nationals pursuing their dreams. Lack of such basic amenities as electricity, water, transportation, health, education and security, had dampened initiative and zeal. Unemployment rates soared, food was lacking, disease pervasive, fear of destruction by the corrupt rich and absence of the rule of law all characterized the land. Everyone was eager to "check out" of the country. The more rejections people received at embassies, the more vigorously they fought for visas to foreign nations. They seemed intent on at least leaving Nigeria.

Maeze again blamed Americans. How could they give citizens of other African countries five years of student's visa, and only two years to Nigerian students? Students were obliged to go to American embassies in Nigeria when their visas expired, although they might still be in good status. Applicants at embassies looked like refugees from the Biafran war queuing for rations of corn meal and powdered egg. Why did America allow those who stole their nation's funds to bring the loot into America and America's economy, granting stays to them and their family members while the rest of their people were stuck in squalor?

On that night of anguished reflection, Maeze decided that he would no longer pursue his immigration application. Even if it proved his life's worst failure, he would return to his country and face its realities. As for Jenny, their marriage had ended with her slapping him. He no longer cared what anyone in America or Nigeria thought about his not having a green card. His overriding concern now was to complete his doctoral program, then leave the country. He was still in good student status; he would toil to complete his program as soon as he could.

Maeze had of course stopped the dispiriting process of lodgments into the joint bank account for payment of bills and paid directly for everything. That should have proved to Jenny that for Maeze, the charade was over. He stopped all activity with her, and merely shared the apartment. After a few days, Jenny made overtures to him, greeting and being friendly and solicitous. Jenny bought good food and made vegetable salad, Maeze's favorite evening meal, but he was unmoved. Jenny played pop music and did strip-dances, but Maeze was not aroused. She twerked vigorously and boasted that her buttocks were gorgeous, but to Maeze her form might have been a mildewed stone wall. When all her ruses failed, she came to beg forgiveness for her actions. Maeze proceeded to educate her about his culture. He made her feel his masculine assertiveness as an African man.

"Do you know that in my culture, it's an abomination for a woman to slap a man?" He asked.

After a lengthy discussion, Maeze told her that she would need to beg forgiveness with a cockerel. That was the customary sanction for the offence. She promised to comply. The situation deteriorated further when Maeze's income ceased to be regular. In that month of August, rent was paid on the 5th with a penalty. By October, the situation had become so bad that electricity was affected. Bills' payments had fallen behind deadlines. Shortly, Maeze came upon Jenny one evening, with two young men helping her to move her property out of the apartment. He was amazed. Jenny had not indicated she was leaving, neither mentioning it nor leaving him a note. He called her to the side of the sitting-room and asked: "What are you doing?"

Jenny replied briefly. "I'm done. I can't continue like this. I have to move on, bye."

If she had expected Maeze to plead for her to stay back because she was processing an outstanding immigration application for him, she was mistaken. He merely ignored her. Jenny sometimes came to the house, probably curious to see how Maeze was surviving without electricity. He for his part was preoccupied with how to pay his overdue bills. He went through his diary and considered which friends to call. He had met a certain Nigerian at a Nigerian restaurant a few years earlier. He had not recognized the man, who introduced himself as one of Maeze's former students at the university satellite campus in Port Harcourt. The man, Chinedu, had struck Maeze as kindhearted. He gave Maeze his business card – he was an auto-mechanic and director of his own business. At the time, Maeze had felt it inappropriate to take the first step in renewing telephone contact with his former student, so had not called Chinedu.

Maeze now did not mind calling Chinedu. He found the business card and dialed. Chinedu was manifestly excited by the call. After pleasantries, they agreed to meet the following day. Maeze was received at Chinedu's office in the afternoon. He was running an auto-workshop in the heart of the city which was considered an ideal office location. Chinedu had acquired a big auto-workshop in that choice location in the southwest of the city and had six employees at work in the workshop – two Hispanics, one black and three Caucasians – in addition to a secretary who was also Hispanic. All sorts of machines had been installed. From all indications, Chinedu was doing well. Parked at the carport were as many as ten cars waiting for pickup, and about six awaiting repairs. He introduced the secretary to Maeze as his wife, Jo Ann. He took Maeze round the workshop, at each stage informing people that Maeze had been his lecturer back in Nigeria. Finally, the two retired to Chinedu's office for discussions.

Maeze was candid, telling Chinedu of his bills' predicament. Chinedu expressed surprise at Maeze's experience. He had known him to be well-to-do in Nigeria. He remarked how America could make the poor rich and could also make a wealthy person look like a trash. He understood the dynamics of living in

America. Maeze had had considerable wealth back in Nigeria. His businesses had been thriving. Then his bank had problems with the Central Bank of Nigeria, on account of which all the customers of the commercial bank were unable to withdraw their money. Chinedu unhesitatingly gave Maeze a five thousand Dollar check, to be paid back whenever Maeze was able to resolve his financial issues.

Maeze duly learnt that Jenny, who had obviously grown used to grand neighbourhoods, had found and rented another upscale apartment. She had dropped the keys of the one she shared with Maeze, having obviously lost interest in an apartment without electricity, burdened with unpaid rents. When Maeze asked for her new address in case he needed to contact her, she refused and told him: "My cell phone is always there in case." Maeze of course would not tell her of the loan from Chinedu. He paid all outstanding bills. To avoid further contact with Jenny, Maeze decided to move to one of the dreaded, very low-scale apartment complexes. It was one of the places that did no credit checks, and the rent was three times lower than where he had lived with Jenny. Maeze wanted a place that Jenny would not like to visit.

He contacted some of the former friends with whom he had stopped relating on account of his marriage, and they were all happy and keen to assist him. With many other familiar Nigerians living in his new neighborhood, Maeze settled down well. He had just one goal in mind – his education – and faced his studies with single-minded zeal.

13. COMPLETING ACADEMIC WORK

At the university, Maeze was vigorously pursuing his goals. He completed his comprehensive examinations; did his residency and his doctoral candidacy successfully. Maeze's dissertation necessitated visits to many universities, for surveys and data collection. After the terrorist attack of 9/11 in America, it became a herculean task for international students to obtain information from Americans for purposes of research.

Maeze spent weeks without any universities indicating that they would cooperate in his surveys among human elements of the population he targeted. It was not until Dr. Robert, the chair of his dissertation, contacted his many ex-students in high positions in many universities, that Maeze made meaningful progress with his survey administration. After weeks of serious meetings with the school's statistician on his work, other doctoral students were referred to him by his dissertation committee members for help in data analysis and interpretation. Thus, Maeze was one of the first students to complete his dissertation work. English was the sphere that rattled him. Coming from a Nigerian-British educational background, Maeze's grammatical structures were inconsistent with American-style written English. His final work required many revisions. A young but tough woman at the graduate school also proved an obstacle for him. He was uncertain of the cause of her hostility towards him but suspected she might have had sad encounters with some Nigerians in the past. Her reasons for being particularly unreceptive of Maeze could not be explained, but Maeze suspected the woman could have also had some unhappy encounters with Nigerians in the past.

Maeze was greatly assisted by being in a study team led by Mark, one of the best in their discipline, endowed with awesome organizational skills. Mark was effective in effacing barriers in Maeze's path. Thus, Maeze completed his dissertation defense in record time. Mark's assistance was the key that helped him through the many challenges on his way at both the faculty and graduate school. Whenever he was at a deadlock, Mark sprang forward to provide the essential leeway. He made Maeze have a reading group that became like a family to him. However, they did not know what he was struggling with at the home front.

In that period that Maeze worked on his dissertation, he was anticipating his reunion with his family in Nigeria after six years. He was also working towards a neat and final parting from Jenny. They had been separated for over six months and needed to divorce officially and get on with their lives. Jenny obviously had already moved on. He called her on her cell phone and received no response. The next day, Jenny returned the call. They arranged to meet at the Walmart store car park on Westheimer after her day's job. Surprisingly, Jenny did not come in her car. Maeze imagined that she had decided to ride with her friends to work as she sometimes did. As was her wont, she requested money to help with her rent. They agreed to end their marriage properly as they were separated, and Maeze could leave the United States anytime in the future. Maeze promised to bring her three thousand dollars when they met for signing the divorce document. The next day, Jenny began to call Maeze's cell phone, nonstop. It was her irksome habit whenever she needed cash. Maeze's mention of three thousand dollars had obviously made her salivate! She could not wait for the time agreed for the gift before she began to swamp him with tales of her landlord's efforts to eject her. Jenny's greed made Maeze recall a story of his community's. It was that the python, sighting any prey, would not take its eyes from the prey until it devoured it.

Jenny's many calls would begin with her impatient query: "Where you at?"

Despite her demands, Maeze tried hard not to give her the promised sum until the agreed date. She began again to threaten him. Four days later, Maeze fulfilled his part of their agreement and sent the money to her. On the date agreed for signing the divorce deposition, Maeze waited where Jenny had instructed him, at a gas station near her work place. He waited for hours for her to come and sign her portion before she finally appeared. Jenny took her pen and the document, then held it as though reading through before she could sign. After studying the document for a while, she seemed reflective, then withdrew her hand. Maeze was sitting next to her on the driver's seat, while Jenny was on the front passenger's seat beside him. Maeze was dismayed at the drama Jenny was enacting.

"What is the problem?" Maeze asked.

Jenny said nothing but refused all entreaties to sign so that the lawyer who had already been paid could go ahead with court processes. They had of course agreed to end their union and had been separated for many months. And Jenny had of course collected money from Maeze. Now, she refused what was necessary for each person to proceed lawfully with life. After a long time, she said they would meet the following day at a shop near her house to sign the document. Maeze wondered what difference there might be between signing on that day, and on the following day. Jenny finally left the car for her work. The next day, Jenny refused to pick her phone or appear at the place she had suggested. Maeze was familiar with her telephone attitude. If she was called when she was not interested in speaking, she would act as though the caller was in desperate need of her and ignore the calls. In Maeze's situation, he had no choice but to persist. The lawyer was waiting, and the time within which the signed divorce deposition could be submitted was limited to thirty days. Jenny was aware of the rules and was willfully frustrating the process. When the allotted period expired, Maeze accepted that the sums paid to the lawyer and to Jenny had been wasted.

Jenny called Maeze about a month later. He initially ignored it, but after the calls became persistent he answered her. She began to plead for forgiveness and asked to see Maeze that evening. He refused to let her know where he lived. The next day, as he was keying in his apartment's security code to open the gate, someone suddenly sprang to his side. It was Jenny! There were many vehicles behind Maeze, so he was compelled to let her into his car. Jenny refused to leave the house that night. She ate her favorite African spicy rice and soup with Maeze. She pleaded with Maeze, explaining "There are people you meet in your life, and you just can't let them leave you". Maeze, at the final stage of his academic work, intending to leave for his home country shortly, wanted no further distractions. Every other pursuit in America had failed save his doctoral aspiration. He was resolved that this woman would not destroy that or even know his plans for leaving America, because she might somehow thwart his plans.

Maeze told her plainly that he wanted nothing more to do with her. She begged him to have her back, if only as a girlfriend, whining that she had no one else to go to.

"Where are you living now?" He asked.

"I'm living with Cynthia in the North of the city," She replied.

"With her husband?" Maeze queried.

"No, Cynthia has separated from Rex," She answered.

Jenny told her story of meeting another boyfriend who she discovered was a pimp. He would take her to Louisiana at weekends and collect money from other men to have sex with her. They had lived like that for several months.

"What?" Maeze shouted.

She said that that was the guy's business. Pimps would pick pretty sexy girls from one city, go to another city and get them to do all sorts of bad things with other men for money. Jenny was actually hiding from this guy to avoid him taking her to Louisiana again. Maeze asked her whether the so-called boyfriend put a spell on her or kidnapped her against her wish. She explained that there were "bad guys" who could kill. "Why then did you have to think about my place and nowhere else?" Maeze asked.

She was seeking pity. That night, Maeze suppressed all sentiment and sensuality, refusing to share the bed with Jenny. He slept on the couch in the living room, with one eye open all night. In the morning, although Maeze had no engagements, he pretended to have important meetings at school. He hurriedly dropped Jenny off at her work place and returned to the house. At about the time she would close at work, Maeze left his house for the library and stayed outside till late before going home. Jenny started calling regularly again.

Maeze knew that if he again yielded to Jenny's overtures, he would be on a course of certain self-destruction. He recalled his people's adage: "an insect killed by an *okpoko* is merely deaf, considering that *okpoko* is attended by an alarming noise."

Maeze was on the verge of completing his doctoral degree program, his reason for spending six arduous and eventful years in America. Should he be so daft as to resume his relationship with Jenny in order to assuage his lust, he might not complete his programme and leave the United States happily. Then Jenny could become more obstructive if stopped from reaching Maeze, as they had an outstanding divorce matter. In America, citizens have great advantages over immigrants in the resolution of disputes. Maeze had never forgotten Jenny's threats concerning her brothers when she lived with them in Richmond, Texas. She bragged about their feats of violence as people of the street.

Recalling a fable told him by his grandmother about intrigues in the animal kingdom, he felt it was apposite to his situation. The lion, king of all animals, would borrow from other animals when in need. He was however notorious for killing creatures who dared to come to collect the debts he owed them. The king's requests would always be granted promptly by his subjects. Those foolhardy enough to seek repayment suffered for their rashness! The lion would literally make them his dinner. Animals could neither refuse to lend to the lion nor ask for return of possessions lent to the lion.

It happened that Tortoise lent his property to Lion. Knowing it would be suicidal to ask for it back, he summoned his kinsmen and asked them one after the other, who could volunteer for a risky debt-collection assignment. He promised to bequeath his entire property to the volunteer. He did not tell them they would have to brave the lion's lair, knowing no one would accept that challenge. He rather asked them one after the other: "How many times would somebody do something bad to you before you learn your lesson?" Some answered, "Ten times." Others said, "Nine! Eight!. Two! One!" When it was the turn of Ram, he answered, "As the person plays his own game, I'll play mine at the same time, and turn things to my advantage."

Tortoise was very happy with Ram. He sent him to go to Lion the King to demand his properties which were long overdue for return. Ram embarked on the life-threatening task. As Ram approached the King's gate, he started to arouse the king sexually by bleating. It happened that the Queen Lioness had not allowed king Lion access to her bed for a long time because of some domestic issues. Both King and Queen were aroused, and they went indoors to copulate. Ram sneaked into the compound and collected all of Tortoise's belongings there. After enjoying himself, Lion came out to realize that Ram had collected all the belongings of Mr. Tortoise in his house. King Lion and his wife realized how effectively Ram had tricked them. Lion went berserk searching for Ram. And that was why Lion had always hated Ram. Wherever Lion saw Ram or any creature that looked like Ram, no matter the circumstances, he would descend on him with murderous intent. Conversely, Tortoise and Ram remained fast friends.

Maeze concluded that in order to successfully complete his academic work and return to his home country without harm or disappointment, he would cooperate with desperate Jenny. He told Jenny that he would have to visit his home country, seek money and return so that they could continue their marriage. Maeze prepared himself, completed his program, and promptly left the United States. He reflected that in Africa, Jenny would have been publicly abhorred for admitting she had engaged in prostitution and having the nerve to tell her husband that she had cohabited for months with another man, a man who hired her out to countless men for their sexual gratification.

Jenny would have suffered the public disgrace of being stripped and paraded in the village square. What abomination and grime she had plunged him into, just because he was an immigrant. Those nauseating facts further fuelled Maeze's resolve to leave that beautiful country that the entire planet was flocking to.

PART III

14. ARRIVING IN NIGERIA

Airplane officials, both at the American airport and the transit one in Europe, must have been surprised by his one-way ticket to Nigeria. They searched Maeze rigorously and asked him more questions than they usually would.

On arrival in Lagos, he encountered surprises. There were throngs, noise and disorderliness at the baggage collection point, added to the blast of heat. The air-conditioning at the airport had obviously broken down. He had been used to all those conditions before he left Nigeria. However, many representatives of government had come to America to proclaim the new Nigeria, which was supposed to be functioning beautifully. Their town hall meetings were aimed at encouraging Nigerians in Diaspora to return to motherland and contribute to the nation's improvement. Now Maeze wondered if the change vaunted by those visiting officials did not include improved infrastructure at the airports. Any first-time visitors would be appalled at their experiences from the international entry points.

At the Customs desk check, they turned Maeze's suitcases upside down. He was baffled about what they might have been searching for. When they appeared satisfied that he had nothing incriminating, they started to beg him for money. Returnees were usually advised by family and friends to have some change in Nigerian currency before departing from America. They were advised they would have to tip corrupt customs and other security officials at the airports, whether or not they were in possession of contraband! Otherwise, the traveler might be delayed unduly or even robbed, whether or not they had violated any laws. Returnees were also urged to have phone numbers of the good and great in Nigeria, to rescue them from nightmarish encounters at the airport. There were stories of returnees who, asserting in Nigeria the civil liberties they had enjoyed in foreign lands, got killed by security agents.

Consequently, caution and meekness were required of Nigerians returning from overseas. Maeze handed some cash to the customs man that begged him for money. Realizing that Maeze was actually returning from America, the man requested Dollars instead of Naira notes. Maeze ignored him and walked on with his suit cases. He had asked his best friend, Chuks, to pick him up at the scheduled arrival time, but did not want his return disclosed to his family. Chuks was waiting, and it was dusk as they drove to a nearby hotel. Returnees had also learnt not to take long trips from international airports to city centres at certain hours. There had been many incidents of robbery.

The hotel Maeze was taken to, was decent but dear by American standards. There were many other guests who also looked like passengers departing or arriving in the country. Many young and alluringly clad women loitered around the hotel premises. They seemed to be seeking overseas travelers. Many returnees, long before their arrival, were warned about those harlots.

They could be deadly. There had been ugly incidents of people drugged and robbed in hotels. Those women lusted after dollars. Hotel guests noted the presence of heavily armed security personnel around. "That's why many people come to a place like this," Chuks observed.

Maeze went to bed that night full of thought. His years in America had given him a different outlook from many Nigerians'. He worried about his family, about having to bribe to achieve almost all his goals and living without electricity in the tropical weather.

After all those years away, how would he work his way back into his family's lives? When his wife divorced him, he had started the relationship with Jenny in America without his family's knowledge. He had concealed that affair from even his closest friends in Nigeria. When he and Jenny parted, he had continued to chat with his former wife without mentioning that incident. He had forgiven her whatever harm she did him but would need to tell her of his affair with Jenny. It was going to be tasking especially with the children who would never understand. Maeze decided that if he could win back his former wife, she would help with the excuses or explanations to the children. Of course, he had no choice. Well, he reasoned that the life of a journey man, is left to be told from all angles. It didn't really matter from whose perspective the story is told; but the authentic and one story is the one by the journey man himself. In Maeze's Igbo nationality, it is said that "warfront is meant for the brave, but the war story is for the women."

Maeze took the first local flight the next morning to his home in Port-Harcourt. The traffic situation in Port Harcourt was dreadful that early morning. Since he did not wish anyone to know he was returning, he boarded an airport taxi and arrived at his house at about 11am. The gate was manned by an elderly man. He must have been in his sixties, was dark-complexioned, of average height, neat and alert, with a good command of English. A Rottweiler at the other side of the compound roared as though its privacy had been violated. The spruce and articulate man asked Maeze: "Who are you looking for?"

Maeze paused. The dog raged still. When he mentioned his name, the gatekeeper seemed skeptical about his identity because he had not been informed that such a "big man" as the house-owner would arrive on that day. He went to the window to announce to the children that their father was back. Meanwhile, Maeze and the taxi driver were still outside. He duly learned that there had been many robberies in the neighbourhood. The wily thieves feigned familiarity with the house owners only to attack and steal once they were let into the compounds. Now, the four children raced towards the gate, screaming "Daddy! Daddy!! Daddy!!!" It was no surprise they were all at home as it was a Saturday morning.

Maeze stood there, dazed with the reality of his folly. He went for a doctoral degree and abandoned his treasures. Now, equipped with that certificate, how would he make up for lost time? How would he start afresh to bond with his children? He began to call the children by their names, one by one. They were all transported by the poignancy of the reunion. The driver loudly reminded Maeze that he had to discharge the taxi, and he promptly paid his fare. He learned his children's mother was out of town, and quickly called her. She was in another state about four hundred miles away, attending a funeral. The children in Port Harcourt with a sister.

The following day, Maeze travelled to his home village to see his old parents. They lived about a hundred and fifty miles away and had of course been worried about his long sojourn in the United States. Tears of joy flowed freely as the reunited as a big family.

Over the following weeks, Maeze tried to re-familiarize himself with his house. The chairs, carpets and other furnishings in the house were worn by age or rough use by boisterous children. He had many question-and-answer sessions with the children. The happiness in everybody's face was affecting. The next morning, Maeze accompanied his children to school. They were delighted to be driven to school by their father. The atmosphere was festive, many staff members coming to say "welcome sir" to the returned proprietor.

The school was vibrant with activities. Many managerial issues had to be addressed. Everybody understood the proprietor to be a seasoned administrator, equal to the challenges facing the institution. After addressing the school that first morning, Maeze spent the rest of the day inspecting the institution's physical structures for repair or replacement. Challenges abounded over students' and staff discipline, software management and reporting system, electricity supply, treated water, salaries, maintenance, vandalizing of equipment and fittings.

Most disheartening were the bad roads in the school's vicinity. Those roads were impassable in places. All the school's vehicles, purchased at exorbitant cost, had been damaged by those horrible roads.

The premises and buildings were in urgent need of repair. Many schools had sprung up in every direction. In fact, nearly all the houses surrounding the school had been converted to schools. It did not seem to Maeze that regulations over the operation of schools were being enforced. In earlier years, the inspection and approval unit of the Ministry of Education had made it hard for people to casually open schools. How could educational institutions be left to operate without monitoring of standards? Maeze realized he would need time to accomplish all he had to do. In the meantime, all he could do was plod on as best he could.

Maeze's two eldest children were now teenagers, and in high school. They were preparing for entry into university. Maeze was always keen on his family's education and general wellbeing. He naturally immersed himself in their studies and preparation for the transition from high school to university. When the family moved from Port Harcourt to Abuja, Nigeria's federal capital territory, Maeze's first son who was completing his secondary schooling that year had to remain in the dormitory in Port Harcourt. Even while Maeze was living in America, many friends had called to advise him to move his family to the fast-rising and beautiful city, Abuja. Abuja was said to look and function like a Western metropolis. Maeze was further advised that Abuja was a better location to run a school than Port Harcourt.

Maeze made an abrupt decision. Rather than struggle to upgrade the amenities in the Port Harcourt school, he would move his family to Abuja. Militancy, a new brand of agitation for resource control in the Niger Delta, had ravaged the serene and beautiful garden city, Port Harcourt. Sporadic shootings occurred in the state. In the neighbouring state to Rivers, Abia, kidnapping and robbery flourished. Those disasters could be unleashed anytime and anywhere. Maeze's home state, Imo, was suffering the same blights, as indeed the entire South-East and South-South regions of Nigeria. Many of the elite had moved their families from the beleaguered states to the safer zones like Lagos and Federal Capital Territory, Abuja. In Lagos and Abuja, many who were conspicuously wealthy – and consequently endangered – in the southern states, would be unnoticed amidst the staggering wealth of numerous members of those communities.

Professionals like medical doctors and lawyers, educators like Maeze, and big business owners, were deserting the region in large numbers for fear of their lives. Those fleeing the Southern States left their businesses and mansions to associates and security guards to look after. Some even left Nigeria to seek better lives overseas, or simply to rest in the case of the retired. There were of course many who had been so successful in Nigeria that they could afford not to seek further paid employment.

The affluent who clung to the troubled states were considered diehards. Mainly tough politicians and gang leaders, they often moved around with official security escorts or other types of guards. In those states, however one strove to be inconspicuous, to avoid being trailed and harmed or murdered by the growing population of hoodlums. The cities had not been properly planned but had simply expanded. No matter how smart one tried to disguise himself, he could easily be traced and trailed by the growing population of bad guys. So, with poor housing plans, it was easy for criminals to cohabit in some shanties around otherwise highbrow neighborhoods. It was not too hard for them to monitor their victims. As a result of declining oil revenue and the shutting of many companies, many were afflicted by poverty. There were reports of incessant killings, abductions, robberies and cult clashes all over the region. Thus, the trend of moving to richer locations like Lagos and Abuja. In those cities, one could run one's business with no additional cost for personal security, and without disturbance from criminals. Electricity supply was also considerably better in Lagos and Abuja than in the South-East and South-South regions.

In Abuja, Maeze rented a five-bedroom duplex and a two-room, self-contained Boys quarters, all with a security house, borehole and very spacious and well maintained, in a high-class estate in the beautiful Gwarimpa district. He settled there with his young family. Maeze reflected on his years of struggle, both as a young man in Nigeria and through the travails of his sojourn in America, and decided it was time to pamper himself with God's blessings. His family, he felt, had suffered enough and deserved comfort and luxuries. The new house was beautifully furnished. Maeze bought three brand new vehicles to replace the second-hand ones, bought at auction sales in Houston that he had used over the years. He kept one of his old cars in Port Harcourt for his use when on visits, and another one in Owerri for his parents' use. He got his younger children enrolled in some of the best private schools in Abuja. At that time too, Maeze began to seek land in a good location to establish his own school. His life was going well.

Maeze however was troubled by a certain factor: his separation from Jenny was not yet concluded. Their marriage had not been dissolved. After all, they had lived apart for over two years, and she had descended into a filthy life of prostitution. Maeze, despite the money and time spent, and abuse and humiliation endured, had decided to drop the craze to live in America, and return to his family like a prodigal son. It was time to close the story.

Maeze pleaded with his ex for forgiveness. He told her his story of America and the relationship with Jenny. She assured him of her support and love, thus giving him the strength he needed at the time. Maeze began to urge Jenny towards the final dissolution of their union. Meanwhile, Jenny seemed to have received information about Maeze's new life with his family in Nigeria and tried to threaten his peace from America. She refused to agree to the dissolution of the marriage, pleading that their relationship should continue, although they were thousands of miles apart. When her pleas failed, she threatened to report him to the government to stop him living with his spouse. Maeze wondered how she thought she could achieve that goal and ignored her threats. Finally, she began to plead for financial assistance. He reflected wryly that in the past, she had taken his assistance for granted.

With the help of Maeze's friends in the United States, a marriage attorney was contacted. Assistance to Jenny was tied to her signing of the divorce petition and the grant of the divorce from the court. Jenny could not resist a monetary offer. After a few months, Maeze received the court's order granting the divorce petition. He was free from marital enslavement.

Maeze sometimes wondered what he had gained from his endeavor to live and study in America. He had struggled to finally acquire the academic degrees, interacted with American course mates and friends, but he seemed unable to emerge from the nightmare of his union with Jenny.

Maeze recalled that part of his professional training discouraged clients from dwelling on the past, but rather to learn from every experience for the pursuit of future good. His inner perturbation did not totally abate. Whatever Maeze's beliefs and professional attainments, it seemed it would take a lifetime to erase that grim phase from his memory. Maeze strove to discard Jenny and his American nightmare from his memory and remarried his sweetheart. He reasoned it was what the family needed for their peace and particularly the happiness of the children. Maeze and his wife while apart had learnt many lessons about marriage. Their earlier childish attitudes, causes of frequent rows, had yielded to maturity, sacrifice and support for each other.

15. SEARCHING FOR A SPACE IN ABUJA

Maeze, fresh from America, was flush with the knowledge he yearned to impart to the youth through lecturing in one of the country's universities. He bubbled with energy and the American "can-do" spirit.

He went to the University of Abuja. The non-academic staff at the front office were distant, indeed, resentful. His assurance and foreign accent seemed to affront them. They did not disguise their abhorrence of his presence. "Please, how may I apply for a lecturing position in your reputable university?" Maeze asked.

The middle-aged man sitting right across the table in front shouted at him: "Nobody is on seat." Maeze looked around the office in disbelief. Here was a staff of the University telling a visitor that nobody was on seat, with the attitude of "I'm not in the mood to entertain questions".

Maeze felt that the man might have been having a bad day. He smiled at the grumpy group and addressed the speaker. "But, Sir you are around. I believe you can help with my enquiry, Sir."

The group in that office was not disposed to receive Maeze. He asked further questions and was ignored. Their behavior seemed rehearsed, an attitude that proclaimed, "you are not wanted here." After standing there for a while without any response from them, he left the office and walked to the car park. He sat quietly in the car brooding over the encounter.

"Is this how I'm going to relate with people in this country?" He wondered, trying to recall every moment of the encounter in case he had been disrespectful. Indeed, that encounter recalled his earlier career experience with the French multinational oil servicing company. Many people treated prospective employees with disdain, but Maeze expected the situation to have changed. He wished to give back, to uplift and enrich the youth from his wealth of knowledge but would no longer tolerate such discourtesy from the holders of public office in Nigeria. That was the first shock Maeze received in his search for work in his country.

The wish remained to impart all he had learnt in management, statistics, research, Diagnostic Statistical Manual (DSM) of Mental Disorders, American Psychological Association (APA) Manual, Psychology and Counseling, and also his wealth of experience in counseling practice. He had had practical psychotherapy with children, teens and adults for four years in America. He was in a wonderful relationship with both his faculty and the alumni association. They had promised to ship books and learning materials regularly, and to maintain that relationship with Nigerian students in universities. Maeze therefore was eager to contribute to the educational development of his dear country, Nigeria. He had not thought of the ethnic and religious sentiments that had marred the country's development since independence, even blighting learning in the ivory tower. Indeed, those retrogressive leanings had permeated all aspects of the nation's life.

In both undergraduate and graduate studies of statistics and research, Maeze had encountered challenges. Now that he had overcome them, he wished to assist students to demolish the myths that had scared even brilliant students away from those subjects. He recognized, by their attire, that the people he met at the university's front office were from a certain section of the country. He had found that in Nigeria, people generally recognized others' ethnic origin. Those hostile people, he was sure, knew that he came from a different part of the country from theirs. Brooding again over their resentment, he wonders how such conduct from the supposed image-makers of a tertiary institution in the Federal Capital City would affect the nation's teeming, talented youth. He realized that ethnic discrimination, rampant and undisguised, was entrenched in the system. Maeze then decided that he would not waste his energy and time complaining about it. He had had enough experience of it when he served in the oil sector. He considered that the country needed people of his training. He should kowtow to no one.

Maeze decided to travel East, as he had worked with a number of professors there prior to his departure for further studies in America. In his years abroad, he had remained in contact with some of them. When, in the midst of his travails in America he contemplated abandoning his doctoral studies to seek opportunities in a Nigerian university, those Nigerian professors had advised him to endure whatever sufferings America offered and complete his studies there. They maintained that ending his studies there abruptly to return to Nigeria would only bring him regrets and frustration. He duly learnt that lecturers in Nigeria never helped those returning students to complete their programs. The reasons for their reluctance were unknown.

Although he had informed those friends in academia of his move to Abuja, he now returned to the East, to Owerri in Imo State, to seek a lecturing position. He wondered how he would cope with the security problems he had wished to avoid and found no answer. He was however determined not to allow all the knowledge garnered in America, and still fresh in his mind, to simply be wasted. Maeze was astounded that those friends in the East were loath to let him get a teaching position near them. He realized that to gain employment in Nigeria, even for a lecturer, was a herculean task. His good friends lecturing at federal universities were declining his calls. One who answered his call said: "No! Go to the state- owned university instead." Maeze was reluctant to teach at a state university, suspecting that academic standards were low because policy was aimed at admitting large numbers of the indigenous population. There was yet another top female professor in another federal institution that Maeze and his American professor had met in both Houston and Owerri. She visited Houston at that time and now had returned to her job. He had approached her also for assistance in case an opening for a lecturer's position arose in her institution. Maeze was surprised to meet her as the head of a department just when somebody else took him to her office. He had thought it was going to work out this time around. To his disappointment, this head of department acted like she had never met Maeze all her life. Her behavior was a complete opposite of what Maeze had observed her to be in the past.

He went to see yet another professor at a federal university. He and his American professor had met her in Houston. Maeze's allusion to their meeting manifestly irked her. She virtually dismissed Maeze from her office. Maeze was more nonplussed than he had been when he had met hostile university reception staff in Abuja. He pondered the situation. "Is this stigmatization? Or is it the system in Nigeria? I have heard that positions are reserved for relatives of people in high places. Obviously, nobody in a position of authority, no matter how deep the friendship, would give an opportunity to someone outside their circle. Is there anything wrong in acquiring a foreign degree? Is there anything wrong in applying for a lecturer's position at a university?"

He went to the state university he had initially rejected. This time, he was introduced directly to the President of the University. He seemed to peruse Maeze's application and résumé with growing impatience. He asked Maeze and the friend who brought him into the large office where many visitors and lecturers waited. As though intent on publicly humiliating Maeze, he asked: "Why did you choose to study counseling instead of the numerous more important courses abroad?" He obviously wished to be heard distinctly by everyone in his office. Maeze was dumbfounded. The atmosphere was still. He silently asked himself: "How could the President of a University decide to disgrace me openly, and probably others present who studied courses he considered "useless?" How could a university's number one employee insult a job applicant in this manner? The man simply turned his attention to others in his office. He was treating Maeze like some irritant come to disturb his morning's business.

Maeze took his application and walked out dejected. It was incredible how some individuals in positions of authority abused and dehumanized others seeking one opportunity or another in their offices. This chief of university could simply have told him, the applicant, that there were no vacant positions, rather than inviting him in order to publicly insult him.

Maeze was discovering a compelling fact. People in positions like the university president's preferred to use their powers to keep positions for family friends and members. It was becoming usual to find the same last names in government records from one generation to another. It was found on investigation that, even where last names differed, many employees of particular establishments had maternal or marital relationships. Further investigations revealed that heads of government Ministries, Departments and Agencies (MDAs), established grapevine exchange programs where the head in Ministry A sent his "own people" to heads in Ministry B, Department C or Agency D, and vice versa, to the utter and permanent exclusion of the general public who had no family members in the MDAs. Maeze found also that those heads used their contacts in high positions to place their kith and kin in the lucrative private oil and gas companies. The lowly ones who slipped unnoticed into the system might be overlooked during the recruitment exercise and might begin to do well in their respective MDAs. However, they were usually victimized and frustrated along the line, often thrown out at the peak of their careers just to make way for the oligarchical heritage. In Maeze's community, the practice was termed 'ima mmadu,' literally 'knowing people,' being connected.

It was crucial to have contacts in high places, whatever one sought – welfare, admission into a government school or university, employment, contracts and allocation, political office, justice, or just protection. Those without such contacts or 'godfathers' were stuck in small ventures and hardly made progress. Their lack of high contacts made every process onerous for them, from registration of business and obtaining loan forms, to taxation, clearing of goods at entry points, and movement of goods and personnel from place to place. Most new businesses naturally collapsed under the weight of costs. Electricity supply was inadequate, and they needed to generate their own power, yet pay for electricity that was not supplied from the national grid, or face disconnection. They provided their own water, repaired their roads, disposed of their refuse, yet paid mandatory bills for those services to local, state and federal establishments. Consequently, many in business ventures were defeated by running expenses. Nobody asked why those in government employment seemed wealthier than mainly business people, and why all accusations of corruption and looting the public treasury ended without convictions in the courts. Everybody in the country agreed that, since the military era, monumental corruption had been going on, yet the police and courts seemed to disagree with the rest of the citizens. The prisons bulged with petty thieves. Those who defrauded Maeze in 2000 hurriedly sought protection of their human rights from the courts, retained his money and faced no sanctions.

Maeze spent a whole day musing on all he was experiencing. He wondered if it was wrong to have gone for master's and doctorate degrees in the United States. In more developed climes, people like him would be wooed by higher institutions to accept teaching appointments from them. In Nigeria, the prevailing attitudes were baffling. Was it wrong to have applied for a position in the universities? Far from it! There could not be anything bad in seeking to teach young people in the nation's ivory tower. Obstacles were created by the sheer wickedness of those who should have striven for the nation's growth. In America, which had more people with higher degrees than any African country, doctorate degree holders were still appreciated, and people urged to study for doctorates.

Maeze now realized the truth of the tragedy of the nation's leadership. The wrong people were holding office. They obstructed the poor minority's channels to progress and advancement. The disadvantaged, trapped in their destitution and subjugation, become habitual beggars. Citizens were excelling at begging. The CEO of multinational corporations who refused to employ you, and the bank executive who could not give you loans without impossible collaterals, pay your children's school fees and proclaim their benevolence all over the community. The politician shares two Dollars to voters during elections and is returned to office to continue exploiting the populace. The governor might fail in his election promise to provide uninterrupted electricity supply and good roads but would promise to do it all in his second tenure. The electorate knew the words were just ploys to obtain their votes but felt powerless because they needed to feed their families.

Meanwhile, the few oppressors lived in opulence, squandering the country's collective resources. They were insatiable and unflagging in their acquisitive zeal, amassing riches that would not be exhausted by their descendants even after twenty generations. Birthdays, marriages and vacations were being celebrated in Europe, America, Dubai and other major cities around the world as a status symbol. Education of their children was pursued overseas, as medical treatment and even routine shopping.

Successful individuals in business aped those very affluent few. Yet, it was no surprise that the very wealthy felt unsafe and uncomfortable in Nigeria, despite their security escorts! Crime still raged in various parts of the country. As leaders insisted on their issue studying abroad, their associates, then the general public would try to emulate them. The leaders' stance was that homegrown education was inferior. Consequently, all parents yearned to send their children abroad. That, veritably, was leadership by example! The leaders had shown they had no confidence in Nigeria's schools and universities, hospitals and shopping facilities. It was no surprise that the institutions should be left to rot.

Maeze wondered what he would have done had there been no educational business of the family to return to. He would simply have been frustrated by compatriots who had gone round the globe urging their nationals to come home, claiming that the government of the day had changed the nation for the better. Now Maeze recalled the attitude of acquaintances in America who were adamant that they would not return home. They said they had undertaken that journey in the past, and found it was futile. After returning to America, they declared they would not go to Nigeria again, and even instructed their family members not to take their corpses back to Nigeria if they died. Those people paid no heed to government agents at town hall meetings in the West asking Nigerians to return home.

Maeze decided to concentrate his energies on operating and developing his personal educational institution rather than sink into the helplessness and hopelessness he was being frustrated into.

16. SHARP PRACTICES IN PUBLIC WORK

Maeze's family had bought property to build a school in the beautiful Federal Capital City, Abuja. Maeze planned a state-of-the-art high school, comparable in standard to those he had seen in America. He was resolved to bring professionalism into the management of the school. Inundated with stories of fraudulent practices in land transactions in Abuja, Maeze decided from the outset to retain an experienced legal practitioner.

The school land was originally allotted to a woman from the local community, a tribal woman who worked with the Local Government Council. A land surveyor was also engaged to help Maeze determine that there were no subsisting claims on the land. After the official search and confirmation at the Federal Capital Territory's land registry, and confirmation of the particular piece of land by the lawyer, the land surveyor who was registered with the Local Government Council, took Maeze and his team on a physical inspection. The conveyor came with her team comprising her lawyer, surveyor and agents; while Maeze was accompanied by his own team of lawyer, surveyor and agents. There were over twelve persons there, and were shown the large, empty piece of land with particular emphasis on the demarcations with other allottees. Having satisfied all present as to the genuineness of the piece of land, the lawyers went ahead for the final documentation and transfer of titles. Finally, payment was made to the satisfaction of all. To Maeze's dismay, when he tried to begin the fencing of the land, he found his land was encumbered! Over fifty people occupied the land Maeze had actually bought, which adjoined the one the surveyors had shown the inspection team. Those who had gone on physical inspection had been deceived! Maeze's land teemed with huts, latrines, water wells and auto shops.

In Abuja, those illegal occupants were called "squatters." Maeze had found there was acute shortage of housing in Abuja. It was a fast-growing city, daily drawing people to its serenity and economic promise. Sometimes, empty spaces already allocated were rented out to unsuspecting tenants by indigenous and visiting land-grabbers alike. With that practice, thriving villages emerged from illegal rentals. Abuja abounded with such housing settlements. Those lands meanwhile had true grantees, properly documented in the lands registry. Numerous land disputes raged, with litigation, demolitions, thuggery, fights and sometimes killings.

Maeze wondered how successive land administrations had allowed such high-level profiteering to fester in the country's capital city. He realized of course that the pains of citizens confronting those man-made obstacles were the gains of unscrupulous civil servants in charge of the establishments, and their political "godfathers."

The civil servants in charge of lands deliberately allowed people to build on lands not planned for houses. They readily accepted bribes proffered by those illegal developers, only to demolish their shacks when the original owners appeared to develop their lands. It was bitterly amusing that the civil servants granted the official approval for illegal developers to build, and afterwards ordered the demolition of the structures. Ultimately, disputes between land grabbers and grantees were referred to the offices of the top civil servants for investigation and resolution. Eventually, vendors, buyers and squatters all pressed bribes on the civil servants at the lands' ministry. Original town planning layouts, surveys, drawings and structures were often altered or mutilated in order to justify one's petition. Sometimes, people actually lost their lands to others because they were unable to afford the bribes demanded. There were cases where whole estates which cost developers billions of Naira, were demolished by regulators who were there from the day the foundations were laid. Why would government regulators who were supposed to halt any form of physical development in the beginning close their eyes to such developments until the estates were completed? Why waste scarce resources that would have been better channeled into more economic and socially rewarding ventures? Owners of empty lands were therefore always eager to occupy their property for development before squatters preceded them. Many had lost their officially allocated lands because they were unable to move in before squatters did so. Again, because of the shortage of housing, people who built even shanties reaped bountifully.

Lands' authorities claimed lack of funds to provide infrastructure for areas where lands had been allocated by government. Furthermore, they did not allow people onto those lands unless infrastructure was available. Consequently, as the population increased, more people demanded the few available houses. With funds severely limited, the government would prioritize a few areas for provision of roads, water, drainage, electricity and sewage with the sparse resources. The relatively few houses available for rental were pursued by crowds of prospective tenants, making rental costs escalate. In a country considered corrupt by its own citizens, a few people in positions of authority allocated lands gratis to their kith and kin, then resold those lands to developers on their own terms. Those people seemed bent on arresting the even spread of housing development until they had sold out their predetermined tracts and buildings.

Maeze wondered what was stopping the government from implementing an economically rational policy. It was simply to provide land and ask numerous low-income house applicants to pay a certain percentage of the cost of one or two-bedroom houses. They would then gradually become owners of the apartments. Financial houses would be helpful in the plan. Those workers would gain a sense of belonging, becoming proud owners of houses, and families' suffering over accommodation would be greatly reduced.

Unfortunately, many in authority seemed to harbor the conviction that good and affordable housing or a comfortable existence should not be available to everybody. Maeze concluded that until people were elected who truly cared, there would be no qualitative change in society.

The wastage was appalling, the carnage on the highways unspeakable. On roads across the federation, potholes were ignored until they become dishes, then gullies and veritable deathtraps. Roads were sometimes completely closed because of gullies. Gruesome and fatal accidents occurred daily on those roads. Those contracted to keep the roads in good condition brazenly disappointed. Many federal roads – Lagos to Onitsha, Abuja to Benin, East-West Road, Enugu to Port Harcourt – had not been in completely good repair since the 1980s. The same was true of state and local government roads. Successive governments tried to make excuses for the situation, yet the deaths continued unchecked. The gallant officials of the Federal Road Safety Commission sometimes took heroic risks to save lives on the highways. Maeze felt they should be commended for the risks they took in order to save lives on our highways. Daily, they put their lives on the line to wage "Save Your Life" campaigns with our careless and untrained drivers who would casually end their lives and those of other road users.

Drivers of government-owned vehicles and accompanying security aides continued to pose a tremendous risk to road users in Nigeria. Claiming to be on important national assignments, they screeched along at breakneck speed, violating all traffic regulations. Kidnappers and highway robbers took advantage of the roads' disrepair to unleash calamity on the citizenry. The Abuja-Lokoja-Okene-Auchi highway over the years became notorious for kidnapping and armed robbery. Nigerians lost count of the number of people robbed, killed or kidnapped on that road. Similar disasters featured on the Owerri to Port Harcourt road, the Lagos to Benin expressway, and indeed all the highways of the country. Whenever news of kidnapping on those highways spread, citizens were moved to ask: "What is the proactive or remedial action government is taking this time around to protect her people from the constant attacks?"

There would be speeches, workshops, sermons and drills given on radio, television and social media sites by supposed security experts. The efficient employment channels appeared to be only among military, police and paramilitary personnel. All sorts of corps were springing up daily, providing employment for numbers of unemployed graduates. Agents went about purportedly collecting bribes for the influential bosses: "*Oga* at the top." Print and electronic media reported the ruthlessness of those agents to impoverished, vulnerable youths. They collected huge sums of money from those applicants and failed to give them the promised jobs afterwards. The immigration service, inundated by innumerable applications for a few advertised positions, decided to hold interviews in football stadia across the nation. An uproar occurred which left many dead or injured. Maeze wondered why the interviews could not be conducted through the internet. He reflected too, that a country like Nigeria, struggling with its economic survival, could not continue to provide employment only with the service industries.

Although not an economist, Maeze felt that if a country was not manufacturing, she could not earn sufficient foreign exchange to finance her imports. It meant the citizens were dependent on importation for all their needs. That constituted a drain on the available foreign earnings. Increasing the number of security personnel to curb criminal activity was commendable. However, it would not create the desired economic atmosphere until the deeds which promote ineptitude and corruption in leaders and their agents were effaced.

As the nation persisted with counterproductive practices, no positive change would be affected. Manufacturing could not succeed in a country where the power and energy essential to manufacturing were nonexistent. Until those important drivers of economy were removed completely from the hands of government and handed to private operators – with the State providing the enabling environment through legislation and regulation – no meaningful development could be affected. It was true that government's regulation and control were essential for checking unhealthy practices. Market forces of demand and supply would then stimulate healthy competition, necessary for bringing quality products to consumers' doorsteps at affordable prices. When the market developed and operated fully, the government would receive adequate taxes to run its affairs and pay for security and other human services.

Maeze had been careful to purchase his land from someone working in government, an indigenous original allottee. To avoid falling into fraudulent hands, he made further efforts over the identification of the vendor, making unscheduled visits to her home and office just to be sure he was not negotiating with a trickster. Despite all his caution, the woman had been able to conspire with a surveyor to convey the wrong piece of land to him, a land that teemed with illegal squatters and encroachers.

After discovering the duplicity, Maeze tried to contact the surveyor, but was of course unable to do so. The surveyor had simply disappeared; his phone was switched off. Maeze wasted much money trying to fence land that was not his. He went to their office and was advised to use surveyors from the municipal office in charge of the area where the school land was located. He saw many desks at that municipal office, but no officials sat at them. The ones he saw were chatting with supposed clients in corridors and on the balconies. He gradually felt it was a misleading scenario: those people were not truly engaged on professional pursuits. When Maeze asked for a surveyor, he was directed to the one that was said to be one of the government's staff, and the man stated that the vendor of the land was his colleague. The vendor also declared that surveyor to be among the best in the council. The surveyor even addressed Maeze in his indigenous language, to earn his trust and prove that he had no tribal affiliation to the vendor. Maeze understood the profound intertribal distrust in the country. He later reflected wryly that the surveyor speaking his ethnic language must have been procured to douse any suspicions of his. Maeze would be decisively deceived!

He paid for the land yet was unable to take possession of it. The land shown by the surveyor was of course different from the one he had bought. The one he had bought teemed with people and could not serve his plan of establishing a school.

Maeze was in a quandary. He demanded his money back, while his lawyers threatened the vendor with a lawsuit. She had no money to refund but brought other people as her co-owners of the land. The impasse dragged on for four years. Maeze was advised to be patient with the woman, and work with her to remove the squatters, or he would lose both his money and the land purchased. It was in the process that Maeze learnt a great deal about how officials in lands' administration operated as criminal cabals over land conveyances.

Land allocations are made in such a way that the cabals received hundreds of allocation letters. Aided by their accomplices in the lands' office, they obtained company registration certificates of organizations directly from agents in the company registration office. The next step would be to get a corporate land allocation. Sometimes, owners of those businesses did not even know that their companies had been allocated lands. The cabals, having fraudulently acquired packets of land allocation documents, proceeded to sell to unsuspecting people at their own prices. The new buyers at this time received transferred titles, were obliged to effect changes of title at the land registry, and as such become the authentic owners. Owners of the companies could be in Lagos, unaware that their businesses and registration documents had been used by others to acquire choice landed property. Once the new owners effected title changes, the names of the original allotees would be off the records, and the cabals would continue to prosper. They and their agents gained such wealth from their illicit deals that they could influence or thwart the nation's progress. It was hardly surprising that such people and their ilk were determined that the country would remain dormant – the corrupt, inept, system benefited them.

Those economic saboteurs were devious and dangerous. Similar deceitful schemes attended crude oil allocations, employment opportunities, opening of bank accounts, granting of loans, importation of petroleum products and numerous other activities. It was no surprise that good governmental initiatives were never allowed to succeed, but always stifled at inception.

Those unscrupulous cabals had much power and money. They could achieve much. Any governmental policy that was not to their advantage was crushed, no matter how beneficial it would have been to the populace. Their pugilistic corruption was termed "corruption fighting back." The police and judiciary were both rendered ineffectual by the mighty network of the cabals. They pervaded the political, economic and social environment, twisting and blighting the course of justice.

Maeze recalled his experience long ago at the hands of the police and courts in Rivers State. He had learned that it was futile to report a crime to the police, when they would abandon the complainant at the court, or ally themselves with the alleged offender if the complainant failed to meet their demands. The cliché that the judiciary was the last hope of the common man contradicted his country's realities. That had been his unhappy discovery before he left Nigeria for the United States. Criminals and offenders seem to prefer that their matter was taken to court instead because it was much easier to twist and pervert justice than local shrines and deities.

Maeze's late cousin, a lawyer, had confided in him that traders in Aba, Southeast Nigeria, shunned going to the law courts to seek redress because of the perceived twists in the system. In place of courts, business people aggrieved over non-payment of debts or some fraudulent acts, went to deities and shrines to lay their complaints. The chief priests of those shrines would prescribe lists of items to be brought by petitioners. Once those items were presented, oracles would be consulted, and the cases promptly decided. Like anything from the devil, results of such decisions were death and destruction for those who believed them.

Good Christians, not just churchgoers, refrained from such practices. For justice in their frays, they trusted only in God Almighty. The cabals in Nigeria ruled the courts. When government policy offended them, they recruited and mobilized armies of unemployed youths, equipping them for agitation, thereby worsening the nation's shaky security and poverty. The protests and marches were given political overtones, and were often acts of barefaced terrorism, vandalism and abductions. They either swerved the government from laudable activities or compelled it to do their bidding. They even retained some morally flexible journalists to defame the government. Consequently, many writers and bloggers, rather than decry the mindless looting of public resources, urged that many suspects in custody or under trial should be freed!

Maeze was sometimes baffled as to who was in the right, the economic saboteurs or the insiders in government.

17. SHARP PRACTICES IN PRIVATE LIFE

Finally, Maeze received a call from the vendor of the school land urging him to occupy the land immediately, as the illegal squatters had been removed. She warned that if Maeze wasted time and another set of squatters moved in, she must not be held responsible for the situation. The tones imparted urgency and sternness – Maeze must take possession instantly and never again complain of encroachment.

Maeze mused upon her obvious ruthlessness. She had cruelly misled him and his lawyer. At some stage in the land-acquisition drama, it was uncertain that she owned the piece of land. She had suddenly introduced another quantity called "Alhaji." Alhaji proved to be the "big man" in charge of the entire layout of that part of the Federal Capital City. When the threats from Maeze's lawyers to return the money paid for the piece of land intensified, the said "Alhaji" had rushed to the layout to construct all the inner roads around the school property. That man's word was clearly law over that district of Abuja, even among the indigenous people.

Now the woman urged: "The school land is free for your possession now. If you leave it and people go in there to occupy it again, that's your business." Her attitude seemed to say: *You either take possession of the land you paid for or you forget the money paid because my hands are off it forever.* Maeze quickly hired a bulldozer to clear the land of the mess left by squatters and the enforcement team of the Federal Capital Development Authority.

In the four years that Maeze had waited to take possession of his land, he lost all the savings intended for the building of the new school. While waiting, he had built a personal house in his home town, on land acquired many years earlier, indeed before he left for the United States. Maeze needed to invest his saved funds to avoid unnecessary waste. The house was rented to a construction company which was quick to renege on terms and payments. The agreement had stated the house was let as residential accommodation, but the company turned it into a workshop! The property became the subject of seemingly interminable litigation. He also built on another tract of land that had not been put to use for many years. The investment in hotel in another long-acquired property in his home state, though outside the scope of Maeze's experience, had helped to sustain him at the hardest time of his need. The land had lain fallow over a long period of time. He thought it was better used for hotel instead of acquiring another land altogether.

Maeze was learning that business ventures often required the owners' daily presence. It was virtually impossible for the proprietors to make any profit if they were not daily involved in the operation of the venture. Otherwise, the employees would loot and leave the business to fail. Maeze, running his small hotel, felt he was sharing income equally with his staff. However, he remained grateful to the Almighty that he was making a little cash.

He had learned that if land was bought and left fallow, the original vendor would either resell it to another buyer, or even build on it as if it had never been sold. Part of the savings Maeze would have spent on erecting the school building was channeled towards investing in property. Shortly after he acquired the land, the community that sold it to him came with an unknown set of indigenes to compel Maeze to renegotiate his purchase of the land! Anxious not to lose that property, Maeze eventually paid an additional fifty percent of the original amount spent on it.

At this time, an infamous kidnapping kingpin called Osisi-kankwu emerged to terrorize the South-East and South-

South communities of Nigeria. He and his gang caused mayhem in those southern regions. That notorious kidnapping kingpin and his gang caused the disappearance of prominent citizens from the region. In the overwhelming fear and destabilization, many businesses folded. By the time soldiers were mobilized to overcome the criminal's might, irreparable harm had been done to public psyche and economic progress. It was clear that it would take decades for the community to recover from the onslaughts of Osisi-kankwu and his accomplices.

Indeed, there was much to dismay Maeze the returnee. To deepen his woes, youths of the community from which he had bought land were enticed by promises of untold wealth by some oil company executives. They trespassed into Maeze's land. Maeze was moved to fence the land in order to secure it permanently. The cost of the project was staggering. The young men destroyed all the building materials and chased the workers away. Maeze fought them through the police and the courts, which of course depleted his funds further.

Maeze tried his hand at trading stock. He bought stock of about ten million naira, then the equivalent of approximately eighty-four thousand Dollars. Ten years later, the value of those stocks had fallen to twenty thousand Dollars in the stock market and continued to spiral downwards. That was about seventy-six percent loss of the original investment after ten years. He felt that it was suicidal and moronic to invest in one's own country that he loved so much.

A cousin of Maeze's cajoled him into investing about another eighty-four thousand Dollars in a printing press. The cousin had been passionate and convincing with his proposal, and Maeze decided to try that venture. The cousin was trusted with the running of the business. In just two years, he became conspicuously wealthy, a typical Nigerian "big boy." He would no longer drive himself, but had a driver and aides, put on airs and was cutting and condescending to people. He cruised about town as a veritable Very Important Person – VIP. What irked Maeze was that the newly rich cousin was telling relatives that he had only borrowed money from Maeze and had long repaid him with interest. Such deceit became another emotional trial for Maeze.

The cousin changed the name of the business that Maeze's cash had begun. It now belonged to him and his immediate family. He was widely lauded for his acumen and success. Maeze felt it would be foolish to seek redress through the police and courts. He did not trust the efficiency and impartiality of investigators in his country. He was also restrained by the knowledge that business disagreements in extended families prompted diabolic acts, extended family resentment and generational curses. He felt it was best for his children not to rouse those forces. He shrank too from a public squabble with someone who begged his assistance only two years previously. The cousin had obviously intended from the outset to cheat Maeze, using the returnee's resources to start a new life. Maeze had of course supplied all the funds for the business and agreed that the cousin should own thirty percent of it. He had also agreed to pay his cousin a salary, as the man had no other means of income than the press. The business was duly registered with the Corporate Affairs Commission as a partnership. Maeze's cousin would maintain full time employment, and work to develop the enterprise. The cousin was quick to divert business to some phony companies, and incoming check payments into his private account. He had obviously forgotten how wretched he was when he came begging for Maeze's assistance.

The first audit report had shown abuse of authority and reckless use of the partnership's funds. Maeze's efforts to inquire into the business's operations were vigorously resisted by his cousin. In fact, he became belligerent.

Maeze reflected on what fraternal tenderness he had been roused to by his cousin's tales of woe. He had not been suspicious of the man. His cousin said his previous employer, an illiterate from one of the Southeastern states, was a Shylock. He said that employer had used him as a manager to make a great deal of money, then sacked him, leaving him empty-handed. Maeze had believed the tale.

He now realized that those sorrowful stories had been ploys to lure him into parting with his cash. The man had obviously intended all along to start the business, set a quarrel with Maeze, and change the partnership into a one-man venture. Maeze had all along trusted his cousin to work for the partnership's success.

His final decision was neither to seek redress from the courts, nor consult deities in shrines. He would face his own ventures and ignore his cousin's aggravating conduct and lies. He had learnt to be extremely cautious with relatives over business arrangements.

18. CORRUPTION IN NIGERIA

The African Development Bank (ADB) estimated that Nigeria needed to invest US$15 Billion each year over a ten-year period, in order to remedy the shortfall in its infrastructural needs. Energy and power shortages, cuts and disruptions were incessant and hampered businesses. Where those amenities were available, they were extremely costly.

Maeze's business was imperiled. Capital that should have been spent in increasing the school's capacity and providing world-class training was spent on electricity generators and fuel for the generators. Generators of course were no substitute for necessary, daily power supply. Yet, the need for them was not occasional, or a few hours every week. Those generators, burning expensive fuel, were in almost permanent use.

Indeed, Maeze had experienced weeks, months and years of total absence of power supply from the national company. Bills were still sent to him, which he had to pay under threat of being disconnected, never to be reconnected. He labored on under that vile situation from year to year, hoping the situation would improve. As a generator was started, or refueled, or repaired, Maeze cursed all involved in the management of the national power supply. Lack of electricity was the worst punishment inflicted on Nigerian businessmen and women.

Maeze equipped his school with two diesel-powered generators. He also provided the electric transformer and substation which served the school's immediate community. It was exasperating to reflect on how the funds expended on the generators and substation could have developed the capacity and quality of his business. It was galling to think that somebody might disconnect the supply of electricity to the school for failure to pay a bill, a bill for power that was never supplied! He reflected on his powerlessness, which impotence was shared by innumerable other Nigerian citizens. The realities of living and investing in the country were indeed grievous.

Others' businesses were burdened. The aggregate effect was that few people could succeed in business in the country. Capacity for assets, publicity and outreach, product quality and income-generation, were all obstructed. Much waste also occurred over information and communication technology, with electrical gadgets often destroyed because of incessant disruptions in the system. Electrical gadgets which had long lifespan in other countries, stalled in Nigeria because of interruptions in the supply of electricity. Modern technology software and computer gadgets were highly sensitive and vulnerable to destruction by unstable power supply. Internet and phone services were similarly affected by power failure. If an interruption occurred whilst one was working online, the work must be suspended, resulting in loss of man-hours. Criminal elements also used the period of interruption of power to hack into gadgets and perpetuate fraudulent acts. Similarly, ruined automobiles littered Nigeria's roads and streets. This was caused not only by bad roads, but because many of the car gadgets were ruined and abandoned as scrap all over the environment.

The avoidable expenses were legion. A journey from Port Harcourt to Abuja would have taken less than eight hours where good roads and bridges were provided, often took sixteen hours and sometimes, more. In Nigeria, it took a whole day. Risks of being robbed and kidnapped remained high in the country. Consequently, most people preferred to travel by air. The combined costs of a taxi fare to the airport from one's residence, air fare, and another taxi ride to one's destination, were enormous. It amounted to about five times what the journey would have cost in a better-operated nation.

As he brooded over his country's numerous discomforts, Maeze contemplated moving to another nation. A voice within asked: "Where is better? Is it Ghana, South Africa, Europe, Asia or America?" He concluded that despite all the problems of living and engaging in business in Nigeria, the country was the most convenient place for him! Any other nation would be hostile to him as a non-citizen. Nigerians had earned a dreadful reputation internationally. In Maeze's travels across the globe, he had often been treated with suspicion and gruffness by foreign immigration personnel.

Maeze shortly read an article which was apposite to his ruminations. It was by Ruth Maclean, West African correspondent of the Guardian, published on Wednesday May 11th, 2016, alluding to Nigeria's new President, Buhari, who for twenty tense months in the 1980s led a fiercely anti-corruption military government. "Buhari's adherents say that it was his first anti-corruption drive that led to his initial political demise in the 1980s. He was ousted in a military coup, because, according to his supporters, the coup's leaders were worried about becoming the targets of his investigation."

Maeze knew that in Nigeria, to speak of bribing one's way through was an understatement. Receipts were not issued for numerous massive payments. Registration, inspection, education, environment and commerce, were all corruptly run. While Maeze strove to fulfill the standards prescribed by the education authorities, employees of the ministry of education worked zealously to jettison those requirements. Two decades earlier, when Maeze was first establishing his school, the education ministry had clear rules for establishing and operating a school. Those regulations, which embraced students as well as academic and non-academic staff, addressed classrooms, walkways, bedding spaces, number of lavatories, change rooms, sick bays, laboratories, playing grounds, assembly halls. Those regulations prescribed qualifications and experience for staff, curricula for schools, and background checks on proprietors to ensure qualitative instruction and learning. Environment and sanitation were inspected and certified before approval was given. He now saw the situation as an "all comers" affair. Over 50% of functioning schools were owned by staff of the ministry of education. Schools abounded in all the major cities of the country, and the quality of instruction was dismal. Uninformed parents moved their children from one school to another because of proprietors' unimaginable ruses to attract pupils to their institutions. School fees were haggled over as though one were purchasing commodities in the marketplace.

Indeed, schools were operating like marketing departments of financial institutions, with staff hired and remunerated on commission basis. Some spent whole working days scouting for "customers." As the quest was primarily for money and numbers, all forms of indiscipline were condoned. Maeze knew that discipline was the bedrock of every school. All over the country, pupils were seen sauntering to school at 9 o'clock in the morning, many dressed untidily. In the past, offended citizens would have asked: "Which school owns that uniform?" Such laxity would have shamed the school and outraged parents and guardians. Late attendance and nonattendance drew no censure. In many cases, teachers, principals and directors were intimidated by students, under the unspoken threats that wealthy parents might withdraw them from the schools or use their status to punish the school staff. Many parents, intoxicated with their wealth, encouraged their children to despise all authority. Some who failed in a class were promoted, for fear their parents might withdraw their patronage. Some proprietors were terrified of their students being instantly accepted and promoted by rival schools. Some schools did not demand transfer certificates of pupils from other schools. Maeze wondered how they could be properly assessed for placement in new classes. Parents, sometimes, helped their children to conceal their academic deficiencies by sorting their entrance into other schools or through some unscrupulous teachers. It was no surprise that standards had deteriorated significantly over the years. Maeze knew the situation in the educational sector merely reflected the nation's state.

He wondered how there could be proper records and statistics when there was poor identity management in the whole country. In an efficient system, births and deaths would be recorded. Personal identity management systems ensured verifiable records, militated against criminality, and provided reliable statistics. He felt there should be personal identification numbers for citizens and emigrants, with records of the bearer's birth date, family name, address, local government area, state and sex. Dependent relatives might also appear on the subject's biometric data. The information should be updated periodically, noting educational, health, employment, banking, travel, litigation, housing, property, and security details.

The bearer would supply the identity number to whichever establishment they had business with. The central identity management system would assess the individuals' information automatically. It would then be easy to check the bearer's background, combating crime and creating greater efficiency and safety for the entire citizenry. Nigeria simply seemed to be in a muddle over identity management. Records of citizens were haphazardly available. Some were with various government establishments, while many could not be traced. Unsatisfactory reasons were given for lack of proper documentation of Nigerians. One establishment blamed the other, and the one faulted declared the flaw was caused by another. The situation did not merely remain unchanged, but steadily worsened. The truth of course was the lack of willpower and funding to execute that essential project. Funds and energy were continually wasted on unprofitable pursuits.

Maeze read and mused on a report in the Nigerian daily newspaper, "Punch," of remarks made by the Vice President, Professor Osinbanjo, whilst on a visit to Rivers State. "It is easy for people to say that times are hard. One of the reasons things are hard in the country is the corruption that has been in the system for years. At the moment, we are investigating the Fifteen Billion Dollars Defence Contract Award. If Fifteen Billion Dollars disappeared when you have a reserve of Thirty Billion Dollars, there is no way there will not be hardship."

Maeze also recalled the frustration expressed by the former President, Goodluck Ebele Jonathan, at the Nigerian Economic Society's 54th Annual Conference in the country's capital, Abuja. The former President was reflecting on the fight against corruption, and his remarks were reported in the Vanguard newspaper of 18th September 2013. "When you talk about corruption, the private sector is involved; the public sector is involved; even the individuals, including other societies, and I wouldn't want to mention names so that I will not be attacked. But I know that if collectively all of us don't reward corruption, people would not be attracted to corrupt practices, but when we all reward corruption, then off course, we will be tempted to go in that direction."

Other memorable remarks came to Maeze's mind. The late former President, Umaru Musa Yar Adua, had attended a dinner in Davos, Switzerland organized by the Partnership against Corruption Initiative at the World Economic Forum Summit on January 23rd 2008. His speech was reported in the

Nigerian Guardian of 25th January 2008. "For us in Nigeria, I want to say that until very recently, corruption had become virtually endemic. In fact, it was threatening to become a national culture and almost a new civilization not only in official government business but also within the private sector business, and you can imagine how difficult it is to fight such a system. It reached that point people no longer cared how anybody made his money, yet I know that when I was growing up, the society in Nigeria cared. If you displayed wealth and it was through dishonest means, nobody would want to be associated with you. But we reached a situation where the means by which you get wealth does not matter anymore. To earn respect and honour, you have to make efforts to get wealthy by any means, whether it is through armed robbery or whether it is through outright stealing of public funds."

A report of the global corruption watchdog's, Transparency International, stated in October 2003: "Corruption in Nigeria remained pervasive, and the failure of Africa's most populous country to improve its ranking was disappointing." The Chairman, Mr. Peter Eigen was quoted as saying it might take generations before corruption was rooted out." For his part, the Nigerian politician, Mallam Nasir El-Rufai was reported to have declared that ordinary Nigerians were "tired of hypocrisy and corruption of some of our elite."

For succinctness, few remarks could match the speech of Nigeria's two-time former President Olusegun Obasanjo. Obasanjo spoke at the public presentation and launch of *The Story of my Two Worlds: Challenges, Experiences and Achievements*, the autobiography of Justice Mustapha Akanbi, on 26th November 2014. "Today, every aspect of our national life is riven and raddled with corruption – the executive, the legislature, the judiciary, the military, the civil service, the media and the private sector. I must hasten to say that there are a few exceptions that stand out and would not succumb. They are unsung heroes. The legislature, which shrouded its corruption in the opaque nature of its budget, has been encouraged through direct payment of money to the legislature to cover up wrongs done by the executive thereby making the legislature fail in its oversight responsibility.

"Apart from shrouding the remuneration of the National Assembly in Opaqueness and without transparency, they indulged in extorting money from departments, contractors, agencies and ministries in two ways on the so-called oversight responsibility. They do so on visits to their projects and programs in the process … Truth must be told, though it hurts at times, but it eventually edifies and uplifts, unlike lie and deceit which are dishonest which eventually brings down and destroys.

"Corruption in the National Assembly also includes what they call Constituency Projects, that are given out to their agents to execute but invariably, full payment is made with little or no job done … They cannot, in full conscience oversight anybody or any section of government in these areas. I must say again that there are still honourable and distinguished men and women in the National Assembly who will do nothing to soil their hands."

"When the guard is the thief, only God can keep the house safe and secure. But I am optimistic that sooner or later, we will overcome. God will give us guards of integrity and honesty with the fear of God and genuine love of their people and their country. Today, there is no institution of government that is not riven with corruption, and not even the Military. As people cry out, where then is the salvation?"

Maeze recalled that at his inaugural speech on May 29[th,] 1999, as a democratically elected Head of State, President Obasanjo had decried the impact of official corruption as rampant, earning Nigeria a very bad image at home and abroad. "Besides, it has distorted and retrogressed development. Our infrastructures – PHCN - Power Holden Company of Nigeria, National Telephone Services, Health Institutions, roads, railways, education, housing and other social services were allowed to decay and collapse. Our country has thus been through one of its darkest periods. All these have brought the nation to a situation of chaos and near despair. This is the challenge before us."

Maeze was moved to continually recall idealistic statements of Nigeria's leaders, which had ultimately achieved little. He remembered reading a speech given by a former Head of State and Head of the Military Government, General Abdulsalami Abubakar, which bore the title *My Transition Agenda for Development.* "This administration is concerned about the level of corruption in our national life. Such concern emanates from lapses in the management of public funds. We are determined to put in place all necessary measures to breathe into the conduct of government, a fresh air of openness and accountability. Therefore, enjoin all public officers to demonstrate transparency, uprightness and honesty in the conduct of government. Machinery will be established in due course to ensure the compliance of all public officers to the principles of transparency, particularly in the management of public funds."

When President Shehu Shagari was overthrown in December 2013, Brigadier Sani Abacha had addressed the nation which had just been returned to military rule.

Fellow countrymen and women, I, Brigadier Sani Abacha, of the Nigerian Army address you this morning on behalf of the Nigerian Armed Forces. You are all living witnesses to the great economic predicament and uncertainty, which an inept and corrupt leadership has imposed on our beloved nation for the past four years. I am referring to the harsh, intolerable condition under which we are now living.

Our economy has been hopelessly mismanaged. We have become a debtor and beggar nation. There is inadequacy of food at reasonable prices for our people who are now fed up with endless announcements of importation of foodstuffs. Health services are in shambles as our hospitals are reduced to mere consulting clinics without drugs, water and equipment. Our educational system is deteriorating at an alarming rate. Unemployment figures including the undergraduate have reached embarrassing and unacceptable proportions. In some states, workers are being owed salary arrears of eight to twelve months and in others there are threats of salary cuts.

Yet your leaders revel in squander-mania, corruption and indiscipline and continue to proliferate public appointments in complete disregard of our stark economic realities. After due consultations over these deplorable conditions, I and my colleagues in the armed forces have in the discharge of our national role as promoters and protectors of our national interest decided to effect a change in the leadership of the government of the Federal Republic of Nigeria and form a Federal Military Government.

Twenty months later, Maeze knew, that government was overthrown by another military government, of which General Ibrahim Babangida emerged as Head of State. General Babangida, curiously, had been Chief of Army Staff in the overthrown military government. It would later be strongly alleged that he had been intent on usurping the government which he had served as Chief of Army Staff because of impending and damning revelations of his misdeeds! However, he assumed the mantle as Head of State of the government created by the coup of 27th August 1985 and addressed the nation.

When in December, 1983, the former Military leadership, headed by Major General Mohammadu Buhari, assumed the reins of government, its accession was heralded in the history of this country. With the nation at the mercy of political misdirection and on the brink of economic collapse, a new sense of hope was created in the mind of every Nigerian. Since January 1984, however, we have witnessed a systematic denigration of that hope. It was stated then that mismanagement of political leadership and general deterioration in the standard of living, which had subjected the common man to intolerable suffering, were the reasons for the intervention. Nigerians have since then been under a regime that continued with those trends. Events today indicate that most of the reasons which justified the military takeover of government from civilian still persist.

The last twenty months have not witnessed any significant changes in the national economy. Contrary to expectations, we have so far been subjected to a steady deterioration in the general standard of living; and intolerable suffering by the ordinary Nigerians have risen higher, scarcity of commodities has increased, hospitals still remain mere consulting clinics, while educational institutions are on the brink of decay.

Maeze's mind again returned to the takeover of December 1983. The speech of the new Head of State, Muhammadu Buhari, had read in part: "While corruption and indiscipline have been associated with our under-development, those two evils in our body politic have attained unprecedented heights in the past few years. The corrupt, inept and the insensitive leadership in the last four years has been the source of immorality and impropriety in our society."

"Since what happens in any society is largely a reflection of the leadership of that society, we deplore corruption in all its facets. This government will not tolerate kickbacks, inflation of contracts and over-invoicing of imports, etc. nor will it condone forgery, fraud, embezzlements, misuse and abuse of office and illegal dealings in foreign exchange and smuggling. Arson has also been used to cover up fraudulent acts in public institutions."

The admission of corruption in Nigeria achieved a global climax at a meeting of the United Kingdom's Prime Minister, David Cameron, with President Muhammadu Buhari in May 2016. Buhari had been elected Nigeria's Executive President the previous year. When asked if Nigerians were incredibly corrupt, he unhesitatingly answered "yes."

Maeze withdrew from his prolonged and exhausting musing. He felt he must concentrate on the present. Yet the present brought more aggravations. Power Holding Company of Nigeria (PHCN) officials were about taking inventories of all existing old meters. Their goal was to avoid missing a deadline decreed by the Nigerian Electricity Regulatory Commission (NERC). That body had ordered that all Electricity Distribution Companies (DISCOs) should provide and install Electronic Prepaid Meter to all subscribers free of any charge before a certain date. Severe sanctions would befall defaulters.

Nigerians had of course suffered greatly from the virtual robbery of faceless officials, implementing the inhuman Estimated Billing System, which obliged people to pay for power that they never used. It was indisputably preferable to have the prepaid meter and not be given power, then live under the previous extortionate system. Budgets of power distribution companies were spread out among their units, with specific amounts to be collected from consumers. At the end of each month, those units were required to make returns to their head stations. Those reports must reflect compliance with the revenue budgets. It did not matter whether or not electricity was supplied. What was considered crucial was the meeting of the target revenue. In order to achieve these targets, grossly padded bills were imposed on non-metered consumers to cover shortfalls in the revenue sought from the unit.   On account of this practice, consumers with meters had a considerable advantage over those without. The non-metered households bore the burden of paying the extra revenue sought.

Maeze felt the prepaid meter operated on straightforward logic. It meant consumers would only pay for what they used. They would not suffer inflated bills, disconnection of light, nor stealing from subscribers. If there was no supply of electricity, there would be no bills to pay, and where bills were not paid, there would be no supply.

The National Electricity Regulatory Commission (NERC) held that consumers' problem with the Power Holding Company of Nigeria (PHCN) was not power supply *per se*, but poor internal administration. With the prepaid meter, PHCN would be focused and efficient, knowing that if they failed to supply power, they would not be paid free money by subscribers. Aware of the obligation to be productive, they continually thwarted the bid to operate with prepaid meters, so that they could continue to cheat and made money for jobs not done.

Maeze was aware of a popular and ironic saying in Nigeria. "It wouldn't make any difference to lay a complaint to the chief executive of PHCN. This is because the generator noise by the side of his office has damaged his hearing. How then could an electricity subscriber persuade him to find lasting solutions to the problem of darkness pervading the entire landscape of the country, when his hearing is bad and he has an alternative electricity supply from his small generator?" It was a situation that applied not only to the top managers of the power supply system, but to all involved in the electricity supply value chain. The ceaseless din and fumes from their generators, both at home and in their offices, had so damaged their ears, eyes and minds, that they held the current state of affairs normal and irreversible. Nigerians might attend conferences and workshops, be regaled by long speeches, learn of huge budget spending all in the cause of providing adequate electricity supply, yet never enjoy satisfactory electric power supply. Consequently, small businesses continued to close and big businesses continued to relocate. Resources which should have been spent on developing industries and capacity would be wasted on imported substandard electricity generating sets, which had incalculably destructive effects on national health, safety and environment.

Reflecting on his return to Nigeria and immersion in the 'Nigerian Project' – the country's business development – Maeze concluded that he had merely taken himself into a maze. Although he could not say he regretted returning to his fatherland, he felt completely disorganized and alienated from the country's business practices. For a business entity to be successful, there had to be fair and equal accommodation of all competitors in the same sector so that the forces of demand and supply could play out in the open market. That would create rewards for all participants. However, where some participants were strictly, even excessively regulated, while others could flagrantly disregard rules, the outcome would only be detrimental and destructive to the system. Citizens eager to operate within the laws of the land would be discouraged, while the fraudulent would be encouraged. The country was certainly lurching towards annihilation. Yet, Maeze reflected that he would not have chosen his life abroad as a second-class citizen, with his green passport an embarrassment or liability, forever held suspect by immigration officials at all nations' entry points.

Maeze mused over a copy of letter he had, by mere chance, received from an anonymous Nigerian sitting next to him in one of those numerous town hall meetings organized by Nigerians in Diaspora for visiting government officials in the city of Houston in 2007,

February 24, 2007.
The Honorable Minister of Information and Communications
Federal Republic of Nigeria
Town Hall Meeting – Houston, Texas

I attended the Town hall meeting at the Standford Convention Center tonight. Your effort in promoting our nation's brand assets and tackling the negative image confronting us as a people is commendable. The point, however, is that Nigerians seem to have received a lot of disappointment in the past from their leaders that it would take more to convince them that the present leadership under President Olusegun Obasanjo is different from other leaderships in the past. Let me give you a scenario.

I lived in Port Harcourt and my family is still there as I write you. I have been out here in the United States since 2001. My effort is geared towards how to bring my family out of that country. In the year 2000, our family's attorney collaborated with some other fellows to dupe our family business of the sum of seven million Naira (N7M). Since I was at the head of the family business, and since all entreaties to resolve the issue peacefully had failed, I personally reported the case to the police. And that was the beginning of my problem.

The police merely interrogated him and abandoned the case. It was at the police office I realized that the lawyer had instituted a case against one of his collaborators on my behalf. That was done ostensibly, in preparation to defend himself in a case he carefully orchestrated. From that point the lawyer took over. He turned to his friends at the Rivers State judiciary who are judges to manufacture warrants. He would go to the judge's house to claim that I brought in police at the court premises to arrest him in spite of a court's injunction. The judge would pretend that the matter was done in the court and would issue him with a warrant of arrest in his bedroom. Even when we knew all that the lawyer and the judge were doing was wrong, we have no way to stop them. So, the victim and complainant would turn to be the accused. The accused turned to be the complainant and would be chasing the duped around the state. As God would have it I was out of town and ignorant of the set-up going on. At one of the meetings organized by a pastor to reconcile the matter the lawyer boasted that he had equally planned with some prison officials to poison me if eventually I was brought in. He boasted further that the cases would remain in the court forever while I would be forced to spend our savings until the business would not be able to support itself and the case.

Some of my friends asked me why I should be wasting my time in the courts. They said that traders and business people no longer rely on the courts for justice. They rely rather on deities and shrines to adjudicate their cases. So, I lost my money to a lawyer thief; my property was lost; our business was threatened; my life was threatened; police cannot help me; and court cannot help me. I decided to check out. Since 2001 I have been here, I have studied for two different Master's degrees, after the one obtained in Nigeria and now a doctorate. Meanwhile, the cases are lying about at the courts in Rivers State being tossed from one court to another; and from one judge to another. This scenario is a typical example of what goes on in the Nigerian justice system. And how can a citizen be happy to go through this kind of torture in the hands of government officials? And what can the younger generation learn from a system where the last hope of the citizen is also corrupt? And what story can I tell about my country to my classmates, students, and friends from other parts of the world? Of course, I love my country and would do anything I can to contribute my quota to its development. But is there any way I can keep this and many other stories from being told?

Many of the Nigerians in Diaspora have similar stories like this to tell; it's very heavy in their hearts. So, while you are going around telling a story of a new image about Nigeria, some people are still embroiled in painful, tragic and embarrassing stories like my own. Since stories like mine are common and therefore inconsequential to the Nigerian people, we are forced to tell them in classrooms, workplaces and professional conferences around America. Honorable Minister, Sir, you cannot make a significant impact in the image laundry campaign you are currently undertaking without the government addressing these anomalies in our system. Ordinarily, I would have preferred to teach in a Nigerian university for a lesser pay than to teach in American university. The abuses and degradation that Africans face in the West is just too much. Ironically, even when most of our leaders are trained abroad, and understand these things we are saying first hand, yet they seem insensitive, ignorant, or handicapped to the plights of their citizens. When you are faced with two evils, naturally you would choose the lesser one. Many of the hardworking and responsible Nigerians in Diaspora who are professionals and some business tycoons who still have something in terms of good image left do not hate to live and do business in their fatherland. They are just being forced to live outside the country. Personally, I want to return home. Regardless of the injustice and abuses going on in our national life, I agree that East or West, Nigeria my home, is the best.

What is the way forward? Sir, we cannot pack our new clothes on top of the dirty ones and claim that everything is clean. We need to start first by washing the old clothes. Our judicial system needs to be cleaned up. When the system can provide hope for the common man, then trust can return, and confidence will return. You as an agent of government don't even need to go around selling the new image, rather our relatives and friends will tell us that things are changing for good. I bet you, many in foreign lands would not wait for a perfect situation before they return home. Of course, there is no perfect situation. What we need is just a practical sign that things have started changing. Like somebody pointed out tonight, none of the histories of India, China, United Arab Emirate and South Africa showed that their leaders stole their money and stacked them in European and American banks. They are not in the habit of going abroad for health and education reasons. Now, Nigerian leaders are adding shopping and birthday celebrations too. When Nigerian leaders depend on the West for such services, other citizens are encouraged to tow the same line. It, therefore, looks contradictory when you are saying one thing, and the practice is another thing. The trust can only be established when what we say, and what we do are the same.
Anonymous Nigerian Citizen
Houston, Texas – USA.

Virtually, all citizens of Nigeria, including presidents, agree that there is massive corruption going on in the polity. What is not settled is that each government that is enthroned, fails to do what is necessary to provide the much-needed solutions to bad leadership. In fact, the deterioration seems to get worse as a new government takes over reins of power. The elites mesmerize the world with eloquent speeches but do little to provide the needed good life citizens yawn for. That has been the plank of our political practice.

Instead of engaging in programs and policies that would redefine leadership as is done in developed and developing countries, our political leaders chose rather to be deceitful and retrogressive to development. They are quick to state that without power, the much talked about industrialization is a mere hoax. Everybody understands this. So, why waste precious time and scare resources to be repeating speeches upon long speeches across conferences and retreats that don't produce nothing. They seem to make the speeches to further their deceitful dispositions.

Why should top government officials be hobnobbing the entire globe in the name of image laundering, and be inviting home Nigerian professionals in diaspora who are seeking to provide better life for their families? The few of these citizens who return home quickly discovers that they had been led to regrettable mistakes by these image makers. There was a story of a professor from one of the top universities in America that returned to Nigeria following one of those town hall meetings in his city of residence. He was doing an important research in an epidemic disease. That night, while in his study, Power Holding Company had suddenly interrupted the electricity supply. In a bid to continue what he had in his hands, he had dashed across the room to switch off the water heater in his room before the security person would start the standby generator. This is because some appliances needed to be turned off, thus enabling the electric generating set capacity to carry the remainder of the gadgets in the house. He ran into the open door of the closet, mistakenly left open. The man's face was badly damaged. Luckily, his cousin, who was on a short visit, was in the adjoining room to render a help. He was driven to the nearest government hospital in the vicinity. The hospital was also shut down because the interruption also affected them. Good spirited hospital staff, with the combination of their torch lights, provided a haphazard aid as they could humanly give. He was urgently arranged for an emergency trip to Europe for medical treatment. The professor spent six months in the hospital before things returned to normal for him. He had to rejoin his family finally and permanently in America.

This man was merely lucky to have survived. There was somebody in the house to readily help him to receive medical emergency aid at that point in time. This happened in the city where there were available medical personnel. He had the means to be flown out of the country immediately for proper treatment. And he could leave the country to seek a future abroad. What if the professor had been a poor teacher in one of the numerous rural communities around the country where there is no good housing, roads, good transportation, health centers and so on and so forth. That is the fate of millions of citizens of Nigeria. They are dying for lack of infrastructures, bad policies and insensitivity of their leaders. To worsen matters, these leaders and their families steal public revenues made possible by the sweat of these nobodies and receive all the good things of life money can buy abroad.

This is the reason for the anger and hate Nigerians carry about in their daily lives across the country and the world. This is the reason for the hostility going on between the elites and the poor masses; between government officials and voters; and between one ethnic nationality and another. This accounts for the criminal actions of many young people across the country. This also accounts for the agitations, hostilities and extremism rearing from all fronts in the country's national life. The suspicions, mistrusts and disappointments are just too weighty to be ignored. When a people have been disappointed for too long, they would decide to determine their destiny by themselves. Their confidence in the sincerity of purpose of their leaders is seriously in doubt. All sorts of agitations are currently taking place. It would only take the grace of God to win back their trust. Nigerians are being deported in large numbers from across the globe, sometimes without very good reasons. The challenge that the government and people of Nigeria has to address is building strong political and economic institutions to cater for the growing youth population.

New Telegraph (February 23, 2017, P.35) reported about the killing and inhuman treatment being meted out to Nigerians in all parts of the world. Save for the assistance of International Organization for Migration (IOM) that brought one hundred and sixty-one deportees back from Libya, many more would have been killed. Some of them narrated how they were made to drink urine by that country's immigration officials. They urged the Federal Government to speedily intervene to rescue over 350 Nigerians trapped in Libya before the mindless immigration officers would kill them (Metro, February 15, 2017, P.8).

Worried by persistent xenophobic attacks of Nigerians in South Africa over the years, (New Telegraph, February 2, 2019, P.11), reported that the House of Representatives passed a resolution calling on the ministry of Foreign Affairs and national Assembly to send a strong message to the government of South Africa to stop their nationals from attacking Nigerians. Daily Trust (February 25, 2017, P.4) stated that the case of the persistent attacks is because South African nationals felt that Nigerians were taking away business and employment opportunities from them. Permanent solution to the problem remained a more responsible, responsive and corruption-free leadership that ensures national resources are utilized productively for the sole benefit of her citizens and reduce the tide of emigration currently going on.

John Kerry, former United States Secretary of State, on the occasion of World economic Forum, held in Davos, Switzerland, called for a conceited effort to address the issue of corruption in Nigeria thus, "When Nigeria's President, Buhari took office last spring, he inherited a military that was under paid, under fed and unable to protect Nigerian people from Boko haram. One reason is that much of the military budget was finding its way into the pockets of generals. And just this week, we saw reports that more than 50 people in Nigeria, including former government officials stole 9 Billion Dollars from the treasury."

He stated that, "We have to acknowledge in all quarters of leadership that the plaques of violent extremism, greed, lust for power, and sectarian exploitation often find their nourishment where governments are fragile, and leaders are incompetent and dishonest."

Maeze had always been reluctant to wade into Nigeria's muddied political waters. Since his return from America however, friends and associates had been lauding him for possessing the integrity, ability and briskness required in the current political milieu. He kept recalling his discussion about political involvement with his former academic supervisor in America, and the revulsion he had felt for it. Yet he sometimes asked himself if he should continue to act as though he were a lone saint among his people. Politicians had long roused distaste in him. He could not shed his deep-seated appraisal of them as objectionable. Yet, the calls by his community to represent them were persistent, and sometimes strident. Maeze, still abhorring the political system, was finally persuaded to participate in politics.

Maeze sought elective positions in his state constituency and failed. The Nigerian political landscape seemed thronged with the utterly untrustworthy. It was discouraging for worthy citizens who wished to be politicians. Maeze wondered if the political parties were totally devoid of decent Citizens intent on giving honest leadership to the country and felt that could not be the case. The problem, he told himself, was that such trustworthy persons were a very small minority, continually fought and suppressed by the barefaced looters. Those corrupt elements were often hailed by subdued and bribed electorates – the masses – trapped by those leaders in illiteracy, poverty and powerlessness. Some of those fraudulent politicians were pathological liars and captivating orators, concealing murderous urges in badinage and fellowship. They excelled at the infamous "419" and cultism. They were like trained performers, indeed like most professional actors playing their roles superbly.

In well-ordered societies yearning for development, those elements would not be leaders. However, in Nigeria, where integrity was no longer expected in public life, the wolves held sway, grinning as they gnawed into lambs. He sometimes wondered why the downtrodden lack the will to resist oppression over their own survival.

Maeze joined the race to the state legislature. He spent three years consulting and campaigning in his constituency. In that period, he routinely left his family in Abuja, spending his life savings as he campaigned against a pack of aspirants to the legislative seat. His political career would prove unforgettable, acquainting him with staggering depths of human trickery.

On the day of his party's election primaries, the leaders informed Maeze that they had narrowed their choice. They had decided on another aspirant as the party's candidate. A question that remained unresolved was, "Why did the leaders pledge to provide a level playing ground for all the contestants until the last minute?" The party's explanation was that they usually tried to stimulate the contest in order to publicize and market the party. When many people were engaged in seeking positions in a party, people would see that party as where the action lay, and so the party would be popularized. So, to lure interested aspirants to the party, they made it look like, "This is the party to belong to." Maeze's incredulity at the perfidy remained. How could leaders of a party have an advance, chosen, candidate, yet send their agents to recruit aspirants across the federation?

A few leaders in Maeze's ward of a particular political party, sought him as an illustrious son of the community. They expressed delight that he had decided, after many failed entreaties, to work directly for the political good of their community. They remarked the strange fact that their hometown, although close to the state capital, was conspicuously lacking in various amenities. The exception were the villages where some villagers, by their own efforts, constructed some roads and provided access to water and electricity. The roads maintained by the villagers were of course only earth roads. Maeze had helped to provide his hometown with what the government was doing for other towns with the state's resources, after government officials had taken their cuts from contractors, and contractors, siphoning all they could, had provided cheap and shoddy amenities which were neither qualitative nor durable.

Maeze reflected on a Socratic dictum. Socrates had held that until good people joined in the political process and stopped criticizing from the sidelines, their fate would continue to be determined by those considered inferior to them.

It was then that political scouts zealously urged Maeze to join their party. They arranged meetings with their party leaders in the state and local governments and took Maeze to the homes of their party leaders. Maeze was elated to hear those leaders tell him stories of his own numerous acts of philanthropy. He would later learn that those leaders had been primed by political scouts, all determined that Maeze should join their party. On those visits, the leaders vowed that at the party's primary elections, they would choose Maeze as their candidate for the state legislature. They added that, at the very worst, they would work for "a level playing ground" for all aspirants. They were all determined to pull Maeze into a political life.

Maeze had fears even then. He had heard of people inveigled into political activity, only to be abandoned by their declared supporters after all their life's savings had been squandered. He therefore retained some skepticism as he was taken to meet the important people in his local government council. He did not know how advanced in the game of deceit those leaders were. Their agents were highly skilled in inveigling people into politics. Maeze noted that he was taken to visit over two hundred party and community leaders for "consultation." They were all approbatory of his candidature. Indeed, the agents, acting as wise advisers, made him scour all the twelve wards of their local constituency. They declared themselves the ideal persons to "market' Maeze to opinion leaders who in turn would "market" him to their people when it was time to cast votes. On each visit, he parted with cartons of wine, bottles of spirits, and cash. Much money was also spent on petrol, motor repair and maintenance. Some of the trips were arduous, on almost impassable roads, and dreadfully eroded terrains. The community had indeed been neglected by the government. Maeze wondered why so many political leaders appeared on television and radio to relate their feats of development in their villages. His visits to – and through – interior communities belied those boasts. His resolve to enter the political arena grew stronger. He must contribute to his people's wellbeing.

Of course there were many other aspirants seeking to become the party's candidate. He learned later how they were all wooed and cajoled and assured by the leaders that they would be chosen, just as he was! They also were being made to spend large sums. Many of the agents were party executives. Their game was motivated by the knowledge that the greater the number lured into elections, the greater would be their takings as agents. At primaries, local government, state governorship and legislative aspirants as well as presidential and national assembly hopefuls would also bestow their largesse on the agents and party executives, as people who would decide their fate. They were of course statutory delegates who would vote in the party's candidates for all elective posts. Maeze learned that in the previous election, about thirty people vied to become the party's gubernatorial candidate. Each of those thirty hopefuls gave about six thousand Dollars to each delegate! Similar events occurred with local government and national assembly aspirants. It was no surprise that party posts were so fiercely fought over that the novice wondered what gains there were in those posts.

Winners did indeed take all. If one's supporters, one's "own people" occupied important positions, one was sure to win the party ticket at the primary elections. In like vein, followers wooed the important people in the party in order to gain positions in the party's executive body. They would then enjoy all the bounties dispensed to executive members, casually disregarding the party's constitution's stipulations for election into party positions. The party's cohesion and integrity would be continually diminished. Consequently, leaders' individual programs' override the party's. Parties were often plunged into crises because members had manoeuvred to appoint rather than elect executives. Sometimes after election primaries, party members whose preferred candidate was not chosen, would join other political parties to discredit their previous party and its chosen candidate.

Considering the astronomical sums dispensed by candidates, the eventual winner would seek reimbursement of their expenses from the public purse. They could not be expected to be scrupulous over cuts in contracts awarded, indeed in amassing riches from all available sources. It was known of course that most elections were farcical. Rigging and destruction of voting papers were rife. Those declared winners were candidates with the greatest wealth and most adroit hoodlums in their pay.

The lack of internal democracy in Nigeria's political parties was wrecking the political process and governance. Leaders eventually would merely be appointed by party leaders rather than by adherence to the democratic process. Those leaders would of course strive to gratify the people who had brought them into eminence. Power was gained through the manipulation, bluff and violence of a relative few. Merit was jettisoned.

It was no surprise that in Nigeria, appointments to public office and contract awards were concentrated in a few families and their cronies. Of course transparency and accountability were no longer valued. The checks and balances in the constitution, aimed at protecting citizens, were disregarded. Even the ultimate arm and last hope of the commoner, the judiciary, had been trammeled by the damning nepotism of judicial appointments, and allegations of corruption of judges. Maeze was shocked to read of charges of corruption against judges even in the ultimate appellate courts. Such tales were unthinkable in the western world.

Because of the failures and disappointments from the military in the previous republics, many good Nigerians, in observing caution, stayed away from active politics when the present fourth republic was announced. This is true because the era of Shagari, though fraught with great challenges looked very much on course to put Nigeria in that developing democratic pedestal, was punctured by the same military that handed power over to civilians. Many of the military officers were actually interested in controlling the oil resources of the country and didn't really want to leave power. So, they toppled the civilian government not minding all the attendant waste that they brought the nation into. In the third attempt at installing civilian government, General Babangida struck and cancelled an election that was hailed across the globe as the fairest and freest ever. By the time they sermonized another civilian government, not everybody was enthused to believe them. That was the opening that many men of easy virtue seized the opportunity to grab the many elective positions yawning for people to fill them up. Like anything they do, deceit which is the core of their life principle, has taken over, and taken a toll on the political progress the country deserved. They are working hard to ensure those that might take the shine out of them do not have the chance to be discovered by Nigerians. They have taken distinguished, honourable, religious, royal, academic, and military accolades that in the present-day Nigeria, it is difficult to determine who is and who is not what is claimed. The few truly men and women of honour in positions of authority are under suffocation of the "smart" antics of the many disingenuous leader colleagues. They recruit their associates who have over these years, and under the involvement of their "friends" now in power, branched into all sectors of the political and economic lives of the country to perpetuate their dominance.

The popular opinion was that once power was relinquished by the high handed and corrupt military officers, things would change for good. But the suffering of the people seems to be getting worse since the coming of democracy. Unless and until leaders with conscience and fear of God emerge on the scene, the sacrifice of the founding fathers of the country will rather seem to have been in vain. Rascality and impunity are the order of the day in our national life today - behaviour well identified with the so-called leaders. They ply our roads dangerously in convoys displaying ignorance, lack of civility and ruthlessness. Young people from Malaysia with their own brand of questionable wealth have followed suite acting up in public in ways reminiscent of the 419 era. Even ritualists, yahoo yahoo boys and young school people are imitating the dishonorable lifestyles of these *nouveau riche*. The looming security problems of cultism, armed robbery and some political youth gangs are disturbing trends to be contained if the country must move forward. The decay in our political life has affected all professional life of our people.

Organizations that traditionally fought the cause of the oppressed had gone sadly silent, as everyone scrambled for morsels from the politicians' table. Such organizations as the Nigerian Bar Association (NBA) and the Nigerian Union of Journalists (NUJ) seemed to have abandoned the crusade for justice and equity. Even the human and civil rights organizations were no longer effectual. They seemed to make intermittent and half-hearted barking sounds yet remained unable to bite! All bastions of decency had been assailed and destroyed by the might of the corrupt.

Maeze considered his participation in politics divinely ordained. It gave him invaluable insight. He found that those who observed the democratic process from the sidelines remained unaware of the rooted dysfunction of the system and misguided in their criticism and blame. There was no substitute for taking part. It proved to him that the leaders were only taking advantage of the collective apathy of the populace. He saw the aptness of a dictum of Edmund Burke's: "The only thing necessary for the triumph of evil is for good men to do nothing."

On learning that Maeze was going to join a particular political party, some agents of a rival party exerted themselves to draw him to theirs. As many of those who approached him had been his childhood friends, he heeded them, and was promptly introduced to the party leaders. They were heartily encouraging, vowing that they would ensure his being chosen to represent their party at the state's constituent assembly elections. Maeze was again drawn into an orgy of unrestrained spending.

He was urged to visit and consult many influential "opinion leaders." Each of those visits obliged him to dispense cash and crates of wine and spirits. At some stage, the city's largest importer of liquor and beverages, was moved to rise above a trader's normal gladness at selling his merchandise. He told Maeze that he was spending too much on drinks. He related how many aspirants had become rudely disappointed by the people who had consumed their drinks and grabbed their cash. Political leaders, he explained, remained active for decades. They seemed to be presiding over a continually replayed movie. Ardent young people would arrive, play their parts in the scripts given them, and disappear. Some, panicking, on the brink of destitution after spending all they had earned and borrowed, rushed back to their previous occupations, abjuring politics. Those who remained on the political arena would be tested by further disappointments, given impossible assignments, and end up trapped in the political arena. On the other hand, those who fled the scene were viciously maligned, to ensure they would never have a future in politics. Any aspirant who remained interested after failing in the primary election was quickly promised a lofty post if a preferred candidate won the main election. It was, Maeze later found, a ploy to retain the failed candidate to work for the party's success.

Maeze stayed behind to help his party and its candidates to win in the general election. He deemed it injudicious, as a new man in politics, to move from one party to another – a practice termed "carpet crossing" – just because his initial bid had failed. During his campaign, he had declared that his seeking the party's nomination was not a "do or die" affair. If he had left the party subsequently, he reasoned, he would have been proved to have been insincere. He valued his reputation for truthfulness and believed politics should be played with seriousness and sincerity. The political tricksters of course dangled the prospect of a lofty future appointment before him. They had called Maeze on the very day of the primary election to step down for an anointed candidate. Curiously, the leader that gave Maeze that directive to withdraw had been doling out Maeze's money to delegates and non-delegates until 3am that morning, preparatory to the convention that should have upheld Maeze's nomination! The same man later came to Maeze to declare that the entire leadership would support him in the next election. Maeze now had no interest in the duplicitous man's assurances. He had so deceived him that he would be demented to again believe him.

On the eve of that next election, Maeze was not surprised when the leaders produced a list of candidates for posts. His name was not included, and he deduced that those leaders were in accord over his exclusion. By then, he had become too experienced in politics to feel betrayed or disappointed. That they could want to prevent his progress despite his loyalty, zeal and respect to them and the party, was simply in character. They were even working to make party members loyal to Maeze, turn against him. The party leader who had been directly duplicitous exuded satisfaction. His attitude to Maeze was "we have done our own thing; go to blazes if you don't like it." The assembly became so unruly that the woman leader chided the party leader openly, telling him his behavior was childish.

That night, Maeze took the solemn decision to leave the party. Those opponents were powerful, commanded state recognition and numerous followers, and intent on frustrating his political career, turning even his supporters against him. Above all, they were past masters of an art in which he was a novice: duplicity. It appeared futile to battle them. It was wiser to flee their circle before his reputation was further besmirched.

Many people, both within and outside the party, sympathized with Maeze, denouncing his treatment as unjust. Yet, they would not speak out openly for fear of reprisals from the mighty transgressors. Maeze considered moving to another political party, then reflected that the group there would have the same character as those he had left. They would certainly be masters of doublespeak, unabashedly treacherous and extortionate. His business beckoned compellingly.

Apposite to Maeze's feelings was a poem he was sent, **Nationalist Retrospection**, written by a Nigerian, Reginald Chiedu Ofodile.

Nationalist Retrospection
They saw esteemed compatriots shamed and jailed
denied employment and ignored in queues
for no defaults save happenstance of race.
Mau-Maus of Kenya suffered vile abuse
in Africa's South, rank apartheid reigned
its West was faced with Jim Crow style taboos.

They'd cause enough to rage, orate, project
resources vast abounded, coal and gold
diamonds, bauxite, cocoa, palm and salt
extent of crude oil still a tale untold.
The peoples swelled in numbers, learning, skill
once freed, we'd be a marvel to behold.

They knew that once "imperial might" with-drew
we blessed peoples would astound the West
as shooting eagles soar beyond the skies.
Now from their graves, they'd look at us aghast
our radiant realms in failure's fog obscured
by devious packs and rank corruption caused.

19. AN ANGEL ON A LONDON TRIP

Maeze was at Guangzhou province of China when he realized he could no longer walk with ease. He and his wife had arrived in China that afternoon, after two days of flights via Dubai. His wife's company would prove a boon. He had brought her along to familiarize her with the operation of the business, in case she had to come alone in future. Maeze's pain grew excruciating.

He considered his options. Communication with their business partners in China was labored. It was inadvisable to seek medical treatment there. He could not explain his symptoms to the doctors properly, and they, not understanding English, might give him treatment opposite to his needs, or even fatal. Such incidents had been known to occur, caused by a doctor acting in irreproachable good faith.

Leaving their business undone, Maeze and his wife hurried back to Nigeria. Maeze went for MRI and other tests at one of the country's esteemed Indian hospitals. Immediate physiotherapy and surgery in a couple of months were prescribed, and assorted medicines dispensed. He knew that before undergoing the prescribed surgery, he should seek a second medical opinion in the United Kingdom.

A momentous meeting occurred on that first trip to Great Britain. Maeze encountered someone he later described as an angel. The woman was of average height, and he surmised she must have been in her 50s. There was, predictably, disorder at the airport. As fate would have it, they found themselves standing next to each other in the queue.

The woman voiced her dismay, "Why are our people always in the habit of not forming a queue?"

"Well, sister, I don't know," Maeze replied.

"It seems we enjoy proving who has the greater strength all the time. It's a shame, though."

Their conversation continued. They talked about sources of cheap accommodation in the United Kingdom, and stories of Nigeria and Europe. Maeze told her he was going to England for treatment, and she said she was in Nigeria to worship at the Church of God for All (COGFA), founded and headed by Prophet U.C. Eleazar. She had come to Nigeria with her work colleagues a week earlier to seek spiritual wellbeing of the prophet. The lady said she was originally from Eastern Nigeria but had lived in the United Kingdom for over thirty years and become a British citizen. She wondered how Maeze could be going to England for treatment costing huge sums rather than receiving free healing from the Almighty under the anointing of His prophet in COFGA. Maeze must have looked skeptical, or even amused, because she proceeded to explain that there was no affliction or infirmity that Prophet U.C. Eleazar was not anointed to heal.

She told Maeze how she became a regular visitor to the Church, taking her friends and colleagues along. She had sent monies to her family members when tussling with life, doing multiple menial jobs to support her family in Nigeria. Many years passed before her residence in the United Kingdom was regularized. She then happily visited Nigeria. Her glee vanished when she learnt that the sums she had sent her brother had been squandered. Her brother had lived in luxury with the money she toiled and sweated for. Indeed, he spent like a rock star. Her indignation precipitated a family feud that had never been resolved.

She had reported the matter to paternal and maternal families and friends. Their wading into the fray only worsened it. They were unable to make him either refund part of the money or douse the fierce rancor that the feud had spread in the family. At some stage, her siblings seemed bent on assassinating her. She managed to return to England and had not visited her hometown in Eastern Nigeria since then. She had forgiven her brother but had no wish to associate with her family on her visits to Nigeria. She would go to Lagos, arrange for accommodation there, and after worshipping at COGFA, return to Great Britain. Maeze was sympathetic, having heard of many such situations, and had worse experiences from his own people. The woman maintained that Maeze must visit the Church for his health challenges and referred him to the COGFA YouTube site on Joseph Television. In all their discussions, neither Maeze nor the woman had asked each other's identity.

In the United Kingdom, Maeze began regularly to watch Joseph TV. The trip was of course purely for medical reasons. He felt however that he should take advantage of the uninterrupted power supply to work more on the book he had been writing. Nigeria's epileptic electricity had brought vexations. He did his research and study at night but hated the sound of the generator which he often had to use.

Maeze was riveted by the miracles and spiritual power demonstrated at COGFA and shown on Joseph TV. The feats were awesome. The more he watched, the stronger was his conviction that the Almighty was truly working through the Prophet, U.C. Eleazar. As the evil spirits which fettered people spoke through those being delivered from bondage, Maeze realized how foolishly he had lived all his life. The areas of his life held captive by Satan were assailed by the spirit within him. He felt stripped naked by the words and work of the Prophet.

Maeze had watched Joseph TV in the past but had not been as moved as he now was. The discussions with the angel woman on his flight made him watch and listen with a new intentness and spirit. He had been among people who thought miracles simply did not occur in the present world. He had attended both orthodox and Pentecostal churches, and heard reverend fathers, pastors, evangelists, prophets, spiritualists and traditionalists preach and cast out demons from people. However, as he watched the videos and heard the messages of COGFA on Joseph TV, Maeze knew that he had not been living as a Christian should. The humility, devoutness and generosity of the Church's work convicted his spirit.

Maeze's entire body was racked with acute pain. He went to hospitals and eventually got an appointment with a neurosurgeon. After tests and a review of his medical history, it was determined that he would undertake procedures in two stages. The first would be done at once, and the second, depending on the outcome of the first, over a period of time. Maeze wished to do the first, then return to England later for the second. He was impatient to visit the Church in Nigeria to receive deliverance and healing. He felt in dire need of that church and the touch of the prophet.

Over his two-month stay in England, Maeze became an addict to Joseph TV with the messages of deliverance from the Church. Curiously, many to whom he enthused about the work of the Almighty through the man of God, dismissed the prophet as phony, and even declared the miracles he procured diabolic. However, Maeze's conviction that God was working through that prophet grew ever stronger. He remembered when he used to doubt spiritual healing, so could understand those who daily read the Bible but did not understand the power for remission of sins in the blood shed at Calvary by Jesus Christ.

A miracle of sorts now occurred in Maeze's life. His lustful yearnings and zest for fornication vanished. Those had burdened him from puberty. When he left for London, he had promised himself lavish sexual gratification: he would meet many women and fulfill all his sexual fantasies and more. At the time, he had idly wondered how he could ever rid himself of attraction to women and pornography. Those urges had manacled and almost destroyed him. All his previous efforts to drop them had failed. Now, suddenly, he seemed to have received a power to reject every urge that might becloud his faith. He realized how filthy lust and fornication were.

The human body, he now fully understood, was the temple of the Holy Spirit. Whenever one defiled that temple through fornication, the Holy Spirit was repelled. The sinner would become vulnerable to temptation, and lose the spiritual protection conferred by the spirit of the Lord.

Maeze, in self-revulsion, realized how hollow his life had been, as carnal sin had made him live out of the sight of the Lord. He accepted the Bible's words in John 3:24. "And he that keepeth his commandments dwelleth in him, and he in him. And hereby we know that he abideth in us, by the spirit which he hath given us." In Exodus 20:14, God warned against adultery. Among the commandments of God, that sin in particular had held Maeze down. He asked himself, "To what end am I called a Christian when I don't hearken to His laws?"

It dawned on Maeze that he had lived a most sinful life. For the first time in his life, he realized how wrong it was to be physically intimate with a woman who was not his wife. He acknowledged his sins and asked God to forgive him. Maeze vowed never again to commit the sin of adultery. He was having a personal encounter with God. He saw how one sin bred other sins. One involved in infidelity would try to conceal it by telling lies, claiming the decency that he lacked, calling the name of the Lord in vain, committing more sins and crimes to cover the first and remain in his league of racy friends. The Bible told how King

David, greatly loved by God, brought calamity upon himself by instigating murder consequent on his adultery with, and impregnation of Uriah's wife. He suffered the wrath of the Almighty subsequently.

The Lord, however, is ever merciful, and forgave those who confessed and truly repented of their past misdeeds. Leafing through the Bible, Maeze read 1 John 1:9. "If we confess our sins, he is faithful and just to forgive us our sins, and to cleanse us from all unrighteousness." He read in Ephesians 1 of how St Paul the apostle spoke to humanity about the love of God in human lives as his chosen people through Christ Jesus. Humanity was redeemed according to the riches of his grace. It should therefore be understood that until humans gave their lives to God and shunned sin, the main purpose of creation would not be fulfilled. As Maeze continued to study and absorb the scriptures, he was continually shocked at how adrift he had been, how lost to sin and stupidity. He again vowed to overhaul his spiritual life.

Maeze became more conscious of, and thirsty for the message of Christ. Prophet U.C. Eleazar's work of miracle and humility, and messages, all infused Maeze with wholesomeness. Although he had been a lifelong Christian, he was now properly converted to Christ. Maeze recalled that he had twice encountered the Holy Spirit in his dreams, and both encounters indicted his infidelity. The first had been in Eket town in the South of Nigeria twenty years earlier. He had been young, flush with the impunity of sin, on an official trip to a worksite of the French company he was working for. When he awoke that night in tears of contrition, he knew that the experience was real. The second dream occurred a few years later, in similar circumstances to the first. Maeze knew that the Almighty had been reaching out to him in those dreams. He knew that God loved him greatly and was calling to him to give him peace. By the time he stepped through the portals of the Church of God for All, Maeze was already enjoying such peace as he had never known.

20. THE CHURCH OF GOD FOR ALL

He arrived in Nigeria from London early in December. Rather than proceed to his base, Abuja, Maeze remained in Lagos to find the Church. Lagos and Western Nigeria were foreign territory to him. After two days of fruitless searching, Maeze decided to go to the family he had left two months earlier and return to Lagos later.

A week later, Maeze was back in Lagos. Before arriving, he had contacted a friend in Lagos and arranged for his accommodation and transport. He anticipated a fairly long stay as there was currently a convention in the church. Christians appeared to have converged from all nations on earth. The crowds were huge, hotels filled, and traders and agents were all over the venue, engaging in brisk business.

Maeze and his friend had arrived in the church about one O'clock in the dead morning. The screening arena was already half-full. Many groups of overseas worshippers were present, most of them in uniforms. Reservations had been made for them. The COGFA's workers were phenomenal in their organizational expertise. Maeze, a first-time visitor, pondered how that huge crowd could be managed. He marveled at the skill with which the workers got everyone screened, then seated for the service. In the five days that Maeze and his friend participated, there were bigger crowds every day. At some stage, people were advised to skip some days of worship if they had been admitted once.

Maeze was luckier than his friend, for he made it into the main worship hall on one occasion. His friend did not progress beyond the overflow arena but received instant healing for a chronic shoulder pain he had suffered for years. He would give fervent thanks to the Almighty long afterwards for that relief. Maeze's friend, although a high-ranking member of one of the orthodox churches, had never been serious in his devotions. He found the revival at COGFA a wonderful spiritual experience.

When Maeze appeared before the man of God, he was racked with spinal stenosis pain. It seemed to burn his entire back from neck to heels. The Man of God laid hands on him, and the excruciating pain began to lessen.

Maeze later went for an X-ray. Doctors confirmed that his lumbar discs, once said to have shifted after an MRI test, were now in their normal position. As the pain continued to ebb away, Maeze increasingly performed many physical acts that had been beyond him. He was at peace with his life, his marriage, work and general relationships. He had learned to entrust his fears and hopes in the Lord.

Reflections of Mr. Sedrob

Maeze was suddenly moved to long reflection on his encounters with Mr Sedrob. He concluded that the unseen hands of the Almighty had saved him from self-destruction, and that if the circumstances he faced then would occur again, his reactions would be different.

When infuriated by Mr Sedrob at the French Multinational Oil Servicing Company, he had driven for half a day from Port Harcourt to Warri to harangue Sedrob. He reflected that the reasonable course would have been to write to the Managing Director. Although Mr Sedrob's deeds were deplorable and rightly challenged, the confrontation he went for was wrong. There was of course Mr Pierre, the Managing Director who definitely did not support Mr Sedrob's oppressive highhandedness. He could have been aware of the racism propagated by the Head of Finance and Administration under his leadership but ignored it. Mr Pierre therefore was well disposed to Maeze, and also in a position to help him save his job, which was Maeze's prime concern at the time.

Maeze's fear of losing his job was real, along with the conviction that, being black, he could not overcome the net of victimization and humiliation that Sedrob and his acolytes had thrown over him. Maeze reflected further that at that stage of Nigeria's industrial development, all non-blacks – Caucasian, Hispanic, or Asian – were widely deferred to in Nigeria. After all, in that organization at that time, people from other African countries, even as non-citizens, were made to handle immigration matters, and those of them Nigerians were made to keep away from anything concerning immigration matters. At some stage, the company's chairman was recommending associates who were non-citizens for high and sensitive positions which should have been reserved for Nigerians. The Immigration office was also happy that senior Nigerian employees were excluded from dealing with their department because those Nigerians would have been offended at the duplicity of the French Administration Manager. It was vile for the country's immigration service to teach aliens – including illegal ones – how to manipulate "the system." Those officials were of course motivated by their selfish pecuniary interests. They taught aliens how to give false information on immigration documents. They used the few expatriates on the quota to cover the unqualified and visiting ones, moving them from one work location to the other within the country.

Some Nigerian staff of course knew of the dishonesty, and were outraged by it, but kept silent in order to keep their jobs. A few mustered the nerve to send anonymous petitions, but those petitions ended up with investigating officers' pockets swelling with financial inducements! Indeed, after each massive inquiry, those suspected to have sent the petitions would be dismissed from the company. That practice was a powerful warning to the remaining staff to suppress their scruples if they wished to remain employed. Indeed, the company had its own "whistle-blowers" that informed against the disgruntled and their external collaborators.

Similar ruthless deceit and repression pervaded other multinational companies in the country. Some of the deified expatriate employees had neither education nor training in their declared spheres of specialization, for which they had obviously been hired by the organizations. They were actually learning "on the job" from highly skilled Nigerians! Some of the expatriates had been brought purposely to Nigeria as watch dogs, since the management did not trust Nigerians to protect their interests. At worksites, they functioned as security men rather than in the roles officially designated to them.

Now, many years after leaving the company, Maeze felt he should have acted with greater caution and maturity whilst at the company.

21. REFLECTIONS ON A JAGWUDA

Maeze remembered vividly the day he watched a scene created by a certain lanky fellow in Warri, a town noted for its brawny men and women, who could hold their own in fisticuffs in the street. Those days, there were musical shows that featured popular artistes like Tony Gray, Chris Okotie, Jide Obi, Onyeka Onwenu, Majek Fashek, Orits Wiliki, Felix Liberty, etc. There were entertainment centres like Palm Grove hotels, Enerhen Hotels, Midwest Inn, and many others. Most of the shows then ended in brawls where bottles, chairs and every available object would be used freely.

There were popular hotspots like Enerhen junction, Giniwa, Okere, Estates and the notorious Mcdermott and Agbasa areas. There were street urchins that regaled in "Tie Neck". Thus, it was part of daily life then to be surrounded by a group of young boys in the street, right in the presence of passer byes, and dispossessed of personal belongings. One's money, pen, hats, jewelries, shoes and even clothes could be forcefully taken away in daylight without the next person on the street intervening. These young attackers were usually armed with dangerous items and were ruthless in their approach. On some occasions, victims would return to their loved ones only in their underwear. They were more fortunate than many others who were injured or killed in the process of attack. Maeze remembered vividly the day he watched a "Jagwuda" at Upper Erejuwa Street destroy a taxi cab with bare hands. By the time the lone attacker had gone half way into reducing the car to a rubble, a sizeable crowd had gathered around as though they were on a movie theater. Nobody could ask him to stop …just watching. He put on a pair of trending jean pants with a jean long sleeved jacket, just like some of those seen on American movies. He was a tall fair complexioned and handsome young man in his thirties. You could tell he was high on some substances, given the brutality and measured demeanor. He went about the action calm and relaxed as though the owner of the cab had paid him handsomely to do a demonstration test. He started the assignment with the driver. When the poor fellow received the beating of his life, he managed to run away from the hands of this monster man. It seemed his escape incensed the Jagwuda so that he decided to reign terror on the vehicle. As the mob watched in apathy, and almost at the end of his callous engagement on the car, the driver had returned with about four policemen. The presence of the policemen did not deter him from his concentration on the destruction. By this time, the car had been so dismembered and disfigured to know the make, model or type. It was one unrecognizable heap of metal scrap by the road side.

Initially, the police officers were afraid to approach the huge figure of a man. The four inches shoe he wore even added more awe to his size and physique. After much endearments to stop without a reaction, one policeman had summoned the needed courage to step forward against his next step towards what remained of the car. The crowd had expected him to "finish" the policeman. Everybody was just waiting to see what would happen with the policemen sent to arrest him. There was no reaction from him. He acted like he was returning to life from a trance. Like a little boy would pick a chicken, the other policemen helped their colleague and held his hands behind him. He was subsequently hand cuffed. To everybody's surprise he busted into a bout of tears like a suckling. His action left everybody in more bewilderment. What did he think he was doing all along? What substance did he use that led him to such a wilful destruction of a citizen's property and himself? Nobody was touched by his hang dog episode anyway. The driver was by

                                                    Gabriel C. Onyekuru

this time crying by the roadside, narrating what happened earlier on with the Jagwuda man. The Jagwuda accused him of driving his car too close to where he was standing. As he appeared by the driver's door and threatened him. The driver was forced out of the steering and off his seat. He had told the man that his car didn't come near him. But looking at how well dressed the guy was and his size, the driver had said sorry to him. The guy just descended on him and started beating him. He managed to extricate himself from his hold and ran to the police station to make a report of assault. It was evident in his behavior that substance of abuse was the cause. At the station, he had no explanation but just sobbing.

Drug use is dangerous to self and others. It costs societies a lot to manage both the substance abuser and the destruction to society caused by the use of a substance of abuse. There have been links between substance use and criminal conduct in many studies. Continuous use of substance affects the brain and could result in psychiatric condition. Many people who engage in violence also use a substance of abuse. It could come in form of alcohol, drug or other intoxicants. People might start gradually to introduce the use of substance as a way to escape physical or psychological pain. Once the use is not prescribed by some medical personnel, the tendency is for the user to slowly increase the dosage. He might get to a point where the user becomes completely dependent on the substance. It means that that person's anatomy is now in a normal state if he is high on the substance and abnormal when the substance is not acting in his body, a case of reversal. Addiction has occurred. The person needs that particular substance to function on daily basis. The tendency is that the body tolerance may continue to reduce, necessitating incremental use of the substance, until it begins to alter seriously with the internal workings of the individual's cells and organs. Now this is the point: for daily functioning of the user's body, he needs the substance. And for the interference of the substance with the internal body system, what is formerly normal has been altered and in a state of disequilibrium. Withdrawal is difficult because the functioning is now dependent on the drug. The mental, physical, emotional and psychological functioning continues to deteriorate steadily. Non-daily use of the substance of abuse knocks the addict off functioning, and continuous use affects the physiology of the person's complete being. Studies have linked substance use to violence. And violence has been linked to crimes. That is the danger of abuse.

22. REFLECTIONS ON SONNY
THE GIANT

Sonny the giant, greatly resembled the Jagwuda. The man lived in the same apartment complex as Maeze, had a well-paid job as a senior security personnel in one of the country's major oil companies in Warri, and was also a part-time footballer training with one of the state football teams.

Sonny, then in his early 40s, was a lovable fellow. He had two bosom friends. One, a man of about his age, worked in the same company as Sonny. The other was about ten years older. An offshore man, he would return regularly after two weeks' absence, spend another fortnight off-duty, then leave for another two-week stint. Although all three worked flexible schedules, they did not often have their leisure times simultaneously. However, about three or four times a year, they would all be free at the same time. Then the entire street would seem to be crackling and exploding!

They seemed to revel in their aura as "big shots." Only few people in the town owned private cars, and the offshore man owned a car. His prestige was not diminished by the fact that his car was the lowest-priced motor vehicle then on the market – a Toyota Corolla wagon. The elderly man also lived in a three-bedroom flat. His life seemed blessed with luxuries exclusive to the rich and powerful, and unattainable to all his neighbors. The trio were graceless, loud, and inconsiderate in interactions with other residents of both the street and the apartment complex. Many must have been envious of the status and possessions of those three men. Maeze however cringed at their disrespect to both landlords and poor neighbors. They would get drunk, dance and disrupt the neighborhood's peace, even late at night. Nobody dared to express open indignation at their excesses.

The building was a straight block of six two-bed room apartments, up and down. The kitchens, toilets and bathrooms were located at the far end of the block. At each level, there were three kitchens to be shared by two apartments, one toilet and one bathroom for the males and another set for the females. The flats were located at the other end of the block. Sonny's friend that worked offshore lived in the upper three-bedroom apartment with his family while another family occupied the flat downstairs. There was a walkway that stretched from one end of the building circling all the apartments through the kitchen, to the other side of the building. So, no matter where one was, one could access any part of the building. The second building in the compound was partitioned into flats, housing the landlord in the front and two other tenants. Those flats were for high income earners. There were a borehole and a concrete water well in between the two blocks. The entire compound had a concrete floor and was fenced to provide both comfort and security. It was one of the best living complexes at that period of development in Warri. The house was located well away from the town's frenzy. The landlord's wife had a provision store in front of their own flat, serving the tenants and the neighborhood. Sonny and his friends all lived in the same block as Maeze. Maeze was about twenty, single, and shared a two-bedroom apartment with a friend. Their middle door was permanently locked so that each used only the front door.

One evening at about seven o'clock, Maeze was returning to their compound from work when he noticed people clustered by part of the fence. He saw a cotenant held by Sonny's younger friend, with whom Maeze was not on speaking terms. On enquiry, he learned that they were quarrelling over a general electricity bill accumulated over the years. The fact was that Sonny, his friends, and many of the other tenants had lived in the building since it was built. They had not been paying electricity bills until apartments became vacant upstairs and they moved. Now, the Public Electricity Management Company was undertaking disconnection of debtor customers, the current occupiers sought contributions from those who had lived there previously and caused the high payment being demanded. Sonny's friend, highhanded as usual, sought to punish the cotenant for demanding their contribution. Maeze, a few meters away, muttered "Why is he bullying him? After all, they were the ones that incurred the huge bill. Why is he bullying him?" The bully overheard Maeze.

He let go of the cotenant and descended on Maeze. It seemed he had long yearned to harm Maeze, and Maeze's comments were the calls for the battery. He addressed Maeze: "You little boy! I'm going to discipline you today in a way you will remember all your life." He was trying to grab Maeze's shirt. The people who had been trying to part him from the cotenant he was beating were stopping him from reaching Maeze. Some of them had not even heard Maeze's needling remark. Maeze was defiant, telling the bully he could not do him any harm. His scorn of course incensed the man further. Then Sonny arrived on the scene.

Sonny the Giant didn't ask what the problem was. He merely said: "Who is that?" His friend pointed at Maeze, saying: "It's that rat." Sonny shoved away everyone that stood between himself and Maeze, jerking his shirt off, then grabbed Maeze's collar. The group was pleading with him to leave the collar, but he was heedless. Some began to tell Maeze: "We had told you to leave the arena before this time but you refused. This lion is going to eat you today. This young man, you are stubborn." By this time, Sonny was rattling and pushing Maeze about, while still holding him by his shirt collar. Maeze did not have a chance to utter a word anymore. He held to Sonny's waist, choking, praying that Sonny would relax his strangulating grip. He heard Sonny raging that he would kill him and suffer no penalties, as they were in Nigeria and he had contacts in the highest places. He heard voices urging Sonny's friend: "Don't hit Maeze. Leave that bottle. Drop the bottle." Then Maeze's hand touched a bottle. He felt its neck being put into his grip. Maeze was looking for a way out of the stranglehold of Sonny. Sonny must have been unaware that Maeze had been handed a weapon. Maeze mustered all his strength and struck Sonny, hitting his face. Sonny immediately released his hold of Maeze. Maeze saw blood trickling, then rushing from Sonny's face, the group dispersing, as Sonny made a wild rush at him. He picked up a concrete block used to wedge a flower bush and threw it at Sonny, striking Sonny's chest. As Sonny groaned and staggered, Maeze escaped, running into the compound. He felt Sonny and his friends would shortly be after him to deal him some deathblows and made an instant decision to run to the back of the kitchen. The fence was high and reinforced with six-inch nails on top to prevent thieves from scaling the wall. Warri was notorious for local thieves and house breaking. There was no time to think about the lateral effect of the injury to be sustained. He placed his palms on the nails and jumped over.

Maeze learned later that Sonny and his friends searched for him throughout the compound, then from one apartment to another believing someone must be hiding him. No cotenant had the nerve to tell them not to invade their living quarters. They turned people's furniture and closets upside down in the bid to find Maeze. Of course, it never occurred to them that Maeze might have scaled the wall. It was a risk they considered beyond human daring. Maeze, in the mean-time,had run to a pharmacy to have his injuries treated.

When the bleeding of Sonny's face became too profuse to be ignored, Sonny and his friends accepted neighbors' advice that he should should seek treatment to stop the flow. Later that night, after his cut had been stitched up, he and his friends resumed the search for Maeze. They declared they would kill Maeze once they found him.

They all met at the police station the following day. Sonny and his friends were unable to give a coherent account of the events that precipitated the fight. Maeze related his experience, and how he had been almost choked to death by Sonny's strangulating grip, and how he had miraculously been handed the weapon that saved him from extermination. He had acted in self-defence. Friends, neighbors and Maeze's relatives all pleaded with Sonny to withdraw the case from the police station. By the time Maeze ventured into Sonny's apartment for a conciliatory meeting, Sonny was calm and cordial! He told the people present that he had always loved Maeze and thought him a nice young man who always minded his business. Sonny admitted that he blamed himself for the incident because he had had too much beer before the incident. Maeze agreed to pay all medical bills associated with the fight.

For his part, Maeze expressed regret for ever getting involved in a clash that could have claimed his life or Sonny's. What if the bottle or concrete block had given Sonny a mortal injury? What if he had been caught by Sonny and his gang that night? What if he had landed on a sharp object when he scaled the fence? What if neighbors had mistaken him for a thief when he was running away from Sonny that night? He would have been remanded by the police and charged for murder or manslaughter. His life and achievements would have been unrealized. His life's career would have been cut short at the age of twenty. What if what happened at that time had happened in today's globalized world, with law enforcement greatly improved, and criminal records well-kept and retrievable within seconds? How would that have affected Maeze's career, family and education? It was true that one might not understand the import of some actions taken in one's youth, but those deeds impact one's future. How easy it was, whilst growing up, to make irreparable and irrevocable mistakes which would be regretted for the rest of one's life. Such records would cause emotional and psychological disorders in adult life. Life, Maeze concluded, was like a one-way high-speed train. A stop once passed would never be encountered again. Whatever is picked up at the train stop, will accompany one on the journey. The good items would of course shape one's life positively, while the objectionable ones would obstruct one's path to greatness.

He watched many Nigerians take the law into their own hands. Some asked in rhetorical arrogance: "Do you know who I am?" Those people exuded smug conceit. Others of their ilk would proclaim their close acquaintanceship with the highly placed, bragging that even if they committed murder, they would suffer no penalties. Many, Maeze found, lied about those contacts, claiming kinship and friendship with people who did not know them. However, those lies often proved effective, making listeners kowtow to the speakers.

23. REFLECTIONS ON A GENTLE ARMY GENERAL

A bar incident in Owerri left many people perplexed. The bar was very popular with night clubbers in that serene and beautiful city in the Eastern heartlands. The town was noted for its irresistible delicacies. At weekends and on holidays, young and old, craving delightful diversion trooped to the city of Owerri. Night crawlers from every part of the world brought and shared their diverse experiences of fashion, dancing, and food, enhancing the entertainments in the city. Returnees from America, Europe and other parts of the world were emulated.

Owerri's nightlife was believed to have begun in earnest in the early 1970s, when highlife music of the Bongo brand was in vogue. The Owerri that Maeze thought of was not the collection of five aboriginal clans that comprised Owerri township, but the territory known as Owerri Province in the colonial past. It embraced Mbaise, Mbaitoli, Ikeduru, Ngor Okpalla, Ohaji, Mbano and the many towns in between them. All those communities were included in what was currently the Owerri Senatorial Zone of Imo State.

Owerri people are gregarious, fun-loving, and hospitable. They were so cordial that violence was hardly ever encountered in their centres of socializing, unlike in other cities of the country. Indeed, Owerrians were reputed to prioritize their social lives, unlike other Igbo communities who toiled to amass wealth. A popular Owerri adage held: "Once I've eaten my oil-bean dish and stockfish and drunk palm wine, others may go for wealth and building storey houses." Over the years, they pursued education and eschewed trade and artisans' apprenticeship and military service. They had a history of teachers, judicial workers, lawyers, doctors and other professionals. That attitude however was changing as many were engaging in various spheres of human capital development. However, even the poorest families took pride in educating their children and wards to the highest possible levels. It was hard to find a family whose members had not been to university. On occasion, people had to forego their schooling in order to sponsor their siblings to a high level of education. Maeze found that Imo State of Nigeria, of which Owerri was the capital, had more institutions of higher learning than any other state in Nigeria, and more candidates seeking admission into higher institutions. Maeze wondered whether the city's vibrant social life was the result of the high number of higher institutions, or droves of visitors arriving every week. Some held that people streamed into Owerri to entice the innumerable beautiful girls studying there. Whatever the reason, Owerri harboured some of the most beautiful women in the country, and its entertainment centres were thronged with women. "Wherever there is honey, bees are also found." Every weekend, male visitors swarmed like bees. Some Bongo artist joked that the hotel business was the only business in Owerri. Streets teemed with hotels and guest houses, and more were being built. The hotels were often full, despite their high rates. "This is the Las Vegas of Nigeria," Maeze sighed. A first-time visitor would think carnivals were held every weekend. Predictably, social miscreants sometimes plied their trade of scamming, stealing and troublemaking.

It therefore struck an odd note when a nouveau riche young man decided to vent his dissatisfactions on a gentleman seated next to his table. The bar was filled to capacity when the young fellow had a shouting match with his girlfriend. The beautiful young woman had gone over to another table to greet the gentleman. She returned to her circle of friends – five men and two women. When her boyfriend's fury would not be contained, she must have felt embarrassed and began to leave the bar. On her way out, she stopped to speak to the man she had greeted earlier. Her man sent two of his bodyguards to bring her back. An argument ensued between the gentleman and the guards. The nouveau riche, in a classic show of power, called in his police escorts hovering outside the bar. It emerged that one of the other four men at his table was a police officer. He reeled out commands to the escorts. They should take everyone at the gentleman's table out of the bar. The gentleman and his friends pleaded for peace, but all their entreaties were ignored. They were roughly shooed out by the escorts and bodyguards.

It was not known then that the equable man was a serving Army General. He sent a signal to the Army Commander at the Brigade Headquarters, and another to the State Commissioner of Police. His signal to the army commander at the brigade headquarters was for a team of soldiers; and that to the state police commissioner was for a team also. He had quietly explained to them the developing saga at the bar and the treatment he had received. He also cautioned them not to harass the rest of the guests at the bar when they arrived.

In a matter of minutes, a twelve-man police suicide squad in plain clothes arrived, followed immediately by a truckload of army men. They had parked their vehicles some distance away from the bar. The Army team laid siege outside while the policemen entered the bar. They were just in time to witness abuse from the nouveau riche and his group. First, they announced, on the public-address system, that they did not plan to embarrass anybody or the bar proprietor but wished to ensure that the peace of the state was maintained. They solicited the cooperation of all at the bar. It was at that point that the guests realized that the gentleman was among the Country's topmost, who had served on foreign peace missions. He had arrived in

Nigeria the previous day and was just relaxing with friends at the bar. The young businessman, his police escorts and guards were all whisked away for questioning at the Brigade Headquarters. People marveled that Nigeria still had someone, so self-effacing as the gentle general in the topmost ranks of the military profession.

At the brigade commander's office the next day, the media publicized the news of the arrest of a kidnap kingpin and his criminal gang. Their network, including international links were exposed. Assorted arms, documents and stolen property were discovered in the process. The lesson Maeze drew from that incident was that criminals were usually quick to employ violence and flaunt their power. They might be clever, but they would leave incriminating acts in their path.

Maeze also mused on other instances of exemplary behavior he had witnessed among Nigerians, despite the challenges of the environment. He reflected that it was not honourable of him to have lived the kind of life he had engaged in while in the United States. Unwholesome peer pressure must be resisted. To blunder into muddles just because others claim it is right was deplorable. To tread on ignoble paths would destroy his dream of becoming a successful man. Most aspirations that failed at the later stage of a man's life foundered because of impulsive and careless decisions at a much younger age.

24. AFRICAN INTERNATIONAL STUDENTS IN AMERICA

The primary purpose of this review was to relate this story to existing knowledge regarding international students in general, and more specifically, to African international students studying in United States of America (USA) colleges and universities. To assess the adjustment problems and processes, an examination of the literature was necessary. The literature attempted to review existing studies on cross-cultural college adjustment as it related to spirituality, communication, finance, health, counselling, social and personal relationships, as well as academic advising.

Several researchers (Coleman, 1997; Tomkovich & Al-Khatib, 1996) had attributed the increase in the population of international students to the active recruitment by colleges and universities, for educational and utilitarian purposes. Living in another country creates problems of adjustment to the host country for the migrant, and overseas students were not exempted from this process (Mehdizeh & Scott, 2005). Recent research suggests that adjustment is influenced by various cross-cultural variables, such as the amount of contact with host nationals, length of residence, finance, country of origin, country of study, economic factors, psychosocial factors and accommodation (Mehdizeh & Scott, 2005). International students, as long stay tourists, often tended to have a significant injection into the host country's economy due to the fact that they pay full tuition fees and also their expenditure on produced goods and services (Kelly, Marsh, & McNicoll, 2002). In addition, non-economic benefits arise from international students such as English language course as well as culture and understanding among races (McNamara & Harris, 1997). They recognised that, on a global basis, universities in US, Australia, and Canada have undertaken most of the researches on sojourner adjustment. Nevertheless, a lot more studies still need to be done, because of the import of the adjustment process of international students for their academic success in the host country (Maundeni, 2001).

The presence of international students on different campuses would often bring to student affairs administration, a whole new set of responsibilities for providing a range of services for international students and faculty (Ping, 1999). International students, including Africans generally contributed meaningfully to scholarship, globalisation ability, and finances of US institutions of higher education (Woolston, 1995). Indeed, their financial impact is so great that higher education had been called an export commodity because of its ability to attract international students who would bring new money to their US institutions (Woolston, op. cit). African international students, who returned home after a successful sojourn in the US, were expected to become "ambassadors" and political allies. For this reason, (Hughes, 1992) urged that we need to educate our students to become world citizens. Casazza & Silverman (1996) suggested that international students should be seen as a resource for learning about cultural diversity. Their work suggested that personnel on campus assistance programmes should provide workshops in which international students could share information about cultural issues. Boylan & White (1994) described the beginnings of developmental education as rooted in an effort to help members of different groups prepare themselves for successful higher education experiences.

International students contend with the same problems that confront anybody living in a foreign culture, such as racial discrimination, language problems, accommodation difficulties, dietary restrictions, financial stress, misunderstandings and loneliness (Lin & Yi, 1997). These authors maintained that exposure to an unfamiliar environment can create anxiety, confusion, and depression. Adjustment was defined as a process of examining the interaction between personal characteristics of the students with the structure of the host community (Lin & Yi, 1997). In other words, the more the similarity between the characteristics of international students and that of the nationals of the host country, the easier it would be for interaction (Mehdizadeh & Scott, 2005). The work of Logan & Glenna (1996) suggested that older people around the globe would prefer to grow old in the place where they have lived out their lives. This is an indication that older people in a foreign country would find it more difficult adjusting to a new culture. Lin & Yi (1997) recognised that financial pressures were serious problem among international students because they were legally prevented from assuming a part-time status or dropping out. Apart from the fact that international students had little or no access to welfare benefits, loans and scholarships, as well as have the awesome responsibility of paying out of state tuition, they would have to forfeit their student visas if they didn't assume full time status (Lin & Yi, 1997).

The initial challenges of African international students in the United States, included finding a place to live, learning where and how to shop for groceries, transportation and how to use a public transportation system, registering for classes, and setting up a communication medium to reach loved ones back home (Poyrazli, Kavanaugh, Baker, & Al-Timini, 2004). Those with good English skills might have an easier time during their transition to the new setting, while those with low levels of language communication might find it more difficult (Poyrazli et al., 2004). These challenges might have an impact on their academic success, psychological well-being, and the educational institution's effectiveness in retaining these students (Poyrazli, Arbona, Nora, Mcpherson, & Pisecco, 2002). To help African international students reach greater academic achievement and attain their goals, encouraging students to interact with faculty members had been suggested (Anya & Cole, 2001). In addition, helping students increase their English proficiency would likely lead to higher levels of academic self-efficacy (Poyrazli et al., 2002).

The similarity between the students' home culture and the culture of the host country, perceived discrimination, being extraverted, high communication skills in English, and a positive approach to forming relationships with Americans were noted as variables affecting the international students' attitude (Ying, 2002). Depending on the international students' native culture, participation in classroom discussions could assume extremely difficult and intimidating position (Lu, 2001). Ying (2002) found that students from Southeast Asian countries and Africa might considered it impolite or that they were wasting the instructor's time if the class was interrupted with a question. This group of international students might feel distant to the American culture and experience more adjustment difficulties (Triandis, 1991). Strandholm (2002) proposed that the ethical orientations of older foreign students would exhibit convergence towards the ethical orientations of the host culture. Further, as the level of perceived prejudice increases, so would be the likelihood that international students would identify with other international students rather than with the host nationals (Schmitt, Spears, & Branscombe, 2003). Once international students commenced building relationships with Americans, their experiences might be more positive, and they might experience an increased level of social support (Poyrazli, et al., 2004).

During their initial transition, international students might feel lost, confused, overwhelmed, helpless, and become isolated; they might also feel stressed in their academic pursuit like their domestic counterparts as they struggled to settle into their new environment with the start of the semester (Poyrazli, 2005). Meanwhile, unlike the domestic students, international students usually do not have similar resources-related problem in combating this stress (Sandhu & Asrabadi, 1998). Poyrazli (2005) reported that the culture of international students determines the amount and type of psychological reactions they show. European students for example tend to report experiencing less acculturative stress than students from Asia, Central/South America, and Africa (Yeh & Inose, 2003). Non-European international students may also experience more discrimination, which in turn, might lead to lower self-esteem (Schmitt et al., 2003). African international students have a peculiar problem because they come from a collectivist-oriented culture, quite different from American culture; largely considered more individualistic. Degges-White (2005) found that when adults shift from a rational focus on the present day, which essentially is materialistic world to a more universal and transcendent perspective, the shift would be accompanied with a desire to move towards the end of life, with a sense of integrity and acceptance of one's choices.

The interdependence of all parts of the world underscored the likely outcome that those students who have studied abroad would be more likely be hired in and be readier for a global marketplace (Nasr et al., 2002). The process of cross-cultural transition had been of interest to researchers who attempted to uncover factors that often lead to sojourner adjustment and cross-cultural effectiveness (Arthur, 2001). The purpose of Arthur's (2001) study was to investigate the perceived stressors and coping strategies of Canadian post-secondary students during a seven-week cross-cultural seminar programme in Vietnam. The study tracked the common and unique experiences of students. Specific critical incidents were collected from students at six time points regarding stressful experiences, selected coping strategies, use of social support, as well as shifting views of self and perspectives about international development. Results from the study were discussed with suggestions for pre-departure training programmes and the use of critical incidents as a tool for understanding cross-cultural transitions. To be an outsider or stranger in a foreign culture was always a challenge (Hartung, 2002).

Hoffa (2000) noted that it was difficult to know what life was really like in a country whose culture one had never experienced directly and pointed out that simple "knowing about" another culture was not the same thing as knowing what it was going to feel like to be learning and living there in reality on its terms. Apparently, it is difficult to learn new ways of doing things or living life in another culture (Snoke & Long, 1998). For international students, adjustment issues took place most of the time inside the classroom, but these adjustments had to do with the cultural differences between the international students and their new surroundings. The more informal style of studying in the US was discovered to be the main source of dissatisfaction that international students reported, when citing reasons for poor academic performance (Sakurako, 2000). Hoffa (2000) maintained that one of the difficulties students and other travellers have had in adjusting to a host country's culture was bringing too many of their own cultural problems with them. Attempts to categorise cultural characteristics often ended in cultural stereotypes that were rather unfair and misleading. Most often, international students and Americans bring into their relationship stereotypes capable of worsening and obstructing a free flow of communication.

The mission statements of most American universities today include a commitment to international and multicultural education (Smith, 1998). He maintained that the positive reactions of professors to the presence of international students gave us cause to believe that acceptance and appreciation of diversity were becoming more a reality. Nonetheless, there is still a degree of dark tunnel vision on the part of American educational system and the roles teachers and students play in the system. In an attempt to determine how American professors on the campus (Utah State University) view the presence of internationals in their classrooms, Smith (1998) conducted a university-wide survey covering 1995 to 96. Professors were asked to show degrees of agreement or disagreement to position statements concerning: 1) acculturation ("it is incumbent upon the international student to adjust to the United States' educational system and not to expect special accommodation from the university teacher,"); 2) diversity ("In a multicultural classroom, cultural differences should be minimized and similarities enhanced."); and 3) instructional modifications ("It is necessary to modify materials and methods to accommodate the instructional needs of the international student").

In the above study, respondents wrote comments beside their answers to give additional information about their choices ("strongly agree, agree, disagree, and strongly disagree"). The results of the survey indicated that American professors saw acculturation (adapting to the ways of the host country) as the preferred way to integrate the international student into the American classroom. Many participants responded that adaptation to the US educational system was essential in order to succeed academically and agreed with the position that "over accommodation" was a disservice to the student who planned an extended educational stay in the host country. In the post-survey interviews, it was reported that many of the non-accommodating behaviours were simply due to normal job constraints. According to Smith (1998), professors reported that they don't take time to find out what particular problems internationals were having because they have to give priority to their own academic commitments (tenure track demands, committee work, service assignments, and others). Others explained that the imperative to cover the course materials and demand the same standards of achievement from all students obviates any kind of special treatment.

Some developing countries invest in international education to improve their technological capabilities (Grady, 1996). The author in question looked at the contribution of international education to technology transfer with specific reference to Libya. He undertook an investigation into the concerns of postgraduate students. The participants comprised Libyan postgraduate students studying science and technology in United Kingdom (UK) universities. Grady (1996) found that the main problems students identified was with visas and getting extensions to complete their researches or studies, academic issues like choosing a research project as well as finding a suitable supervisor. Sometimes, the areas of research they can go into tend to limit foreign students' academic achievements, and also the social relationship required in carrying out an in-depth research.

Sussman (2002) used a new theoretical model, which explored the cultural identity and repatriation experience relationship. In this study, the researcher used the model in testing one hundred thirteen American teachers who sojourned in Japan. Results indicated, unexpectedly, that overseas adaptation and repatriation experiences were not directly associated. Rather, home culture identity strength inversely predicted repatriation distress with repatriates experiencing high distress reporting weak cultural identity. Findings also indicated that repatriation experience was related to shifts in cultural identity. Ratings of increased estrangement from American culture (subtractive) or feeling "more" Japanese (additive) following a sojourn were correlated with the high repatriation distress. Further, Sussman (2002) stated that the more the global identity shift, the higher the life satisfaction.

Altbach (2001) investigated the internalisation and exchanges in a global university. The study found that internationalisation in higher education is an inevitable result of the globalisation and knowledge-based economy of the 21st century. Other trends affecting the universities, including diversification, expansion, and privatisation also have implications for the international role of academic institutions. The intersection of the logic of globalisation and other pressures facing universities make a reconsideration of international programmes and strategies necessary. Exchanges, university linkages, patterns of mobility, as well as international and regional arrangements among universities were all changing.

Halpern (1992) compared the adjustment difficulties of American male and female students in Israeli institutions of higher learning. Six hundred seventy-one American undergraduates in Israeli institutions were surveyed to determine how difficult it was for them to make 53 specific school-related adjustments. Each participant completed the questionnaire on the Study Abroad Adjustment Inventory (SAAI), created by the researcher specifically for the study. The SAAI categorised the adjustment difficulties into four general areas: Hebrew language, academic matters, personal situations, and living arrangements. It utilised four extents of difficulty response alternatives: 1.00 = none, 2.00 = not serious, 3.00 = serious and 4.00 = very serious, to assess student difficulty with each adjustment. Study findings indicated that the sample of students in the research reported the most serious and most frequent adjustment difficulties in the "living arrangements" problem area among the four problem areas considered. A significant disparity in adjustment difficulty was found between males and females for eighteen of the fifty-three adjustments. Males had more difficulty than females adjusting to matters in the "personal situations" problem area. Female students encountered significantly more difficulties than males adjusting in the "academic matters" area. No significant gender difference was found regarding the "living arrangements" or "Hebrew language" problem areas. The study concluded that understanding of language was not essential to adjusting to the host university's cultural environment. Rong & Preissle (1998) postulated that the rate at which international students acquire English language skills depends on a variety of factors such as age, length of stay in the host country, socioeconomic status, parental education, and residence location.

Allen (2002) carried out a study on "Does study abroad make a difference: An investigation of linguistic and motivational outcomes." This investigation sought to determine if significant changes occurred in two linguistic factors, oral and listening French skills, and two affective factors, integrative motivation and language anxiety, after students studied abroad. This study also investigated whether pre-study abroad affective differences existed for the participants versus non-participants. Results revealed that significant improvements occurred in French linguistic skills and significant decreases took place in classroom and non-classroom language anxieties after studying abroad. Integrative motivation levels of those studying abroad group were unchanged after the experience. However, integrative motivation levels of students with more than two years of college French were significantly improved. Pre-study abroad affective differences did not exist between those studying abroad participants and their non-studying abroad peers (Allen, 2002). Implications of this study include: (1) the need for greater pre-study abroad emphasis on non-academic factors by administrators; (2) the necessity for study abroad programmes to include contact with native speakers as part of in-class as well as informal learning; and, (3) the imperative for foreign language teachers to infuse the curriculum with cultural competence by integration of authentic materials, technological resources, and contact with native speakers.

According to Zambito (2002), studying abroad is oftentimes considered a life-changing experience for young men and women, one that adds depth and quality to their lives and future careers. Zambito (2002) discussed a case study which examined the positive impact of studying abroad had on student participants, as well as explored the under-representation of students of colour in studying abroad programmes. Higher education professionals have been advised to concentrate their efforts on marketing studying abroad opportunities towards encouraging students of colour to change held perceptions, which discouraged them from studying abroad. The ability to effectively compete in the global environment was linked to many factors; one of which is the knowledge and understanding of the cultures involved (Henthorne, Miller, &Hudson, 2001).

Though research confirmed the intuition that most students make significant linguistic strides while abroad, ethnographic studies revealed that such gains were not given to every overseas participant (Wilkinson, 2002). Through an examination of data from a variety of descriptive studies, the presentation explored the complexities surrounding such a failure (or perceived failure) to make progress. Within the framework of Giles and Byrne's speech accommodation theory and Bennett's intercultural sensitivity model, the case study findings of Wilkinson (2002) suggested that participants eschewed opportunities for language use because the perceived costs to their self-identity and emotional well-being outweighed the potential benefits of linguistic gain. The avoidance of such costs may also be precipitated from an individual's stage of cross-cultural adjustment. These findings raised salient issues for consideration in the design of overseas programmes and the recruitment of participants.

Weting (2002) presented results from a survey involving students who participated in an island study abroad programme in London, England. Students were invited to respond to questions regarding interpersonal and intrapersonal developments as well as how their experience abroad had imparted those areas. Further questions asked the students were on how to determine what they felt contributed most to the change. Additionally, they answered a number of background questions; this ensured the surveys analysed all met certain criteria. Participants must have completed, at least, a semester of study in London to qualify to participate in the study.

Findings revealed that students do make interpersonal and intrapersonal gains by having studied in London on an island programme (Weting, 2002). There were greater gains in the following areas: awareness of intra-dependence, becoming more sociable with peers, being more sociable in groups, making friends more easily, better listening, extrovert and introvert. The students all showed high growths in the study on self-esteem, self-confidence, independence and understanding of selves. Students that went abroad for a semester or quarter made larger gains than those abroad for a summer, with very few exceptions. Most frequently, personal change was attributed to the challenges a student overcame while on their study abroad programme.

In a study conducted at a large, public, mid-western university by Booker (2001), applicants who applied to study abroad and interested non-applicants were compared with respect to personal characteristics, study abroad preferences, and perceptions of institutional support for international education. Additionally, they were compared with respect to the influence of perceived outcomes or consequences of study abroad, perceived social pressures from important referents and obstacles to study abroad as related to the decision to apply or not apply. Factors that made significant independent contributions to separating and defining the two groups were identified. Booker (2001) concluded among others that academic constraints and the amount of influence of academic relationships became independently significant when the directional social factors were ignored.

Fordham (2002) was a culmination of three years of participant observation of a Rotary International District in New England. The researcher explored the ways a group of adults taught teenagers about cultural differences. More specifically, this ethnographic project, which utilised narrative, discourse, and content analyses, examined the complex pedagogical machinery used by this Rotary International District to interview and recruit American high school students for study abroad. Rotarians' narratives surrounding teenagers were juxtaposed with dominant discourses extant in the US regarding American teens. The study then examined how Rotarians talk about and represent travel, particularly educational travel and cultural immersion. Lastly, it discussed Rotary's discourses of culture and how Rotarians talked about culture, itself, and the ways in which they represented specific cultures to students and to one another. The study asserted that by recruiting and sending middle class kids to live in upper-class environments re-inscribe race and class privilege underscored the virtue of the Rotary Youth Exchange Programme. The Rotary's programme, for American kids in particular, was a form of cultural capital that prevailed to reproduce a global business class (Fordham, 2002). It was also posited that Rotary Youth Exchange Programme for students, however, have agency as they resisted and transgressed the specific boundaries of Rotary's programme and negotiated cultural adaptation and personal change.

Many students, undergraduate and graduate, look for scholarships and grants to travel and study abroad (Truong, 2002). Truong (2002) stated that those who wish to travel and conduct their graduate research have spent months and years gathering information on their respective choice of countries, learning the appropriate language, and seeking a scholarship grant to support their endeavour overseas. The study maintained that in the US, college students who wished to receive one of the prestigious Fulbright grants as a financial support while they study, teach or research abroad, compete against other students nationwide. Though the selection process was rigorous, the quality of those selected does not guarantee success (Truong, 2002). The researcher stated that they encountered daunting challenges once they entered the overseas environment and in some cases completion of their planned period abroad might be problematic. The purpose of this study was to uncover and analyse the successes, challenges and difficulties of Fulbright students during their time in China and Vietnam and beyond. Truong (2002) found that many Fulbright students had a limited time to complete their research. From the respondents' suggestions, Truong (2002) suggested that future Fulbright students should be prepared for all the experiences while conducting research in China or Vietnam. Storti (2001) reechoed that adjusting to a new culture and getting along with the local people were two common challenges for nearly everyone who lived and worked abroad. Storti (2001) made a case for those students returning home after studying abroad. The writer advised that the shock might come back to one's home country with the student. The researcher warned that the returnee might be in for a shock if the returnee expected things to be the same! Indeed, the returnee might discover that he/she and the home have changed (Storti, 2001). Suggestion was made to integrate the process of returning home into the overseas experience, and by so doing reduce the stress of making the transition home. Park (2001) compared her experiences as a Korean American in Los Angeles and working and living in South Africa and Kenya with her African-American spouse. The study concluded that racial identifications were based to a large degree on political and class categories.

United States Department of State, Office of Policy and Evaluation, Bureau of Educational and Cultural Affairs (2002) conducted a two-year outcome assessment of the US scholar component of the Fulbright Educational Exchange Programme, the US government's flagship international educational exchange programme. The study surveyed a stratified random sample of US Fulbright Scholar alumni whose grants began between 1976 and 1999. Evidence was found that the programme was achieving its mandate of promoting mutual understanding and cooperation between the US and other nations, as well as on their colleagues, students, friends and families.

Spirituality and the Adjustment Process of International Students

Spirituality was defined by Parks (2000) as a personal search for purpose and meaning in life, it was considered an important, yet often neglected aspect of student development. Recently, attention has been devoted to ways in which students would explore and address spiritual issues and how educators could better assist them in their spiritual quests (Jablonski, 2001; Love & Talbot, 1999). Parks (2000) identified interacting components of faith: self, other, world, and "God." The manner in which each of these elements was viewed and related to each other undergoes the change experienced as the person's faith develops (Komives & Woodard, 2003).

Parks (2000) suggested that the experiences of young adults in college were shaped by: (1) forms of knowing (cognitive processes); (2) dependence (affective aspects focusing on relationships); and (3) community (social and cultural contexts). Spirituality was an intensely personal and subjective concept (Corey, 2001). It was described as a capacity and tendency innate and unique to all persons. This spiritual tendency moves the individual towards knowledge, love, meaning, hope, transcendence, connectedness, and compassion (Corey, 2001). Spirituality included one's capacity for creativity, growth, and the development of value system. It encompassed the religious, spiritual, and transpersonal (Summit on Spirituality, 1995). Now, interest in the topic of spiritual and religious beliefs and how such beliefs might be incorporated in therapeutic relationships was widespread (Miller, 1999). Evidence of this interest was found in the increased number of articles in this area in professional journals and in presentations at professional conferences (Corey, 2001).

Recognition of the strength and support people draw from spirituality often contributed to its acceptance as an important dimension of the counselling process (Miranti & Burke, 1995). Spirituality was considered to be endemic to all people, whereas religion can be used to create a structure and focus for the spiritual realm (Ingersoll, 1995). Zinnbauer and Pargament (2000) identified four helping orientations to religious and spiritual issues in counselling: rejectionists, exclusivists, constructivists, and pluralists. Rejectionist and exclusivist present two rigid, extreme positions and were not considered useful perspective for counsellors to use when relating to religious/spiritual issues. Rejectionists were essentially atheists rejecting the notion of God and religion and, therefore, restrict opportunities for addressing spirituality and religion in counselling. Exclusivists took an "orthodox" religious position by embracing a rigid definition of God and religion. Exclusivists contended that counsellors and clients must share the same religion or spiritual worldview to be able to effectively work together in counselling. With the exception of pastoral counselling, most counsellors have viewed the client's religion as personal, private matter; not necessary or appropriate to be explored with a client (Nystul, 2003).

Porterfield (2002) examined student sojourner's spirituality post study abroad. The study explored the essence of spirituality after the student sojourn abroad experience. It utilised the phenomenological and constructivists' paradigms to capture the essence of the lived experiences of students after their return from a sojourn abroad. The study allowed the meaning of the experiences to be constructed and understood as the study emerged. An artefact analysis of photographs and scrapbooks was added and utilised to aid in highlighting students' experiences. According to Porterfield (2002), measures taken to insure trustworthiness of the data was maintained in alignment with the phenomenological method, data analysis, as well as textual and structural descriptions. The textural themes that emerged from the study were: influence and history of family, spiritual practices, mentor relationships, impact of country visited, spiritual experiences abroad, relationships with others abroad, personal significance of religion/spirituality, greater sense of self, struggle upon returning to the US, increased desire for travel and adventure, and influence of education. The structural themes that highlighted the essence of the phenomenon of spirituality included: foundation of religion or spirituality, student sojourner reflection on the experience of studying abroad, cognitive dissonance upon returning to the US, and experiences of adversity, while abroad (Porterfield, 2002).

The holistic health movement also recognised the value of addressing all aspects of the mind and body (including spiritual issues) in fostering health and wellness. In this regard, Westgate (1996) suggested that spiritual issues could contribute to a holistic approach to prevention and treatment of depression. According to Westgate, 1996), spiritual void could be associated with depressive symptom such as meaninglessness, emptiness, alienation, and hopelessness. The spiritually well person could draw strength from religion to gain meaning and a sense of direction in life.

Communication and the Adjustment Process of International Students

American Council on Education (2002) stated that thirty-three higher education, scholarly, and exchange associations endorsed the new proposal for a national policy on international education. The report outlined United States' (USA) needs for international and foreign language expertise and citizen awareness; it examined the shortages in those areas, and proposed strategies and government policies to meet them. Leask (2001) studied how one university was internationalising all its courses so that all graduates would demonstrate an international perspective as professionals and citizens. The researcher focused on courses and their teaching, learning, as well as assessment. The work investigated how these processes would promote international education, multiculturalism, and the recognition of intercultural issues relevant to professional practice. The first section dealt with structural options and pathways for course designing when internationalising the curricula and defining the characteristics of such options. The second and final section of the article outlined ways in which an internationalised curriculum would broaden the scope of the subject to include international contents and/or contacts and sets up teaching and learning to assist in the development of cross-cultural communication skills. Leask (2001) found that internationalising university curricula was a powerful and practical way of bridging the gap between rhetoric and practice to including and valuing the contributions of international students.

Adams (2001) studied the different methods of language assessment and their impact on the understanding of second language learning as well as summarised salient issues on studying abroad. Also, empirical evidence was presented in support of the use of multiple methods of assessment, including self-assessment, for accurate, reliable and valid profiles of language learners. Howard (2001) compared the relative effect of studying abroad as opposed to foreign language instruction. Based on a cross-sectional quantitative analysis of oral data elicited from Irish advanced learners, a number of differences and similarities emerged between the learners' development in the community and in the foreign language classroom. On the one hand, the more beneficial effects of studying abroad were evident insofar as the beneficiaries attained a higher level of accuracy. On the other hand, similarities were also evident between the learners in both domains of acquisition. Based on a variation analysis, which controls for the effect of a number of linguistic factors on the learners' choice of grammatical aspect, inherent lexical aspect, and discourse grounding; the learners' contextual use appears to be relatively similar. The results of Howard (2001) were first discussed in relation to existing researches' evidence concerning a learner's grammatical development during study abroad, and second, in relation to the question of the manifestation of grammatical development in the learner.

It is commonly believed that language study abroad was the most effective and efficient road to proficiency in a foreign language (DuFon, Churchil & McMeekin, 2001). Yet, while the empirical researches on learners in study abroad programmes had revealed a strong positive effect on the development of fluency, communication strategies and sociolinguistic competence, many questions pertaining to second language acquisition in studying abroad context remained unanswered. For example, with a few exceptions, the findings of studies to date revealed little about actual language use or the nature of the social interaction between learners and competent native speakers of the host culture and their effects on the process of language acquisition. Further, attempts to measure changes in inter-language development often yielded divergent findings (Freed, 1995). In order to advance knowledge in these areas, this colloquium began by taking a critical look at various measures of language assessment that have been used to measure learner gains in study abroad contexts and then presented empirical evidence in support of the use of multiple methods to obtain accurate profiles of language learners.

Then three more studies were presented which have incorporated multiple methods to examine the nature of the social interaction between the learners and native speakers of the host culture and the effect of this social interaction on the acquisition of linguistic and social information. Study two primarily utilised diary data to examine socialisation into American culture via participation in routines. Study three focused on conversational data to compare the negotiation of meaning in classroom and home stay situations in Japan and the fourth study examined the socialisation of taste by study abroad learners in Indonesia, using microanalysis of discourse and learner journals. Moreover, the pedagogical implications of all the studies were discussed by (DuFon, Churchil & McMeekin, 2001).

Davidson (2002) examined the student records database of the American Council of Teachers of Russia (ACTR) on study abroad learning. The records contained more than 3000 learning histories of study abroad participants with varying backgrounds and immersion durations. Davidson (2002) updated previous studies on the effects of varying durations of immersion on typical post-programme language outcomes for speaking, reading and listening typical for summer, semester or academic yearlong programme durations. According to Davidson (2002), data collected over four years showed that the specific interventions produced statistically significant improvements in oral proficiency gains in comparison to learners of equivalent background and initial levels of language competence in control groups.

Olson & Kroeger (2001) examined how educators can enhance their global competencies and intercultural communication skills so they can better educate students from increasingly diverse societies? The researchers conducted a survey of fifty-two New Jersey City University faculty and staff to assess the relationships between their international experience, global competencies, and levels of intercultural sensitivity. The study found that second-language proficiency and substantive experience abroad increased the likelihood that an educator will be more advanced on the scale. The findings revealed that there would be the need for global, intercultural, and professional development for faculty and staff that would be ongoing, substantial, and inclusive of work in another language and culture.

A recent survey by "Open Doors" showed that Hispanics constituted approximately 5% of the student population that study abroad each year (Millington, 2002). According to Millington (2002), this statistic was disappointing given the growing prevalence of the Spanish language in today's world. One would expect Hispanics, with their bilingual and bicultural "head start," to be at the forefront of the study abroad population. The study mentioned that financial constraints, familial and academic responsibilities at home and lack of motivation accounted for this low number.

Weeks (2002) presented a series of essays designed to educate overseas study administrators, supervisors, counsellors, and staff about the legal implications of decisions they make. The writer stated that knowing the law and adopting preventive measures were the best ways to reduce exposure at this period in our educational development when more and more people were taking to foreign study. Overseas programmes' administrators often make decisions that could lead to difficulties in pursuing the study abroad programme (Weeks, 2002). For example, administrators who worked with study abroad students developed working relationships with overseas and foreign institutions; counselled students and parents; applied rules of conduct and enforced disciplinary standards; employed risk reducing strategies by using releases and waivers; and might be called upon to interface with the media in the unfortunate event of a crisis overseas. In sum, administrators significantly affect the effectiveness and exposure of the overseas study programme.

Study abroad in recent decades had become more visible in the landscape of American undergraduate education as witnessed by the surging numbers of participants and programmes (Manley, 2002). He stated that research about the educational practice of those studying abroad, on the other hand, had lagged behind the development of the activity itself, creating the need of scholarship for students learning in this setting or context. The subject of this study was a pedagogical technique designed to foster and assess intercultural learning. "Field book" employed an integrated and diverse series of writing assignments, which students were to complete during their semester abroad. Created for use in a Pitzer College programme in Italy, it was revised extensively over a decade, as it was adapted for programmes in eight other countries (Manley, 2002). Feedback from students and staff provided the information critical to improve the "Field book", making it a malleable tool for facilitating intercultural learning and a central feature of the Pitzer study abroad model. The study concluded with suggestions for strengthening the Field book's design and practice as well as with recommendations for how research on applied pedagogy could enhance the quality of experientially oriented study abroad and other types of non-classroom learning.

In studying the impact of globalisation and internalisation on education abroad programmes, McCabe (2001) asserted that there would be the need for educators to consider the mission and value of study abroad programmes and their relation to the processes of globalisation and internationalisation. As educational systems increased their emphasis on the need for international education, it would be necessary to consider what types of study abroad opportunities were relevant to current world trends. The researcher attempted to provide a framework for understanding the distinction between globalisation and internationalisation as well as their relevance to the future of international education and study abroad programmes. In a "United States-Africa Cooperation in Education at Northern Arizona University: Unexpected Lessons", a total of one hundred and fourteen African educators came to Northern Arizona University (NAU), in Flagstaff, from 1988 to 1992 to attend a 45-day Summer Institute sponsored by the United States Information Agency (USIA). The programme's year-by-year evaluations were analysed in the light of interview responses. The study showed that the programme helped the academic and surrounding communities discovered other facets of African education and life that the media often misrepresented (McCabe, 2001). Participating African educators were very appreciative of the innovative curriculum and instructional methods they learnt and were mesmerised by minority inclusion policies on campus. The interviewees and the African educators deplored the United States' lack of awareness and interest in cooperation with Africa.

The influence of self-construal and communication styles on sojourners' psychological and sociocultural adjustment was carried out by Oguri & Gudykunst (2002). The purpose of the study was to examine the influence of self- construal and communication styles on psychological and sociocultural adjustment. It was hypothesised in the study that a close fit between sojourners' self-construal and the self-construal that predominated in the host culture would predict the sojourners' psychological adjustment. Similarly, it was hypothesised that a close fit between sojourners' and host nationals' communication styles would predict sojourners' sociocultural adjustment. The independent self-construal, the prototypical self-construal in the host culture, predicted psychological adjustment. The interdependent self-construal was not related to psychological adjustment. Oguri & Gudykunst (2002) contended that the use of direct communication and positive perceptions of silence, prototypical communication styles in the host culture, were related to sociocultural adjustment and consistent with expectations. In addition, sensitivity to others' behaviour predicted sociocultural adjustment.

Academic policymakers and administrators were charged with the responsibility of articulating and applying appropriate threshold criteria in order to affect desired learning outcomes (Hudson, 2001). The study examined the relationship between the degree of student success on an academic study abroad programme and the independent variables of cumulative grade point average, status, and gender (Hudson, 2001). Participants included in the study were all students who participated in a five-week summer study abroad in a Spanish language acquisition programme in Mexico. There was a statistically significant relationship between the dependent variable of final course grade and the composite set of variables of cumulative grade point average, gender, status, and their interactions. The growing demand for international experiences for students, as evidenced by governmental and institutional policies as well as increasing numbers of participants in study abroad programmes, would necessitate the development of fair and effective administrative policies grounded in outcomes-oriented research (Hudson, 2001).

In a conference paper, Busher (2001) examined the cultural frameworks embedded in doctoral education, which required students to develop new academic literacy as well as a new work-related identity. The study involved twenty students registered at an English university but studying thousands of kilometres away. The students were in their second or later year on the Doctor of Education programme at the University of Leicester and were based on different school sites (Lebanon, Arabian Gulf, and the United Kingdom). Busher (2001) found that coming to terms with new literacy and discourse communities in a host university involved a process of struggling with different identities and power relationships: "the process of adaptation to academic discourse communities involved the participants reconstructing, to a greater or lesser extent, their work- related identities, and possibly their own notions of selfhood".

Financial Needs and the Adjustment Process of International Students

The purpose of the quantitative study according to Chieffo (2001) was to investigate why some students' study abroad and others do not, as well as analyse the factors, which would influence their participation decisions. The primary data collection instrument was a survey questionnaire, distributed to over one thousand students in thirty classes at the University of Delaware during the fall of 1999. Data analysis yielded intriguing results. In general, students reported not being very well-informed about the university's programmes abroad, despite an extensive recruitment campaign. Their participation decisions were greatly influenced by peers and parents, only minimally by faculty, and those who did not go abroad rated programme cost as the major reason for non-participation. Finally, Chieffo (2001) found significant differences between first-year and upper-class students, and among various majors with regard to their participation decisions. Finance had always been noted to be a major factor whenever decision of where and when to seek international education is considered.

Health Needs and the Adjustment Process of International Students

A study explored the relationship between homesickness, stress, social support, personality as well as health in home and overseas students (Kwok, 2002). One hundred undergraduate and graduate students completed a cross-sectional survey eight month into the academic year at the University of Surrey. Kwok (2002) reported that the results showed homesickness was directly related to stress and neuroticism and was negatively associated with social support and health. Overseas students had higher mean scores than home students with regards to homesickness, although the difference was not significant. Regarding social support, overseas students perceived significantly less support than home students. Home students had lower mean scores on health than overseas students and the difference was highly significant. Kwok (2002) recommended that the variables influencing homesickness should be addressed by encouraging better social networks for international students through opportunities for social interaction. Smith (1996) recognised that depression and loneliness were associated with immigration. And, they contributed to the state of mind of most international students.

Counselling International Students and the Adjustment Process

Values and value conflicts in counselling often may be understood within the context of differing worldviews or ways that people see the world (Remley & Herlihy, 2005). An individual's worldview would be influenced by culture and the source of that person's values, beliefs, opinions, and assumptions (Pedersen et al, 2002). Worldviews affect how people think, make decisions, act, and interpret events (Sue & Sue, 1999). Values of cultures might vary in how they relate to nature, time, social relations, activity, and collectivism and individualism, among other dimensions (Hopkins, 1997). When people come from different cultural backgrounds, they might hold differing worldviews, which could lead to misinterpretations, misunderstandings and conflicts (Chung & Bemak, 2002). These conflicting worldviews could lead to misunderstandings, which in turn could lead to people dropping their set goals or premature termination of goals. A growing body of literature suggests that policy makers, like counsellors must develop cultural empathy in order to be reflective when dealing with clients or students who were not from the same cultural background as the professional (Ridley, 1995; Ridley & Lingle, 1996). Remley & Herlihy (2005) suggested some skills or strategies helpful in dealing with people from other cultural backgrounds as follows:

- Expressing lack of knowledge or awareness of some aspects of the client's cultural experience.
- Communicating an interest in learning more about the client's culture.
- Conveying a genuine appreciation for cultural differences.
- Acquiring knowledge about the historical and socio-political background of the client's culture.
- Being sensitive to the oppression, marginalisation and discrimination that clients may encounter on a daily basis.
- Clarifying language and other modes of communication.
- Incorporating culturally appropriate strategies and treatment goals into the counselling process.

Segal (1997) explained that Jung combined functions and attitudes to create a typology of eight personality types with dominant and inferior functions. Accepting and understanding one's type helps an individual to communicate and work effectively with others. Berger (2001) stated that in a large-scale cross-cultural research, the stability of the "Big five" was impressive even as a research on personality occasionally revealed "quite dramatic inter-individual differences" in the direction and pace of personality change. For everyone at every age, the environment continued to play a significant role, and most adults would select an ecological niche that reinforced their basic temperament, but significant changes in that niche could produce changes in personality.

Desimone, Werner and Harris (2002) explained that attitudes would add to our understanding of behaviour by showing another way that thoughts could influence behaviour. Attitudes also, would tend to be stable over time and would be difficult to change. Hodgetts (2002) believed that there were three basic components of attitudes: cognitive, affective, and behavioural. Attitudes tend to govern direction in which psychological energy would flow within the functions, and such energy could be directed inwards (introversion) or outwards (extroversion) (Segal, 1997). Roberts, Caspi, & Moffitt, (2003) provided an analysis of the relationship between personality traits and experiences with a special focus on the relationship between changes in personality and experiences in young adulthood. Longitudinal analysis by the researcher uncovered three findings. First, measures of personality taken at age 18 predicted objective and subjective experiences at age 26. Second, experiences were related to changes in personality traits from age 18 to 26. Third, the predictive and change relations between personality traits and experiences were corresponsive: traits that "selected" people into specific experiences were the same traits that changed in response to those same experiences. The human being (individual) was found to be a complex being, but this complexity would not stop most people from trying to generalise about human behaviour by summing up individuals with a descriptive cliché such as "people are basically accommodating". Segal (1997) explained that Laura Perl, a psychologist, focused on the interrelationship of the total organism, thought and feeling, mind and body, as well as individual and environment, which opens the possibility of increasing the awareness of what might be driving the influencing at a particular moment.

Berger (2001) pointed that genetically-based tendencies would disappear as life experiences accumulate, because life experiences and cultural context would make a difference. Example, "Swedish culture values shy, reserved behaviour and support systems of various sorts. And that made it possible for Swedish boys to enter universities and careers without being assertive". Technically, culture was or had been the vast structure of behaviours, ideas, attitudes, values, habits, beliefs, customs, language, rituals, ceremonies and practices peculiar to a certain group of people providing them with a general design for living and patterns for interpreting reality (Berger, 2001). Culture gives meaning to reality; it is the invisible medium through which all human functioning occurs. It is important to note, in fact, that all human behaviours occur through the influence of one's culture.

All of our training and education were bound by customs; which were nothing more than cultural traits or rituals. Often, educators unfortunately, see culture as the ingredient that enriches their standard educational presentation. The question, then, becomes could we use cultural differences of people to inspire or to create a better method for accessing students into the core curriculum? An examination of the notion of culture would raise questions of how students accessed the educational curriculum. The core curriculum itself should be culturally sensitive. Berger (2001) suggested that the teaching methodology utilised in teaching the core information should also be culturally sensitive. The leadership styles, guidance and counselling techniques, the instructional strategies, and the school climate should also be culturally sensitive to the needs and perspectives of all students. If the real culture was understood as an integral part of the educational process, it would be seen that it was not a social product (something that could be added to what was being done). Rather, it is the sum total of the human processes and experiences of the individual or group to make people "culturally sensitive" to the fact that some people like to dance or that some people like to sing. When this is done, the point would be missed by believing that the question of culture in terms of educational practice or experience would have been addressed.

There was the contention that schools were the most complex of all the social organisations (Roberts, 1998). Like any other social organisation, school faces the tasks of structuring, managing, and giving direction to a complex mix of human and technical resources. The plethora of problems, challenges, and other concerns in today's institutions of learning would make it even important that educational administrators understand the significance of culture and its relationship to education and to the development of viable programmes for their varied publics/consumers (Roberts, 1998).

Abadi (2000) studied satisfaction with Oklahoma State University (OSU) among selected groups of international students. The literature revealed that many international higher education students returned to their countries with negative experiences. There was a little qualitative research done in this area that could elicit from international students their views and suggestions. Six research questions were developed to form a detailed interview guide to cover these four areas (Abadi, 2000). In addition, demographic characteristics were discussed, and the overall picture of the evaluation was reported as perceived by each participant. The study utilised the face-to-face semi-structured interview technique to collect data. Because of the qualitative nature of the study, the sample included only 35 international students from ten different countries. According to Abadi (2000), the major conclusions of that study were: (1) satisfaction of the participants was the most in their academic experience at OSU; (2) Fifty-five per cent of the participants were generally satisfied with their financial situation at OSU; (3) forty-two per cent of the participants appeared to express an overall satisfaction with their personal experience at OSU; (4) only 36 per cent of the participants were satisfied with their overall social life. Combining the four areas of concern in this study, approximately 51% of the participants indicated satisfaction, 29% of the participants had mixed or undecided feelings and 20% expressed some level of dissatisfaction with their overall educational experience at OSU. Sixty per cent of participants' satisfaction with OSU increased with time. Female students were more emotional and more financially secure than males. Some of the recommendations included the following: (1) each department should appoint an adviser for international students to guide and help them in all aspects; (2) advisers should increase their office hours and have closer relationships with students; (3) OSU should organise more activities that foster a better climate of international awareness and understanding between American students and international students such as home visits and host family programmes; (4) the International Student Service (ISS) office should implement suggestions such as the need to include more international students and make some adjustments to the orientation programme; (5) periodic evaluations of international students satisfaction can help maintain and increase that satisfaction; and(6) library and computer labs need a continuous effort of improving and updating their resources to provide a more satisfactory educational experience for all students.

Culture and anxiety: A cross-cultural study was the research carried out by Abbassi (1999). By measuring interactions among and between anxiety and the independent variables of country of origin, gender, level of education, and age, Abbassi (1999) attempted to gain insight into how students from different countries experience anxiety on a US college campus. It was assumed that students with different countries of origin experienced different levels of anxiety. Participants in this study were 158 international students from Thailand, Taiwan, Japan and Korea enrolled in classes designed for international students on the campus of a large metropolitan university in the southwest. The subjects evaluated themselves on how they felt at the moment (form Y-1) and how they generally feel (form Y-2). Results indicated that there was a high correlation between forms Y-1 and Y-2. Results of the multivariate analysis of variance (MANOVA) and the analyses of variance test (ANOVA) indicated that the gender and level of education of the subjects made no significant difference. However, when it came to country of origin, there were significant differences between two of the cultural groups and the respective anxiety level. Findings also support a positive correlation between age and anxiety levels, with the youngest participants having the lowest anxiety levels.

Social Personal Relationships and the Adjustment Process of International Students

The report Hayward & Siaya (2001) detailed the findings of two surveys related to international education. The first examined the public's international experience and knowledge, as well as attitudes about international education, while the second surveyed high school seniors' plans to participate in international activities once they enter college. Hayward & Siaya (2001) revealed that there was a growing public recognition that international knowledge and experience were increasingly important to daily life and global economic success.

As more and more US College students go abroad as part of their studies, it is becoming necessary to look at the experiences of minority students to see if existing procedures and programmes should be changed in any way (Sanderson, 2002). The researcher examined different models of sexual identity formation and culture shock to complement data obtained through a series of questionnaires targeting study abroad participants and advisors as well as foreign nationals. In addition to examining the theories behind these processes, the researcher also based the conclusions and recommendations on intercultural misunderstandings and how they could be explained by the study of pragmatics. Gay-related issues were seldom discussed in the context of intercultural relations, and even less so when young adults were concerned. While those advisors questioned believed that the subject was sufficiently covered in their pre-departure orientations, their students didn't recall this; even if it was covered, it was not done in such a way that the students took notice. Sanderson (2002) greatest recommendation, therefore, was to present a supportive image of the study abroad office and to put maximum information at the students' disposal, such that they do not have to directly ask for it.

Academic Advising and the Adjustment Process of International Students

Faculty culture has a direct impact on the behaviours and attitudes of individual faculty members (Love, Kuh, MacKay, & Hardy, 1993) and thus, on students. For example, the tripartite responsibilities of teaching, research and service make the observance of office hours important to faculty time management, and international students who were often unaware of these responsibilities might interpret faculty reluctance to meet with them outside such hours as evidence of non-caring instead of as a productive issue. The researchers noted that strict adherence to office hours has often been described by international students as uncaring. These students might be unaware of the "publish or perish" pressures on faculty members in the US because the faculty in the home country focused almost exclusively on teaching. Also, different cultural patterns on plagiarism and cheating can complicate the relationship existing between university and faculty as well as the international student (Pennycook, 1996). Similarly, different communication patterns could lead to misunderstanding as described in a filmed conversation (Hodne, 1997; citing Scarcella, 1990, p. 103) in which "in the course of conversation, an American student asks one question after another, and a Vietnamese student responded with one brief answer after another. Each expresses frustration afterward, the American because the Vietnamese showed little interest in the conversation, and the Vietnamese because the American 'kept firing questions at her without giving her time' to respond". Of course, the difference in communication patterns and the stresses involved in trying new ones were exacerbated because many international students were also using non-native language during these processes and might be concerned about making errors in grammar or pronunciation (Johnson, 1997).

Counselling Issues and Student Adjustment

Our increasingly diverse society is reflected in the growing diversity in our schools, workplaces and homes (Hodgetts, 2002). This tends to bring about the leading knowledge that living, working, and schooling successfully with others who didn't share the same background and traditions was a top priority in today's schools and workplaces. Students need help in assessing their behaviour towards people who were different from them and they must understand and begin to change negative attitude and resistance towards others into appreciation and cooperation (Hodgetts, 2002).

The professional ethics and standards of counselling discipline placed a high value on the dignity and worth of individuals regardless of their gender, ethnicity, race, sexual or affective orientation, age, physical and mental abilities, religious beliefs and socioeconomic class (Remley & Herlihy, 2005). Therefore, as part of their professional functioning, counsellors were expected to respect the dignity and worth of the student and strive for the preservation and protection of fundamental human rights of their clients. Part of the goal of counselling was to maintain an atmosphere of respect and trust in which people could feel free to explore and discuss our attitudes, beliefs, values, and behaviours in relation to others who were similar to and different from us (Remley & Herlihy, 2005).

There was the suggestion that a personal approach to counselling should incorporate a multicultural perspective sensitive to the individual differences that reflected contemporary society. Nystul (2003) contended that multicultural counselling had become a fourth force, which follows a psychodynamic, behavioural, and humanistic counselling. The increasing percentage of minorities in school enrolment was compelling school authorities to review their old counselling philosophies to answer the following questions. How can we prepare ourselves to effectively provide counselling services to our students, and in our communities? The days of thinking in terms of a particular large or preferred group were a thing of the past. Tomorrow's counsellors would have to be motivated and lead groups in which women, Hispanics, African-Americans, and Asian-Americans were being enrolled in schools in increasing numbers.

Counsellors would also have to provide services to the older people in our communities. Hodgetts (2002) believed that many institutions in the society were becoming aware of this need to provide for diversified environment in an effective manner. In the colleges and universities, many institutions were becoming more and more interested in the issue of diversity. It was reported that many institutions were hiring diversified personnel that can be extremely useful in providing advice and guidance. In any event, institutions were discovering that they need to develop policies and guidelines for ensuring equality for their workforce. Corey (2001) stated that part of the process of becoming an effective counsellor involves learning how to recognise diversity and shaping your counselling service to fit the client's world. It is essential for counsellors to develop sensitivity to differences in clients if they hope to make interventions congruent with the values of their clients. Counsellors bring their own heritage with them to their work, so they must know how cultural conditioning would influence the directions they take with their clients. Cooney (2001) argued that racism had an inbuilt capacity to make the weak unhappy.

Moreover, unless the social and cultural contexts of clients were taken into consideration, it would be most difficult to appreciate the nature of their struggles. Many counselling students have come to value characteristics such as their own choices, expressing what they were feeling, being open and self-revealing, as well as striving for independence (Nystul, 2003). Yet, some clients might not share these goals. Certain cultures emphasised being emotionally reserved or being selective about sharing personal concerns. Counsellors need to determine whether the assumptions made on populations about the nature and functioning of a therapy would be appropriate for culturally diverse people (Nystul, 2003).

Clearly, effective counselling in schools must take into account the impact of culture. Culture is quite simply, it is the values and behaviours shared by a group of individuals. It is important to realise that culture does not merely refer to ethnic or racial heritage but includes age, gender, religion, sexual orientation, physical and mental ability as well as socioeconomic status. Nystul (2003) clearly captured the essence of a multicultural college environment. Multicultural counselling environment could be used to provide perspective or lens to conceptualise diversity issues such as gender, culture, age and sexual orientation in all phases of counselling. Throughout the counselling process, the multicultural counselling lens must be continuously adjusted to promote a clear understanding of emerging multicultural issues. Once diversity issues were identified, counselling theories and procedures could be modified to reflect a multicultural perspective. Pedersen (1991) preferred the broader definition of culture associated with multicultural counselling, because it "helps counsellors become more aware of the complexity in cultural identity patterns, which may or may not include the obvious indicators of ethnicity and nationality". The research of Sue, Ivy & Pedersen (1996) addressed a wide range of topics, including counselling as a white middle-class activity, social class, gender, the intra-psychic perspective, sexual orientation, stereotyping, communication problems, faulty assumptions, test bias, prejudice, racism, and the efficacy of multicultural counselling. According to Nystul (2003), acculturation was a complex multicultural phenomenon that attempts to measure the extent of adaptation of the customs and values associated with the host culture. Kim and Abreu (2001) went on to note that an individual's level of acculturation would be associated with the degree of change (between the native and host culture) in terms of values and behaviours, cultural awareness and loyalty. Counsellors could also estimate a client's level of acculturation by examining how much the client had assimilated into the mainstream society. Lee (1991) noted factors that influenced acculturation would include educational and socioeconomic levels; length of time lived in the US; and the extent of exposure to racism.

25. COMPETENCIES IN A DIVERSIFIED ENVIRONMENT

Effective counsellors understand their own background conditioning, that of their clients and the socio-political system of which they were a part (Remley & Herlihy, 2005). Acquiring this awareness begins with the counsellor's understanding of any cultural values, biases and attitudes that might hinder their development of a positive view of pluralism. There was a developed conceptual framework for competencies and standards in counselling diversified people in schools. The dimension of competency would involve three areas: beliefs and attitudes, knowledge as well as skills.

First, effective counsellors would have moved from being culturally unaware to ensuring that their personal biases, values or problems would not interfere with their ability to work with clients who were different from them (Welfel, 2002). They believed diversified self-awareness and sensitivity to one's own background or heritage was essential for any form of helping. They were aware of their positive and negative emotional reactions towards other racial and ethnic groups that might be detrimental to establishing collaborative helping relationships. They would and should appropriately seek to examine and understand the world from the vantage point of their clients. They would respect clients' religious and spiritual beliefs and values. They should be comfortable with differences between themselves and others in terms of race, ethnicity, culture, and beliefs. Rather than maintaining the superiority of their heritage, they should be able to accept and value diversity (Remley & Herlihy, 2005). They should realise that traditional theories and techniques might not be appropriate for all clients or problems. They should monitor their functioning through consultation, supervision, and further training or education.

Second, diversified effective practitioners possess certain knowledge. They know specifically about their own racial and cultural heritage and how it affects them personally and professionally. Because they understand the dynamics of oppression, racism, discrimination and stereotyping, they would be in a position to detect their own racist attitudes, beliefs and feelings. They understand the worldview of their clients and learn about their clients' backgrounds. They do not impose their values and expectations on their clients. They understand that external socio-political forces would influence all groups, and they ought to know how these forces operate with respect to the treatment of minorities. These practitioners were aware of the institutional barriers that generally prevented minorities from utilising the mental health services available in their communities (Nystul, 2003). They possess knowledge about the historical background, traditions and values of the client populations with whom they work. They know about minority family structures, hierarchies, values and beliefs.

Further, they were knowledgeable about community characteristics and resources. Culturally skilled counsellors know how to help clients make use of indigenous support systems. In areas where they were deficient in knowledge, they often would seek resources to assist them. The greater their depth and breadth of knowledge of culturally diverse groups, the more likely they would be effective practitioners.

Third, effective counsellors have acquired certain skills in working with culturally diverse populations (Nystul, 2003). Counsellors take responsibility for educating their clients on the way therapeutic process works, including matters such as goals, expectations, legal rights, and the counsellors' orientation.

Multicultural counselling was enhanced when practitioners used methods and strategies as well as defined goals consistent with the life experiences and cultural values of their clients (Corey, 2001). Such practitioners generally modified and adapted their interventions to accommodate differences. They do not force their clients to fit within one counselling approach or framework, but they recognised that counselling techniques could be culture-bound.

Schools were becoming more multiethnic and diverse. The school was only one of the society's agents for learning, education, and training (Knight, 1998). The family, media, peer group, and church were some other institutions that would share this responsibility. In fact, the school may even be seen as a minor partner in the educational process, with the family and media playing the major role in the lives of most children. This vital point should be recognised, though the treatment of education in this paper would tend to use categories most often linked with schooling. It should be understood, clearly, that the "teacher" in the fullest sense of the world might not be an employee of a school system, but a broadcaster, parent, pastor or peer. Likewise, a television programme or an individual home would have a view of truth and reality and a set of values that lead it to select a certain "curriculum" and teaching methodology as it goes about its educational functions (Knight, 1998). In what follows, this idea might not always be explicitly stated, but implicit in the discussion and must be recognised if one is to gain the fullest understanding of education-related processes.

When a crisis hits, we often ask a series of questions: "What"? "Who"? "Where"? "When"? "How"? And then, "What now"? International educators know that responses to these questions might differ from culture to culture. Indeed, the very definition of what is and isn't a 'crisis' might depend upon its cultural context (Burak & Hoffa, 2001). Burak & Hoffa (2001) provided a compendium of experience and expertise from many professionals in the field of international educational exchange. Bura & Hoffa (2001) contended that crisis management in a cross-cultural setting was designed to prepare international educators and others to respond appropriately, expeditiously, and comprehensively to crises that befall students and scholars living and learning a long way from where they call "home". Their thesis was simple: advance planning and cross-cultural sensitivity could make all the difference.

The school exists in a complex educational milieu. To complicate matters, the components of that milieu might not espouse the same message with regard to reality, truth, and value. This undoubtedly would weaken the impact of the school (as well as the impact of society's other "educators") and give children a garbled message about their world and what should be considered important in life (Burak & Hoffa, 2001). It should never be borne in mind that all education, training and schooling would take place in this complexity of forces. The traditional role of the public schools had emphasised individual growth and self-improvement; however, by the turn of the century, social problems began to be viewed from the perspective of the social order as a whole. For public education, this meant that the school as a social institution would also be seen as an institution for promoting the interests of the society, in addition to the needs of the individual (Rippa, 1997). The need for this new approach was especially evident among urban educational reformers. What was originally considered to be the primary role of public education had to be changed; this was premised on the pressing need for a semblance of order in a culture affected by radical socioeconomic change.

During the early decades of the twentieth century, Americanisation meant far more than teaching a new language to new citizens. The approach of World War 1 focused on the question of national loyalty and added a new sense of urgency to the problem. The intent was as Rippa (1997) urged, to:

- break up these groups of settlements;
- assimilate and amalgamate these people as a part of our American race, and to implant in their children, as far as could be done, the Anglo-Saxon conception of righteousness, law and order, as well as popular government; and
- awaken in them a reverence for our democratic institutions and for those things in our national life which we as a people hold to be of abiding worth.

"Americanisation" is an elusive term that defies definition, for its meaning varies with the changing social context (Rippa, 1997). Diversity refers to the variables such as age, gender, culture, spirituality, and sexual orientation, addressed within the context of multicultural counselling. Nystul (2003) suggested a personal perspective sensitive to the individual differences that would reflect contemporary society.

As noted above, our institutions of higher learning and workplaces were getting more diversified. More people from minority cultures were going into institutions predominantly attended by Anglo families in the past. Women, African-Americans, Hispanics, and Asia-Americans were entering communities originally held by Anglo families in record numbers. The result was a major diversity challenge for colleges and universities in these communities (Hodgetts, 2002). Among the reasons for this were the following: (1) Many of today's schools were accustomed to teaching only Anglo children and have had limited experience leading a diverse population; (2) many of the schools have failed to develop the talents of their non-traditional students, thus denying both them and the schools an opportunity to succeed; and (3) many schools have failed to examine the career and family needs of their students as well as work out plans for helping the students and teachers balance both of these demands. What could be done to address these problems? Schools were taking a number of steps, some of which were tied to well-designed diversity training programmes (Hodgetts, 2002). Others were described in the "Ethics and Social Responsibilities" as contained in American Counselling Association's Guidelines.

Personality Traits

The goal of cultural research is seen as developing a universal theory to predict behaviour on a worldwide scale, with individualism-collectivism and other related cultural syndromes serving as parameters of psychological theories that make it possible to explain behavioural variation (Miller, 2002). Berger (2001) maintained that whenever culture was considered as part of the social context, the emphasis would be more on values, behaviours, and attitudes than on the specific foods, clothes and objects of daily life. Gerber (2001) explained that working effectively with clients would require an understanding of how the individual was embedded in the family, which in turn, would require understanding of how the family would be affected by its place in a pluralistic culture. Paunonen (1998) concluded that aggregating personality traits into their underlying personality factors could result in decreased predictive accuracy due to the loss of trait-specific but criterion-valid variance.

An individual's personality, on the other way, would be a complex of mental characteristics that would make the person unique from other people, and includes all of the patterns of thought and emotions that would cause us to do and say things in particular ways (Dennis O'Neil, 2002). Berger (2001) identified the five basic clusters of personality traits that remained quite stable throughout adulthood:

Extroversion: outgoing, assertive and active.

Agreeableness: kind, helpful and easygoing.

Conscientiousness: organised, deliberate and conforming

Neuroticism: anxious, moody and self-punishing

Openness: imaginative, curious, artistic, and open to new experiences.

Rubenzer (2000) analysed and compared the personality traits of forty-one past American presidents using the above characteristics including other factors. Gershoff (2002) believed that a parent's overall style of child rearing, including likelihood to use corporal punishment, was in part determined by the set of parenting beliefs, goals, and expectations inherent in his or her culture's model of parent-child relations - sometimes called cultural capital. One fundamental issue that societies must contend with would be the relationship between the individual and the group, referred to as individualism-collectivism (Gelfand, 2001).

In multicultural counselling, educators were engaged in reconciling the differences among people. The differences included but not limited to race, ethnicity, class, gender, and more. *Ethic perspective*: Some people hold the view that all people were the same, and therapy should, therefore, follow a universal set of rules. *Epic perspective*: Others believe that counselling and psychotherapy should be consistent with culturally appropriate goals and worldviews.

Roberts, O'Donnell & Richard (2004) examined continuity and change in the importance of major life goals and the relation between change in goals and personality traits over the course of college. Participants rated the importance of their life goals six times over a four-year period and completed a measure of the *Big Five* personality traits at the beginning and end of college. Like personality traits, life goals demonstrated high levels of rank-order stability. Unlike personality traits assessed during the same period and in the same sample, the mean importance of most life goals decreased over time. Moreover, each goal domain was marked by significant individual differences in change, and these individual differences were related to changes in personality traits.

Concept of Individualism (American culture) and Collectivism (African culture)

Individualism is "the opposite of collectivism; together they form one of the dimensions of national cultures (Hofstede, 1994). The author posited that individualism stood for a society in which the ties between individuals were loose: everyone would be expected to look after himself or herself and his/her immediate family only. Oyserman, Coon & Kemmelmeier (2002) explained that the core element of individualism would be the assumption that individuals were independent of one another, and their focus would be on rights above duties, a concern for one and immediate family, an emphasis on personal autonomy and self-fulfilment, and the basing of one's identity on one's accomplishments. Hofstede (1994) maintained that people from individualistic cultures tend to think only of themselves as individuals and as "I" distinctive from other people and prefer clarity in their conversations to communicate more effectively and directly to their point.

On the other hand, Oyserman, Coon & Kemmelmeier (2002) explained that the core element of collectivism was the assumption that groups bind and mutually obligate individuals. Hofstede (1994) contended that collectivism was a social pattern that places the highest value on the interests of the group, and they view themselves as dependent and closely linked to one another. And also, they would be willing to maintain a commitment to the group even when their obligations to the group were personally disadvantageous.

Some cultures would tend to embrace needed change, while others were highly resistant. According to Hofstede (1994), three attributes seemed to determine a culture's receptivity to change-sense of a community, shared vision and positive outlook. *A sense of community* would be considered present when people feel as if they belong and trust one another. This sense of belonging includes awareness that others would "care" and that the individual, in turn, would demonstrate the responsibility to care for others. With a sense of community, people would not be viewed exclusively in terms of performing a single role or function. Instead, individuals were seen as unique, complex and evolving, complete with hopes, dreams and personal history. Some pertinent questions were: Do members of the culture really get to know one another (i.e., dreams, special interests, history, etc.)? Do people duly lend support for one another in times of need? Do people feel as if they belong and are welcomed?

A shared vision exists when people recognise that they hold similar value systems. With a shared vision, members of the culture would be enthusiastic about cultural goals and the processes by which they would be achieved. A shared vision implies a sense of inclusion: members of the culture would not be left behind. The people would recognise that they share common values (or at the very least can be enthusiastic about one another's values). The people could describe shared goals and strategies for achieving those goals. They would find inspirational their shared goals and strategies.

With a *positive outlook*, people look for opportunities rather than obstacles and for strengths rather than weaknesses in one another. It wasn't so much that the need for change would be overlooked, but rather there would be a general recognition that cultural and individual strengths would make it possible to improve upon current conditions. People have faith that constructive change is possible. They would recognise individual and organisational strengths and they wouldn't focus on what was wrong alone. The people would view needed change as an opportunity for improvement or wouldn't view change as a problem. They would make use of individual and organisational strengths in addressing needed change. They wouldn't view individual, group, organisational and/or community goals as being in conflict with each other.

Africans believe that a family should live together, share their belongings, take decisions as it concerns them as a group, face their problems together, and remain close-knitted throughout their lifetime. In forming an identity as an African, the child would be trained by every member of the extended family. From infancy through adolescence and adulthood, an African would be provided and cared for collectively as well as supported by the entire family. Naturally, the child would grow to a man and join the system. If one person in a household has the means to support others, he/she would gladly do so. Out of a nuclear family of ten, if only one member has a job, the expectation would be that this member makes a budget for the whole family; this is a convention and considered to be natural. The spirit of "Be your brother's keeper" was very much alive in every African. Any person seen not living his life in this way would be regarded as a lost member. No law or statute was written to enforce the exhibition or exuding of these attributes of this code, but it was well- integrated into the system that hardly anybody violates it, particularly in the rural and suburban areas.

Example: Elemechi was the third son of a Cameroonian family. His mother died when he was only eight years old. The father remarried after ten years of the mother's death. The second wife had three children also. Being a brilliant chap, Elemechi was supported and sponsored through primary, secondary and tertiary education by the first child of the father. The family lives in the same house, and have one kitchen, common sitting room and everything was done communally or jointly as though they were all from the same womb. After graduating from college, Elemechi got a job in one of the top civil engineering companies in the country. He grew fast on the job, and eventually was made the managing director of this big organisation. The elder brother, together with some assistance from other younger ones had continued to train the youngest since their father had no job. At this time, Elemechi was twenty-six and was thinking of marriage. He lived in Yaounde, the country's capital and, therefore, he had associated with elite from different backgrounds.

Throughout this period, Elemechi did not pay attention to the other members of the family. The family had attempted individually and in groups urged Elemechi to render some financial assistance without success. The family eventually invited the larger community to help in making Elemechi listen to the family. Elemechi felt that he was in a better position to take decisions that best suits him, and not the community. He felt that his personal interest should override that of the family. After three invitations without reply, Elemechi was ostracised from the community.

On a fateful day when Elemechi returned with his newly married wife, no person came out from the entire community to interact with him. He tried in vain to reach some old friends, but they won't have anything to do with him. Elemechi could not stand the humiliation. He left hurriedly, since that time he did not return to his home. The above example was taken from the presentation of the researcher at the 2004 annual professional growth conference of the Texas Counselling Association at Fort Worth (Onyekuru, 2004).

This was the typical lifestyle in African society. Marriage process in African communities wasn't the same way it was done in American culture. A young woman going into marriage would be handed over to the parents of the bridegroom to assess her qualities and. give their opinion as to the suitability or otherwise of the woman to be considered for as a wife. In many cases, the bridegroom never makes a choice. The mother may determine whom the son marries. In some other cases and circumstances, the parents of the girl might decide to whom or when to hand their daughter's hand in marriage to a prospective husband to be.

From the perspective of the individual, the life process is regulated by their submission to the rules of life. A person would maintain his/her internal rhythm by the observance of certain basic ideas of self-respect and respect of others. Proper rituals and relationships would reinforce their connection with the "tribe" (community); and, renew the recognition of the universal life force that flows within and through the person as a whole. On a very concrete level this is reflected in the considerable social orientation of African people. The very idea of isolation or seclusion among African people was synonymous with madness. The coming together and sharing with each other in a harmonious manner would tend to reaffirm the rhythmic flow between self and others. This concept should speak to the Pan-African national culture. While close to the African world in meaning, this concept wouldn't be essentially a race-based one but a race conscious one. More importantly, it could be seen as an ideological and culture-based identity.

Family, friends and coworkers often assist one another in a variety of ways. When most people think of peer support, they think about listening and advice giving. In its negative form, such advice is sometimes called nagging. Other forms of peer support include modelling, eliminating barriers to change and celebrating success. Such support could be essential when people attempt to modify their personal behaviour. For this reason, the assessment of peer support systems was considered an important aspect of personality development. Their concerns may include questions like what forms of support were given (e.g., help with goal setting, modelling, eliminating barriers, locating supportive environments, working through relapse, and celebrating success)? What gaps exist in the support system? Are members of the culture receptive to support being offered? Do members of the culture ask for the support needed to accomplish project goals?

REFERENCES

Abadi, J.M. (2000). *Satisfaction with Oklahoma State University among selected groups of international students.* Dissertation Abstracts International, 60 (8-A), 2821.

Abbassi, A. (1999). *Culture and anxiety: A cross-cultural study.* Dissertation Abstracts International, 59 (11-A), 4065.

Abu-Ein, M. (1995). *A study of the adjustment problems of international students at Texas Southern University.* Dissertation Abstracts International, 55 (8-A), 2319.

Adams, R. (2001). *Second language assessment and study abroad.* Paper presented at the Pacific Second Language Research Forum, University of Hawaii at Manoa.

Akbar, S. (1999). *Immigration and identity.* Northvale, NJ: Jason Aronson.

Allen, H.W. (2002). Does study abroad make a difference? An investigation of linguistic and motivational outcomes. (Doctoral dissertation, Emory University). *Dissertation Abstracts International, 63,* 1279A.

Altbach, P.G., & Teichler, U. (2001). Internationalisation and exchanges in a globalised university. *Journal of Studies on International Education, 5* (1).

American Council on Education. (2002). *Beyond September 11: A comprehensive national policy on international education.* Washington, D.C.: American Council on Education.

Anaya, G., & Cole, D. (2001). Latina/o student achievement: Exploring the influence of student-faculty interaction on college grades. *Journal of College Student Development, 42,* 3-14.

Arthur, N. (2001). Using critical incidents to investigate cross-cultural transitions. *International Journal of Intercultural Relations, 25 (1),* 41-53.

Berger, K.S. (2001). The developing person through the lifespan. *Mental Health, 11,* 14 & 83.

Best, J.W., & Kahn, J.V. (2003). *Research in education.* Boston: A Pearson Education Company.

Booker, R.W. (2001). Differences between applicants and non-applicants relevant to the decision to apply to study abroad. (Doctoral dissertation, University of Missouri-Columbia). *Dissertation Abstracts International, 62 (04),* 1337A.

Boylan, H.R., & White, Jr., W.G. (1994). *Educating all the nation's people: The historical roots of developmental education.* Clearwater, FL: H. & H. Publishing.

Burak, P.A., & Hoffa, W.W. (2001). *Crisis management in a cross-cultural setting.* Washington, DC: NAFSA: Association of International Educators.

Busher, H. (2001). *Being and becoming a doctoral student: culture, literacies and self identity.* Paper presented to TESOL Arabic Conference 14-14 March 2001, Dubai Women's College, Dubai, UAE.

Casazza, M.E., & Silverman, S.L. (1996). *Learning assistance and developmental education: A guide to effective practice.* San Francisco: Jossey-Bass.

Chieffo, L.P. (2001). Determinants of student participation in study abroad programs at the University of Delaware: A quantitative study. (Doctoral dissertation, University of Delaware, 2000). *Dissertation Abstracts International, 61 (08),* 3078A.

Chung, R.C., & Bemak, F. (2002). The relationship of culture and empathy in crosscultural counseling. *Journal of Counseling & Development, 80,* 154-159.

Coleman, S. (1997). International students in the classroom: A resource and an opportunity. *International Education, 26,* 52-61.

Cooney, P.L. (2001). *Where class is more important than race. Are they crazy?* Brazil: Theodore Myles Publishing, Brazil.

Corey, G. (2001). *Theory and practice of counseling and psychotherapy.* Wadsworth: Brooks/Cole.

Davidson, D.E. (2002). *When just being there is not enough.* Paper presented at the Conference on Language Gain in the Study Abroad Environment, University of Wisconsin, Madison, WI.

Davis, T.M. (Ed.) (2002). *Open doors 2000/2001: Report on international educational exchange.* New York, NY: Institute on International Education.

Degges-White, S. (2005). Understanding gerotrancendence in older adults: A new perspective for counsellors. *Adultspan Journal, 3,* 4-11.

Desimone, R. L., Werner, J.M. & Harris, D.M. (2002). *Human Resource Development.* Harcourt college publishers: Orlando.

DuFon, M.A., Adams, R., Churchil, E., & McMeekin, M. (2001). *Second language acquisition in study abroad contexts.* Papers presented at the Pacific Second Language Research Forum, University of Hawaii at Manoa.

Fordham, T.A. (2002). Cultural capital and the making of 'blue blazer kids': An ethnography of a youth exchange program. (Doctoral dissertation, Syracuse

University). *Dissertation Abstracts International, 63,* 899A.

Galloway, F.J., & Jenkins, J.R. (2005). The adjustment problems faced by international students: A comparison international students and administrative perceptions at two private, religiously affiliated universities. *NASPA Journal, 42(2),* 175-187.

Gay, L.R., & Airasian, P. (2003). *Educational research: Competencies for analysis and applications.* Upper Saddle River, New Jersey: Pearson Education, Inc.

Gelfand, M.J. (2000). Culture and egocentric perception in negotiation. *Journal of Applied Psychology, 32,* 62.

Gerber, S. (2001). Theory learning intervention counseling. *Journal of Counselling and Development, 59,*16.

Gershoff, E.T. (2002). Corporal punishment by parents and associated child behaviours and experiences: A meta-analytic and theoretical review. *Journal of American Psychological Association,* 4.

Goyol, A.B. (2002). *Adjustment problems of African students at Western Michigan University.* www.wmich.edu/grad/ dissertation/ disarchive/goyol.html

Grady, A. (1996). Technology transfer with special references to international postgraduate education, PhD thesis, University of East London.

Halpern, J. (1992). A comparative study of adjustment difficulties experienced by American male and female students in Israeli institutions of higher learning. (Doctoral dissertation, The American University, 1991). *Dissertaion Abstarcts International, 52 (9),* 3182A.

Hartung. E. (2002). The student as outsider. *International Educator, 11 (2),* 28-34.

Hayward, F.M., & Siaya, L.M. (2001). *Public Experience, Attitudes, and Knowledge: A Report on Two National Surveys about International Education.* Washington, D.C.: American Council on Education.

Henthorne, T.L., Miller, M.M., & Hudson, T.W. (2001). Building and positioning successful study-abroad programs: A ``hands-on" approach. *Journal of Teaching in International Business, 12 (4),* 49-62

Hodgetts, R.M. (2002). *Modern human resources at work. Florida*: Harcourt College Publisher.

Hodne, B.D. (1997). Please speak up: Asian immigrant students in American college classrooms. In D.L. Sigsbee, B.W. Speck, & B.Maylath (Eds.), *Approaches to teaching non-native English speakers across the curriculum* (New Directions in Teaching and Learning No.70) (pp. 85-92). San Francisco: Jossey-Bass.

Hoffa, B. (2000). *Exploring cultural differences.* Study abroad handbook: Unpublished manuscript, University of Mississippi at Oxford.

Hofstede, G. (1994). Cultures and organisations. *Intercultural cooperation and its importance for survival*, 260-261.

Hopkins, W.E. (1997). *Ethical dimensions of diversity.* Thousand Oaks, CA: Sage.

Howard, M. (2001). The effects of study abroad on the L2 learner's structural skills: Evidence from advanced learners of French. *EUROSLA Yearbook, 1 (1),* 123-141.

Hudson, D.R. (2001). Grade point average as a predictor of academic achievement for a credit abroad, language acquisition course. (Doctoral dissertation, The University of Southern Mississippi). *Dissertation Abstracts International, 63 (01),* 38A

Hughes, M. (1992). Global diversity and student development: Educating for world citizenship. In M.C. Terrell (Ed.), *Diversity, disunity, and campus community* (pp. 199-223). Buffalo, NY: National Association of Student Personnel Administrators.

Ingersoll, R.E. (1995). Spirituality, religion, and counseling: Dimensions and relationships. In M.T. Burke & J.G. Miranti (Eds.), *Counseling, the spiritual dimension* (pp. 5-18). Alexandria, VA: American Counseling Association.

Institute of International Education. (2001). *Open doors 2001: Statistics on international student mobility.* Washington DC: Institute of International Education.

Institute of International Education. (2003). *Open doors 2003: Statistics on international student mobility.* Washington DC: Institute of International Education.

Institute of International Education. (2004). *Open doors 2004: Statistics on international student mobility.* Washington DC: Institute of International Education

Jablonski, M.A. (2001). *The implications of student spirituality for student affairs practice.* San Francisco: Jossey-Bass.

Johnson, E. (1997). Cultural norms affect oral communication in the classroom. In D.L. Sigsbee, B.W. Speck, & B.Maylath (Eds.), *Approaches to teaching non-native English speakers across the curriculum* (New Directions in Teaching and Learning No.70) (pp. 47-52). San Francisco: Jossey-Bass.

Kelly, U., Marsh, R., McNicoll, I. (2002). *The impact of higher education institutions on the UK economy: A report for universities. UK, Glasgow:* The University of Strathclyde.

Kim, B.S.K., & Abreu, J.M. (2001). Acculturation measurement: theory, current instruments, and future directions. In J.G.

Ponterotto, J.M. Casas, L.A. Suzuki, and C.M. Alexander (Eds.), *Handbook of multicultural counseling* (2nd ed.) (pp. 394-424). Thousand Oaks, CA: Sage Publications.

Knight, G.R. (1998). *Issues and alternatives in educational philosophy*. Berrien springs: Andrews University Press.

Komives, S.R., Woodard, D.B. & Associates (2003). *Student services: A handbook for the profession*. San Francisco: Jossey-Bass.

Kwok, M. (2002). *Homesickness, stress, social support, personality and health: a study of home and overseas students*. MA Dissertation, University of Surrey.

Leask, B. (2001, Summer). Bridging the gap: Internationalising university curricula. *Journal of Studies on International Education, 5* (2).

Lee, C.C. (1991). Cultural Dynamics: Their importance in multicultural counseling. In: C.C. Lee & B.L.R. Richardson (Eds.), *Multicultural issues in counseling: New approaches to diversity*. Alexandria, VA: American Association for Counseling and Development.

Lin, J.G., & Yi, J.K. (1997). Asian international students' adjustment: Issues and program suggestions. *College Student Journal, 31 (4)*, 473-480.

Logan, J.R., & Spitze, G. D. (1996). *Family ties: Enduring relations between parents and their grown children*. Philadelphia: Temple University Press.

Love, P.G., Kuh, G.D., Mackay, K.A., & Hardy, C.M. (1993). Side by side: Faculty and student affairs cultures. In G.D. Kuh (Ed.), *Cultural perspectives in student affairs work* (pp. 37-58). Lanham, MD: University Press of America.

Love, P., & Talbot, D. (1999). Defining spiritual development: A missing consideration for student affairs. *NASPA Journal, 37,* 361-375.

Love, P.G. (2001). Spirituality and student development: Theoretical connections. In M.A. Jablonski (Ed.), *The implications of student spirituality for student affairs practice.* San Francisco: Jossey-Bass.

Manley, T.N. (2002). Study abroad pedagogy: A case study of the development and practice of the Pitzer College Fieldbook. (Doctoral dissertation, The Claremont Graduate University). *Dissertation Abstracts International, 63,* 878A.

Maundeni, T. (2001). The role of social networks in the adjustment of African students to British society: Students' perception. *Race, ethnicity, and Education, 4(3),* 253-276.

McCabe, L.T. (2001). Globalisation and internationalisation: The impact on education abroad programs. *Journal of Studies on International Education, 5 (2),* 138-145.

McNamara, D., & Harris, R. (1997). *Overseas students in higher education: Issues in teaching and learning.* London and New York: Routledge.

Mehdizadeh, N., & Scott, G. (2005). Adjustment problems of Iranian international students in Scotland. *International Education Journal, 6(4),* 484-493.

Miller, J.G. (2002). Bringing culture to basic Psychological Theory-Beyond Individualism and collectivism. *Psychological Bulletin, 128 (1),* 97-109.

Miller, W.R. (1999). *Integrating spirituality into treatment: Resources for practitioners.* Washington, DC: American Psychological Association.

Millington, T.V. (2002). *Study abroad for bicultural students.* IMDiversity.com –Hispanic- American Village.

Miranti, J.G., & Burke, M.T. (1995). Spirituality: An integral component of the counseling process. In: M.T. Burke &

J.G. Miranti (Eds.), *Counselling: The spiritual dimensions* (pp. 1-4). Alexandria, VA: American Counselling Association.

Nasr, K., Berry, J., Taylor, G., Webster, W., Echempati, R., & Chandran, R. (2002). *Global engineering education through study-abroad experiences: Assessment and lessons learned.* www.asee.org/conferences/internatinal/papers/ taylor.pdf

Nystul, M.S. (2003). *Introduction to counselling: An art and science perspective.* Boston: Allyn and Bacon.

Office of Policy and Evaluation, Bureau of Educational and Cultural Affairs, US Department of State. (2002). *Outcome assessment of the U.S. Fulbright Scholar Programme (SRI International Project No. P10372).* Menlo Park, CA: C.P. Ailes & S.H. Russell.

Oguri, M., & Gudykunst, W.B. (2002). The influence of self-construal and communication styles on sojourners' psychological and socio-cultural adjustment. *International Journal of Intercultural Relations, 26 (5),* 577-593.

Olson, C.L., & Kroeger, K.R. (2001). Global competency and intercultural sensitivity. *Journal of Studies on International Education, 5* (2).

Onyekuru, G.C. (2004). *Culture change and effect on individual personality.* Paper presented at the annual professional growth conference of the Texas Counselling Association, Forth Worth, Texas.

Oyserman, D., Coon, H.M. & Kemmelmeier, M. (2002). Rethinking individualism and collectivism: Evaluation of theoretical assumptions and meta-analysis. *Psychological Bulletin. 128(1),* 3-72.

Park, Y.J. (2001). An Asian American outside: Crossing colour lines in the United States and Africa. *Amerasia Journal, 26 (23),* 99-117.

Parks, S.D. (2000). *Big questions, worthy dreams: Mentoring young adults in their search for meaning, purpose and faith.* San Francisco: Jossey-Bass.

Paunonen, S. V. (1998). Hierarchical organisation of personality and prediction of behaviour. *Journal of Personality & Social Psychology,74(2),* 538-556.

Pedersen, P.B. (1991). Multiculturalism as a generic approach to counselling. *Journal of Counselling and Development, 70(1),* 6-12.

Pedersen, P.B., Draguns, J.G., Lonner, W.J., & Trimble, J.E. (2002). *Counselling across cultures.* Thousand Oaks, CA: Sage.

Pennycook, A. (1996). Borrowing others' words: Text, ownership, memory, and plagiarism. *TESOL Quarterly, 30,* 201-230.

Ping, C.J. (1999). An expanded international role for student affairs. In J.C. Dalton (Ed.), *Beyond borders: How international developments are changing student affairs practice. New Directions for Student Services* (no. 86).

Porter, J.W. (1993). *Michigan international student problem inventory: The manual.* Lansing, MI: John W. Porter.

Porterfield, T.A. (2002). Making meaning of student sojourner spirituality post study abroad. (Doctoral dissertation, University of Northern Colorado). *Dissertation Abstracts International, 63,* 2162A.

Poyrazli, S., Arbona, C., Nora, A., McPherson, B., & Pisecco, S. (2002). Relation between assertiveness, academic self-efficacy, and psychosocial adjustment among international graduate students. *Journal of College Student Development,* *43,* 632-642.

Poyrazli, S., Kavanaugh, P., Baker, A., & Al-Timimi, N. (2004). Social support and demographic correlates of acculturative stress in international students. *Journal of College Counselling, 7,* 73-82.

Remley, T.P., Jr., & Herlihy, B. (2005). *Ethical, legal, and professional issues in counselling.* New Jersey: Pearson Education Inc.

Ridley, C.R. (1995). *Overcoming unintentional racism in counselling and therapy: A practitioner's guide to international interventions.* Thousand Oaks, CA: Sage.

Ridley, C.R., & Lingle, D.W. (1996). *Cultural empathy in multicultural counselling: A multidimensional process model.* In P. B. Pedersen, J.C. Draguns, W.J. Lonner, & J.E. Trimble (Eds.), *Counselling across cultures.* Thousand Oaks, CA: Sage.

Riley, L.A. (2002). *Coming home as strangers: Dialectical transformation of self-identity in the study abroad experience.* Unpublished bachelor's honours thesis, Bridgewater College, Virginia.

Rippa, S.A. (1997). *Education in a free society: An American history.* New York: Longman.

Roberts, B.W., Caspi, A. & Moffitt, T.E. (2003). Work experiences and personality development in young adulthood. *Journal of Personality & Social Psychology, 84(3),* 582-593.

Roberts, B. W., O'Donnell, R., & Richard W. (2004). Goal and Personality Trait Development in Emerging Adulthood. *Journal of Personality & Social Psychology, 87(4),* 541-550.

Rong, X.L., & Pressle, J. (1998). *Educating immigrant students: What we need to know to meet the challenges.* Thousan Oaks, CA: Corwin.

Rubenzer, S. (2000). What makes a good president? *Journal of American Psychological Association, 2.*

Sakurako, M. (2000). Addressing the mental health concerns of international students. *Journal of Counselling and Development, 78(2),* 137-148.

Sanderson, J. (2002). Somewhere over the rainbow: A pragmatic approach to issues of gay youth and sexual identity in study abroad. (Unpublished master's thesis, University of Maryland Baltimore County, 2002). *Masters Abstracts International, 40 (6),* 1351.

Sandhu, D.S., & Asrabadi, B. R., (1998). *An acculturative stress scale for international students: A practical approach to stress measurement.* In C. P. Zalaquett & R.J. Wood (Eds.), *Evaluating stress: A book of resources, 2,* (pp. 1-33). Lanam, MD: Scarecrow Press.

Schmitt. M.T., Spears, R., & Branscombe, N.R. (2003). Constructing a minority group identity out of shared rejection: The case of international students. *European Journal of Social Psychology, 33,* 1-12.

Segal, M. (1997). *Points of Influence: A guide to using Personality theory at work.* San Francisco: Jossey-Bass Inc.

Smith, A. (1998). New survey reveals changing attitudes. *American Language Review, 2 (5).*

Smith, L. (1996). New Russian immigrants: Health and problems, practices, and values. *Journal of Cultural Diversity, 3(3),* 68-73).

Snoke, J. & Long, R. (1998). *Developing and managing a collaborative conversation.* Paper presented at Partners

Program Presentation at NAFSA Region VIII Conference, Pittsburgh, PA.

Storti, C. (2001). *The art of crossing cultures.* Manassas Park, VA: Impact Publications.

Strandholm, K. (2002). American business education: Effect on the ethical orientation of foreign students. *Journal of Education and Business, 77(6),* 351-355.

Sue, D.W., Ivey, A.E. & Pedersen, P.B. (1996). *A theory of multicultural counselling and therapy.* Pacific Grove, CA: Brooks/Cole.

Sue, D.W., & Sue, D. (1999). *Counselling the culturally different: Theory and practice.* New York: Wiley. Summit on Spirituality, (1995). *Counselling Today,* p.30

Sussman, N.M. (2002, August). Testing the cultural identity model of the cultural transition cycle: Sojourners return home. *International Journal of Intercultural Relations, 26 (4),* 391-408.

Tomkovich, C., & Al-Khatib, J. (1996). An assessment of the service quality provided to foreign students at US business schools. *Journal of Education for Business, 61,* 130-135.

Triandis, H. (1991). A need for theoretical examination. *The Counselling Psychologist, 19,* 59-61.

Truong, D.N. (2002). Successes, challenges and difficulties experienced by American students while on Fulbright scholarships in China and Vietnam. (Doctoral dissertation, Virginia Commonwealth University). *Dissertation Abstracts International, 63 (5),* 1747A.

Weeks, K.M. (2002). *Managing liability and overseas programs.* Nashville, TN: College Legal Information, Inc.

Welfel, E.R. (2002). *Ethics in counselling and psychotherapy: Standards, research, and emerging issues.* Pacific Grove, CA: Brooks/Cole.

Westgate, C.E. (1996). Spiritual wellness and depression. *Journal of Counselling and Development, 75(1),* 26-35.

Weting, P.M. (2002). *Impacts on participants of an island study abroad program in London, England.* Unpublished Capstone paper, School for International Training.

Wilkinson, S. (2002). *What if they don't gain?* Paper presented at the Conference on Language Gain in the Study Abroad Environment, University of Wisconsin, Madison, WI.

Woolston, V. (1995). International students: Leveraging learning. In A.S. Pruitt-Logan & P.D. Isaac (Eds.), *Student services for the changing graduate student population* (New Directions for student services No. 72). San Francisco: Jossey-Bass.

Yeh, C.J., & Inose, M. (2003). International students reported English fluency, social support satisfaction, and social connectedness as predictors of acculturative stress. *Counselling Psychology Quarterly, 16 (1),* 15-28.

Ying, Y. (2002). Formation of cross-cultural relationships of Taiwanese international students in the United States. *Journal of Community Psychology, 30,* 45-55.

Zambito, J., (2002). Students of colour in study abroad programmes. *Colorado State University Journal of Student Affairs, 11,* 1-5.

Zinnbauer, B.J., & Pargament, K.I. (2000). Working with the sacred: Four approaches to religious and spiritual issues in counselling. *Journal of Counselling and Development, 78(2),* 162-171